Shelby sucked in a sharp breath

"I'm…pregnant."

Luke stared at her bent head, at the red blotches on her skin and the pulse fluttering rapidly at her throat.

He could only imagine what she was thinking, the surge of panic she probably felt at the shock of it. If his heart pounded any harder in his chest, it was going to burst through his skin.

But his brain was already working, trying to figure out a way to get her to understand he'd meant what he said. They were in this together and no way was she going to deny him his child.

"No, Shelby. *We're* pregnant."

Dear Reader,

Thank you so much for picking up book three of THE TULANES OF TENNESSEE series. Each story stands alone, so no worries about following along. But if you're interested in Luke's other siblings, be sure to check out *Another Man's Baby* (Harlequin Superromance #1477) and *His Son's Teacher* (Harlequin Superromance #1502), and don't forget that Ethan and Alexandra's stories are coming soon.

I've had so much fun with this series. I've been able to develop my fictional town of Beauty, Tennessee, and I've gotten to know my characters with every scene. But just when I think I have them pegged, something jumps out to surprise me. Some of the things are happy, some sad, some funny and all are true to life. It's amazing how life, and stories, work that way, eh? We never know what's going to happen.

I absolutely love to hear from my readers, and I hope you'll write to me at P.O. Box 232, Minford, OH 45653, e-mail me at kay@kaystockham.com, visit my cyber home at www.kaystockham.com or friend me on Myspace at www.myspace.com/kaystockham. I host weekly contests as well as Launch Party Scavenger Hunts through the pages of my books, post book videos, excerpts, blogs and lots more. Come join the fun and keep me company. I'd love to get to know you better.

God bless,

Kay Stockham

HER BEST FRIEND'S BROTHER

Kay Stockham

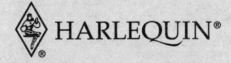

TORONTO • NEW YORK • LONDON
AMSTERDAM • PARIS • SYDNEY • HAMBURG
STOCKHOLM • ATHENS • TOKYO • MILAN • MADRID
PRAGUE • WARSAW • BUDAPEST • AUCKLAND

Recycling programs
for this product may
not exist in your area.

ISBN-13: 978-0-373-71552-7
ISBN-10:   0-373-71552-8

HER BEST FRIEND'S BROTHER

This edition published by arrangement with Harlequin Books S.A.

® and TM are trademarks of the publisher. Trademarks indicated with ® are registered in the United States Patent and Trademark Office, the Canadian Trade Marks Office and in other countries.

www.eHarlequin.com

Printed in U.S.A.

ABOUT THE AUTHOR

Kay Stockham has always wanted to be a writer, ever since she copied the pictures out of a Charlie Brown book and rewrote the story because she didn't like the plot. Formerly a secretary/office manager for a large commercial real estate development company, she's now a full-time writer and stay-at-home mom who firmly believes being a mom/wife/homemaker is the hardest job of all. Happily married for over fifteen years and the somewhat frazzled mother of two, she's sold ten books to Harlequin Superromance. Her first release, *Montana Secrets*, hit the Waldenbooks bestseller list and was chosen as a Holt Medallion finalist for Best First Book. Kay has garnered praise from reviewers for her emotional, heart-wrenching stories and looks forward to a long career writing a genre she loves.

Books by Kay Stockham

Don't miss any of our special offers. Write to us at the following address for information on our newest releases.

Harlequin Reader Service
U.S.: 3010 Walden Ave., P.O. Box 1325, Buffalo, NY 14269
Canadian: P.O. Box 609, Fort Erie, Ont. L2A 5X3

This book is dedicated to my wonderful editor
Wanda Ottewell.
You have no idea how much it means
to know you "get" my characters.
It's a pleasure working with you!

To a hero in the making, C, for helping me
with the gaming industry research, and being
so patient all the times I told you to play it again.
And again. I may be a little biased,
but I think you're very cool.

And to all the computer geeks who make the
world go round.
Where would we be without you?
(Chad, Ryan, Justin—this is for you! Thank you
for being my heroes when I battle my computers
and the computers almost win. You keep me
from throwing them out the window.)

CHAPTER ONE

TOSSING ONE'S COOKIES on gorgeous Italian leather shoes had a funny way of ruining a girl's day.

Shelby Brookes gasped for air and glared at the offending footwear, glad she knew better than to spend her hard-earned cash on overpriced shoes that wore the same as the regular-priced ones. But Luke Tulane had been raised with the best of everything and *he* obviously didn't realize no woman liked seeing a man wearing better shoes than she owned herself. "Sorry."

The word came out as a gasp. A choked *oh, please, not again* groan of undisguised misery as her stomach muscles flip-flopped like circus clowns on a trampoline. This could *not* be happening.

"Bad day?"

Her head whirled, and the ground jiggled in strange, wavy patterns, but the anger in his tone registered. The why-didn't-you-just-pick-up-the-freaking-phone-and-return-my-messages-the-five-times-I-called-you *snap* of a bruised male ego.

Can you blame him?

Shelby swallowed and tried to hold on to what was left of her lunch. Luke had flown home to Beauty, Tennessee, to attend the first family wedding back in June when his older brother, Garret, married Darcy Rhodes. Now it was nearing the end of August and Luke was home again, this time because his twin brother, Nick, had found love with Jennifer Rose.

But instead of avoiding Shelby like any normal person would do in such an awkward situation, Luke had repeatedly sought her out—because of what had taken place between them behind the scenes after Garret and Darcy's rehearsal dinner.

You brought this on yourself, you know. You kissed him, not the other way around. You weren't complaining then.

Maybe not, but she still regretted it. Didn't that count for something?

She'd tried to do the right thing by keeping her distance. It was after the fact, sure, but she'd tried. Yet here Luke stood toe-to-*knee,* and there was no ducking him now.

I puked on your shoes. Your shoes! Haven't you had enough?

"Last night catch up to you?"

Oh, of all the— Even though she'd felt like she could've used the fortification, she hadn't had a single drink last night, knowing her twelve-hour shift would be hard enough to handle given the huge possibility she'd run into Luke. Besides, she rarely drank, having seen how alcohol influenced her mother's behavior. Following in Pat Taylor-Brooke's footsteps wasn't Shelby's idea of a good time. It was bad enough her mother gave the town gossips so much fodder, Shelby wasn't about to add to it.

You mean like now?

She didn't raise her head, not when the slightest movement made the waves of nausea buffeting her that much worse.

How much worse could it be? You're on your hands and knees at the man's feet!

Yeah, well, if embarrassment killed, she would've been dead a long time ago. Growing up with a mother who played the drama queen to the hilt at every opportunity would have seen to that.

"Come on, I'll help you inside."

Inside? To gossip central? No, thank you. "G-go away."

"Shelby, I can't leave you here like this."

He had to. She didn't want him laughing at her misery because he was angry with her. And why wouldn't he be when she was so upset with herself? How could she have been so stupid? Shagging her best friend's *brother?* That ranked right up there with—with—well, she didn't quite know what but it was *huge!* "Contagious."

She had no idea if she was contagious or not, but she'd tell Luke she had the bubonic plague before she'd allow him to drag her anywhere, much less into the wedding reception. The wind created by the gossips' mouths flapping would blow the roof off the building.

Shelby inhaled and got a noseful of roses and wild onions from the woods nearby. *Oh, help me.* The smell had her stomach rolling again and she struggled to hold back a moan.

A white silk handkerchief appeared before her eyes. "Here. Take it."

When she didn't, Luke released a long-suffering sigh, a noise she'd heard him issue many, many times over the years. Usually it was in respect to his sister and her best friend, Alex, though. Not her.

"Quit being so stubborn. Take it."

Since cleaning up boiled down to using either the handkerchief, her shirt or the country club's crested employee jacket, she let go of her death grip on the manicured lawn and accepted the pristine material, finding perverse pleasure at wiping her mouth on the length.

Cheese curls and silk—what a combination.

Another wave of nausea flooded her at the thought of her favorite snack and Shelby clamped her mouth shut, afraid she'd embarrass herself even more than she already had.

"I'll go get Ethan."

"No." She so didn't need his doctor brother witnessing this, prayed to disappear. Where was a sinkhole when a girl needed one? "I'm f-fine."

Oh, what a whopper that was. Her arms hurt from holding herself up, she felt weak and battered, yet all she could see in her mind was how hot geeky-sexy Luke Tulane had looked naked.

You are so *screwed up.*

"Somehow I don't believe you."

Shelby scrambled for a comeback and called herself lame when nothing came to mind. "Something's been going around. A twenty-four-hour thing."

"Shelby—"

"I'll be fine. Don't make a fuss. Mr. Long is watching me like a hawk." Or a buzzard. Which one had the long beak of a nose? *Focus.* "It took me three interviews—" oh, those onions smelled awful! "—to get this job."

And she knew why she'd succeeded. Luke's parents and grandmother had gone to bat for her. There was no other explanation.

And you repaid them how?

She ignored the snippy voice in her head shaming her for jumping Luke's bones, and concentrated on feeling better. "I can't lose it." Mr. Long was a fountain of restaurant managerial experience, something she needed to soak in like a sponge. Getting fired was not an option.

Luke squatted beside her, well out of range, and placed his hand on her back. "What can I do? Would you like something to drink?"

She nodded, willing to agree to just about anything to get him away from her. That night in June she'd considered Luke the perfect person to distract her from her horrendous day. But now what she needed was someone who'd distract *him*. "A soda."

"You shouldn't drink that stuff. It's not healthy."

Shelby rolled her eyes and regretted the movement because of the pain it caused in her pounding head. He'd told her that more than once but she happened to like caffeine and sugar. "It settles my stomach."

The air from his gusty sigh cooled the sweat on her neck. "I hate leaving you here. The least I can do is help you to a—"

"Don't touch me!" Weren't his shoes enough? "Luke, just *go*." She sounded desperate, close to pleading. What woman wanted to do *this* in front of—

An amazing one-night stand?

Uncomfortable, I-can't-believe-we-did-that memories filled her head, but thankfully her order to leave had worked, because Luke's footsteps faded. Feeling better now that she was alone, Shelby lifted her head and watched as Luke disappeared around a statue. When he was out of sight, she slowly pushed herself upright and sat back on her heels.

The boxwood hedges provided a nice shield from prying eyes, but how long would it be before someone came for a stroll? The gazebo in the center of the garden had been a trysting place for more than a few couples over the years.

Rumor even had it Luke's grandmother, Rosetta Tulane, had conceived one of her children there.

Imagining a younger version of Luke's spunky grandmother getting it on in a public place brought a smile to Shelby's lips. Seconds passed, and little by little she felt more human. Until she spied her uniform pants. "No! Oh, no. Oh, *crap!*"

They were ruined! Why on earth would anyone choose white linen as the required uniform for the working class?

Because hugging the grass and hurling isn't in your job description?

Shelby groaned and ignored the quivering inside her body. She grabbed her purse and shoved herself onto her wobbly legs, moving like a hundred-twenty-eight-year-old woman instead of a twenty-eight-year-old one, which gave her plenty of time to take in the bright green stains decorating both knees. "Fifty bucks down the drain."

Maybe she could have the pants altered and convince Mr. Long to let her wear them as elegant summer shorts. Hearing his clipped, British refusal in her head, she brushed the grass blades sticking so stubbornly to her clothing and waited for the world to stop spinning. She couldn't worry about her pants now. She had to get out of here before Luke came back and things got…sticky.

They were hot and sticky that night and you didn't seem to mind.

Shut. Up.

She'd walked that embarrassingly painful mental path every day since they'd slept together, asked herself why. *Why* hadn't she gone home and worked out her upset and frustration by baking? Why hadn't she done something constructive that would have helped her meet her goal? Why had she made such a horrendous mistake with her best friend's brother? Why, why, why?

Because you liked it, her mind taunted. *You really liked it.*

Her entire body flushed with heat. Yeah, she'd liked it—until it was over and the consequences of her actions had walloped her a good one upside the head. Alex would be beside herself if she found out. She was most protective of Luke, closer to him because of the divide that had developed between Luke and Nick growing up. But while Luke might have updated his geeky glasses to the kind worn by business studs photographed for magazine ads and lost the boring shirts his mother had always bought for him, Luke was still Alex's favorite brother because Alex claimed he was more sensitive than the rest, more caring and astute than the siblings Alex sometimes referred to as blockheads.

Shelby stumbled across the rear grounds of the club, trying ineffectively to shove the memory of *doing* Alex's favorite brother from her mind. It was over. Done. A mistake that would not be repeated. It was past time to stop worrying about something she couldn't change and put the incident behind her. She couldn't let what happened cloud her thinking—or make her so nervous she got sick. As soon as she got home she'd…call Luke and apologize? Swear him to secrecy? Beg him to keep his distance?

All of the above?

Shelby made her way to a pea-gravel path, her heels sinking with every step. It would have been a lot quicker to walk through the country club, but with that route she chanced running into Luke or Alex or, worse yet, Mr. Long. Throwing up at home was bad enough, but in public wearing full makeup?

Her foundation was probably gone, her eyes raccooned. Plus her stomach was still rolling like a fun-park coaster.

"Just keep moving." The thought of Luke behind her, closing in and demanding to talk to her *now* made her put one foot in front of the other. She didn't want a scene, couldn't risk someone overhearing Luke demanding answers for her behavior or her having to tell him she'd do anything to take it all back. The night had been wonderful. Perfect. But the fact that she'd done it all with *Luke* bit the big one.

Shelby rounded the corner of the club and continued downhill to the employee parking lot. She'd almost made it to her car when her three-inch heel skidded on a rock. "Ow! Oh, *ow.*" Just what she needed. What else was going to happen?

She hobbled the rest of the way and fell inside the vehicle, absurdly thankful that the pain helped clear her head. Hurry. She had to hurry. She'd practically lived with the Tulanes growing up. If they found out she'd kissed Luke in places his mama hadn't seen for nearly thirty years, nothing would ever be the same.

Shelby fastened her seat belt and took the exit farthest from the clubhouse, checking her rearview mirror for any sight of Luke's tall form and rubbing at the mascara smeared down her cheek.

All she wanted to do was go home, get out of her icky clothes, take a quick shower and—strangely enough—eat more cheese curls.

LUKE SHOOK HIS HEAD with a tight smile as another person tried to halt his progress from the bar. Every second he was away from Shelby, his impatience ratchetted up another notch. It wasn't every day the four-time winner of Beauty's Mountain Queen Pageant was so…accessible. Or vulnerable. And given her avoidance of him, he wasn't above taking advantage of it. Especially when coming home always made him feel like an unwelcome relation who had to be tolerated because he was family.

He shouldn't have left Shelby. What if she felt worse? Passed out? *Escaped?* Luke muttered under his breath. Knowing Shelby, anything was possible, but he'd be ticked if she slipped away again.

Plastic bottle in hand, he forced a smile to his lips and kept going when Mrs. Bumgarner attempted to waylay him. Normally he would have stopped to chat as manners dictated, but time was against him. The moment Shelby was able to yank herself up by her bootstraps, she'd be back to her old self—aloof and unapproachable, spine stiff and attitude in place.

Luke avoided eye contact and wove his way through the crowded ballroom, the tables gleaming with the decorations of yet another Tulane wedding reception. Memories of the first trip home to Beauty bombarded him and his sudden scowl had Mrs. Daughtry raising her eyebrows. The old bat would run straight to his mother and make something of it, so Luke smoothed his features and flashed her a tight smile as he passed.

Luke glanced over his shoulder to see Nick sneaking a kiss from his bride and prayed to God the rumor was true. Maybe Jenn really had found a way to help Nick. Given the look of happiness on Nick's face, it had to be true.

Luke paused a moment to watch the couple celebrate their wedded bliss, happy for them. But what about him and Nick? Would anything repair the damage? He was welcome here, sure, but there was still a mountain of anger between them.

Shaking his head, Luke hurried toward the rose garden via one of the French doors lining the dining room. All afternoon he'd watched for Shelby, but she'd stood in the back of the crowd during the service, avoided his gaze even if it meant staring at her pointy-toed shoes, then disappeared into the throng of guests whenever he took a step in her direction. Quite a change from the woman who'd ripped the buttons from his shirt when she'd stripped it off him.

They'd had sex. Mind-boggling, can't-feel-your-legs sex. Shelby had been wild. Uninhibited. Everything he'd always secretly fantasized she'd be. But when he'd opened his eyes the next morning, she was gone.

So get the hint and leave her alone.

"You *left?* Shel, come on! I thought you were going to stick around and hang out with me."

Luke bit back a curse and paused, searching the greenery for the whereabouts of his sister's voice. He found Alexandra on a bench tucked into a private corner of the garden.

"Oh, yeah? No, I understand completely. I hope you feel better soon. Want me to bring you some leftovers when I sneak out?"

Luke moved closer, pausing before Alex noticed him.

His sister made a face at whatever Shelby said. "That bad? No, I certainly don't want to be sick and trying to fly. Rest up, and I'll call you later… Yeah, I will. Maybe we can get together soon. I have a short assignment lined up this week but will be back in Nashville by the weekend. I'll try to drive down."

She laughed at something Shelby said. "No way. I heard my name mentioned, too. Sounds like the safest place for me is out of town. My brothers are dropping like flies. My money's on Ethan.… No, really. Some nurse will wise up soon, especially if he keeps leaving his scrubs behind in the on-call rooms. Some of the stories I've heard are unbelievable.… I *know!*"

Alex snickered again, this one sounding ornerier than the

last. "Someone today mentioned Luke being next. I don't know who they were referring to, but unless a woman's built like Dolly Parton and animated, he doesn't seem to be interested at all.… Uh-oh, I hear the band starting. I'd better get inside. Look, feel better and take care, okay? And if you need anything, call me. If nothing else, I can drive out and leave it on the porch for you.… Of course I would. You'd get me out of here early. I've had about all the motherly looks and comments I can handle on the subject of settling down and marriage…. Yeah, but try telling her that…. Yeah, I will. Bye, Shel."

Luke waited until Alex ended the call before he cleared his throat. "Dolly Parton and animated?"

His sister started and glanced up at him, color seeping into her cheeks. "Oh…hey."

Luke raised an eyebrow.

"It's just an observation."

"Based on what?"

She smoothed a hand over her skirt. "Well," she drawled slowly, "when I visited you and toured your company last year I saw an awful lot of silicone who seemed very interested in you. But nothing took your attention off your work."

"Maybe I was focusing on showing my little sister a good time."

"Doesn't mean you're *dead*."

True.

"And then there was your boss—what's her name?"

"Anne-Marie."

"She flirted with you bold as you please but you didn't bat an eyelash."

He tugged at his earlobe. "She's my boss. And she only did that because she was having problems with her husband

and he was watching." But if Alex thought Anne-Marie was a flirt then, she'd really think so now. Anne-Marie liked "playing with the boys" as she called it.

"I bet she still flirts with you."

She did but he knew not to read into it. Anne-Marie had gone a little crazy after her divorce and wasn't coping well. Still, she was a good person. Misguided at the moment in what she wanted out of life, but good. He only hoped her recent stint of questionable decisions wouldn't come back to haunt her.

"We're just friends. It's all innocent." Unlike his time with Shelby. He didn't want to discuss his lack of interest in his boss with his younger sister, not when there were more important topics to talk about. "Was that Shelby on the phone?"

Alex physically drew back, her eyebrows shooting up faster than a rocket. "Yeah, it was. Why do you want to know?"

CHAPTER TWO

LUKE REALIZED the switch in topics was too abrupt. The last thing he needed was his globe-trotting journalist little sister on the hunt for a story to get the rest of the family off *her* back for gallivanting around the world all the time. She might be a travel reviewer now, but she'd been a tattletale first. "I heard you talking and thought I caught a mention of her name."

Alex made a face and sighed heavily. "The traitor went home. She was supposed to hang out with me after her shift, but she isn't feeling well. She's been a wreck all week getting the club and the staff ready for the wedding. You know how uptight she gets. She's such a perfectionist, especially if things don't go according to schedule."

Yeah, he remembered. But stressed or not, if Shelby was as sick as she'd been in the rose garden, she shouldn't have driven herself anywhere. Knowing he wanted to discuss that night, he wouldn't put it past Shelby to drag herself to her car by her fingernails if she had to.

Couldn't they approach what happened like two adults? Two consenting, it-was-a-great-night-and-let's-do-it-again adults?

Dream on, loser. You'll always be the geek and she'll always be the beauty queen.

Albeit a reluctant one. Pat Taylor-Brookes had entered

Shelby into every pageant in the state until Shelby had gotten bold enough to flat out refuse to go. He still remembered watching the drama unfold on his parents' lawn after Shelby had snuck out and hidden in Alex's room until Pat had come after her. Man, Shelby's mother was a piece of work. Hard to believe she gave so selflessly to others that she'd do five-K walks for her clients and volunteered to cut hair on the hospice ward.

Luke shook his head. He didn't want an embarrassing scene and knew how much Shelby hated being front and center. Was that why she'd avoided him? Since their night together the only time he'd seen her had been in public.

But what about not answering his calls? He eyed Alex's cell phone. Would Shelby answer if he made the call using his sister's phone? "Didn't Mom give you the no-cell-phone lecture this weekend? I heard that thing vibrating during the ceremony."

Her chin lifted. "She told *all* of us, if I remember correctly, but I've seen you check your iPhone *at least* a dozen times. If not for this big deal you keep talking about, Mom would've confiscated it. Now," she said, crossing her legs as though settling down to do business as Queen Pest, "why are you asking about Shelby again?"

Again? Right. He'd mentioned Shelby just that morning in a bid to fish for info. *Way to play it cool.* "I found her getting sick a bit ago."

"You went into the ladies' room? Oh-ho, what I wouldn't give to have seen that!"

"She was in the rose garden, not the ladies' room," he clarified, pulling at his collar. Used to cargo shorts, T-shirts and flip-flops, he hated having to wear a tie. "And you wouldn't have wanted to see anything. Trust me."

Alex wrinkled her nose at the image. "She did sound miserable, poor thing. She said she'd picked up that nasty bug going around. But let's stay on topic. To see her getting sick in the rose garden, you'd have had to follow her there." Her smile turned sly and mischievous. "Did you?"

Like a dog with a bone. "I did," he admitted but was quick to add, "because she looked sick. What would you have done?"

Luke could tell by his sister's expression that Shelby hadn't shared the news of their night in his hotel room. That was good—because the less Alex knew, the better. But it also confirmed Shelby's lack of interest in him. His sister and Shelby had been friends from the moment they met. If it was important, they talked about it.

Meaning he wasn't important enough to mention?

"No, of course not. But if she was sick, why did you leave her?"

Now that he thought about it, he remembered the way Shelby had practically growled her request for a drink. Then ordered him to go? Sick or not, she'd sent him off in order to make her getaway. *And you fell for it.* Luke lifted the bottle like the idiot he was for believing Shelby's lie. "She wanted something to drink."

"Oh." Alexandra chewed her lower lip and studied him a long moment before looking down at her manicure.

Wait a minute. Was that disappointment? Was he actually reading her right? "What?"

"Oh, nothing. It's just you had that look again and I thought maybe…" Her hand fluttered like she was flicking away the thought. "Never mind. I'm being stupid."

"What look?" For a guy already feeling at a disadvantage where the female race was concerned, this was the kind of detail and fault he needed to be aware of.

"It's silly but— The weird one. The same one you wore the last time we were all home. You walked around in this fog and no one could figure out why."

He knew exactly why. The sight of Shelby for the first time in several years had knocked him for a loop. One glimpse of her long legs and rounded hips was all it had required. That, and Shelby's too-wide smile. Every time he'd seen it he'd found himself smiling.

Then he'd noticed the hives and realized her smile was a fake. She'd been upset over something, so when the opportunity arose, he'd pulled her aside and…the rest was history. "Work has been intense lately, that's all," he said to explain *the look*. "We're almost ready to present this project and things are tense. But while we're playing Twenty Questions, why don't you answer a few? Like why you're out here and not in there with Mom and Gram?"

Alex immediately squirmed and fussed with her hair, guilt written in every movement. He knew movements, actions and reactions. Details were everything in his job. As Lead Creative Director overseeing the entire game development team, every aspect from the original concept ideas, sketches and storyboards to the final touches before a video game was presented to the purchasing powers in charge fell under his umbrella. And one of the reasons he was so good at what he did was his unshakable stance that success was in the details.

The little things gamers probably couldn't identify technically were the very things that got people buzzing about a particular game. Like water rippling as someone walked through it, the murkiness of a bog or the sight of mist rising above water cascading over a cliff, or the ruffled tips of ivy leaves and the deep grooves in the bark on the trees. He made sure everything was visually enhanced and rich in color and texture, detail—otherwise he sent it back to the proverbial drawing board.

"There you went again. You're in Game World, aren't you?"

Once a geek, always a geek. But he could flip between worlds easily and Alexandra's comment did the trick. "Answer the question."

"I needed some fresh air."

Hot, humid, stifling late-August-heat type air? "I see."

"Don't take that tone with me. You sound like Mom."

Her irritation brought a smile to his lips. "Mom bugging you about why you didn't bring David?"

Disgruntlement marked her features. "Yeah. Now shut up about it." His sister released a long, loud groan. "If you love me at all, you will not mention his name in front of her. Mom has this idea that David and I are a perfect match because we're both interested in travel."

"So what's the problem?"

"Hello? Weren't you the one just talking about Anne-Marie being your boss? I love my job. I love the traveling and seeing new places, new countries. David, on the other hand, is an armchair traveler. He's all for reading about it, but he rarely leaves the state." She shook her head in bemusement. "What kind of match would we be? He's a homebody while I have yet to find a place I can't leave."

He thought of the two trips he'd made to Japan and the headaches associated with travel. "You don't get tired of living out of a suitcase?"

"Sometimes, yeah," she admitted softly. "I realize not everyone would like being on the go constantly, but why not see the world while I'm young? The fact I get *paid* to do it makes it all the better."

Alexandra straightened her watch, and he noted that while it was slim and feminine in style, it had three different time zones on the mother-of-pearl face.

Luke opened the bottle of water he held, offering her a drink, which she declined. "Mom alone is one thing, but I'm getting the impression there's more to the story. Good old Dave is putting pressure on you, too?"

Alex blushed and continued to fiddle with the sleek silver. The Celtic pattern of the band links on either side of the face caught his attention. It was the perfect detail to add to Mystic Magi. The door leading into the Scribe's Sanctuary had always struck him as being too plain, but nothing had seemed particularly right for such an important passageway.

"Don't get me wrong, David's great, but I'm seriously not interested. I just need to figure out a way of getting Mom *and* David to back off. Shelby says I need to lie low and take a few consecutive trips until they both lose interest."

"Might work for David but I doubt it'll work for Mom. Parents don't usually lose interest in their children." Especially not their mother. Marilyn Tulane worried about her brood, her single offspring more than the others because they were "all alone." She made a point to call them every Sunday, and Wednesday evenings after church, and sent an e-mail or forwarded a cyber joke almost daily. "Just keep doing what you're doing. They'll figure it out. And if David gives you any major problems, let me know."

His little sister shot him a surprised look that screamed *What would you do about it?* Coming from Nick, Garret or Ethan, she wouldn't have blinked an eye, but him? Mom must have forgotten to mention he'd combated his sedentary lifestyle by taking karate. He was now a fourth-degree black belt with the muscle strength and abilities to prove it. Good ol' Dave wouldn't know what hit him.

"No, thanks. I don't want any more of my family involved in my personal life. I think I'll take Shelby's advice and snatch up all the long-distance trips I can get."

He opened his mouth to go into lecture mode about her staying safe while she worked, but figured he'd get shot down. "Just be careful."

"I am. It helps that I travel as myself and write under a pen name. So long as David doesn't do something stupid and tell people who I am, I'm good. Some of my reviews have been less than complimentary." Alex rubbed her forehead. "Do me a favor, though. If I ever even *consider* getting married, lock me up in one of those games you create and throw away the key."

"You don't think that's a bit drastic?"

"Not when Mom's looking at me the way she is. I'm not a kid anymore."

"You'll always be the baby to us," he teased, knowing he'd get a rise out of her.

"That's even worse. It's only fair that I should be *the last* to have to deal with this pairing-up business. You and Ethan are dateless today, too, but I haven't heard anyone ask either of *you* why. It's such a double standard."

"Most women get into these things and want a date for a wedding."

Alex snorted. "They should know by now that I'm not most women. And you'd better be worried about how you're going to handle Mom. She has grandchildren on the brain, and wants us all attached. With me traveling so much, you and Ethan will have her full attention."

Luke froze, the bottle halfway to his mouth. After several

beers at last night's bachelor party, their eldest brother had shared a bit of news. Ethan planned to head off to do some gallivanting himself.

Leaving only one bachelor for Mom to worry about. In trying to take her mind off Ethan, their mother would throw herself full tilt into Luke. Her first order of business would be to ask her prayer circle to add him and hopes for his future marital bliss to their list and from there the mountain would be moved. "Oh, man."

"See what I mean?"

Luke scowled and drank the water. He did not need that kind of attention. He wanted to get things settled with Shelby and the only hope he had of accomplishing that was to act discreetly, completely under the radar. He thought of how Shelby ignored him, and his blood pressure rose. Shelby regretted what they'd done. He got that. But couldn't they still be…friends? She was too involved in their family for the others not to eventually catch on that something had happened between them if she kept acting the way she was. They had to reach an understanding, set aside the awkwardness and move on.

Maybe he'd go check on her after the reception was over. God knows he didn't want to be in the house after Ethan announced his plans for the future.

Alex had pulled a compact from her purse and quickly repaired her lipstick. "I suppose we need to get in there before Mom sends out a search party. The band's started. Let's go dance."

The plastic bottle popped in his hand. "You want to dance with me? Should I be flattered?"

She lifted a shoulder in a shrug. "Not particularly. It's either you or cousin Richard."

Staring at her and knowing there was a punch line coming, Luke was reminded of why little sisters were often a pain in the ass. "And?"

"He's been taking dance lessons. I picked you because you dance worse than I do."

Thinking of the many dance clubs his last girlfriend had dragged him to during the six months they'd dated, Luke stifled a laugh. His little sister was about to learn how much things change.

SHELBY SPRAWLED sideways across her bed, her damp hair hanging over the edge. She rolled onto her back and stared up at the ceiling.

Nothing. Not even a trace of the lingering nausea she'd had ten minutes ago when she'd dragged herself out of the shower, yanked on clothes and flopped onto her stomach like a dying fish.

Just relax. If you do, the stupid hives will go away and so will the upset stomach.

A bug really was making the rounds at work so it could be that, but she knew her sickness and the hives decorating her skin were more likely due to Luke's return. So maybe she'd had her bout of nervous Nellies over facing Luke and it was over?

That had to be it. It couldn't be anything else.

Sure about that?

Her heart stopped, then began pounding a fast, frantic rhythm, and a muscle spasm made her eyelid twitch. She lay frozen, her body tensed until she remembered her doctor's words. No, it wasn't anything else. Good grief, it couldn't be. The physician had said it would be next to impossible for her to ever have children.

Next to impossible doesn't mean impossible.

Shelby shot up, muddling her way through her spinning senses as she frantically tried to count back the days. Everything scrambled together and she shook her head, desperate to remember last month without having to dig out the journal her gyno insisted she keep. It didn't work. She scrambled for the journal on her bedside table, noticing for the first time that the book was red. How appropriate.

She flipped through the pages until she found the entry. Last month she'd had a light period, spotting really, and cramps. Pain, fatigue and achiness. Not unusual with her diagnosis of ovarian cysts, endometriosis and fibroid tumors. Some months were light, others extremely heavy. Basically it boiled down to pain, always pain.

Her monthlies were never the same. Sort of like a walking flu combined with the period from hell that made her feel like she'd been hit by a truck. Stitches in her side. Sharp, stabbing jabs that came out of the blue and took her breath, stopping her in her tracks because it hurt to take a step. The result of one of the many cysts on her ovaries bursting.

The cysts. That's it! After the cysts burst, she sometimes felt sick. Once she'd even passed out.

Shelby inhaled and breathed a gusty sigh of relief. Oh, thank goodness. Of course that was it. Fingering the thick sheets of paper, she gave herself time to recoup by scanning the entries.

Three months ago she'd had a heavy period that had left her in bed the entire weekend. It was so bad that she'd called and made an appointment with her gynecologist, but the quickest they could get her in was two weeks later, the day of Garrett and Darcy's rehearsal dinner.

The same day you slept with Luke.

Her heart went turbo again because her mind flashed back to that night.

"Oh, my—" She clamped a hand over her mouth and raced for the bathroom, dry heaving into the toilet. Staring into the depths, she moaned because—

The timing was right.

CHAPTER THREE

SHELBY LEANED against the bathtub and gaped at the journal she'd hauled into the bathroom with her. It couldn't be. She knew better. Next to impossible meant *extremely unlikely* to happen. As in it couldn't happen, *wouldn't* happen. It was a *cyst*.

She'd gone to her gyno before reporting to work, and in a somber meeting in his office the man had explained her situation and how her condition was progressing. Like she couldn't tell by the pain and symptoms? But she was only twenty-eight, and to have a doctor say a total hysterectomy was the next step— What do you say to that? She'd reeled from the news, growing angrier and more upset as the day wore on.

But how could she go from being a twenty-eight-year-old in need of surgery because her reproductive organs looked like a battle-scarred war zone to—to possibly being *pregnant?*

"You can't," she whispered, the sound echoing off the tile floor. "Get real, Shel. It's a cyst. You've got enough things to worry about without adding hysteria into the mix."

She was a worrier. Always had been. But her capacity for worrying was already overextended with her job, her plans for the beautiful building in need of backbreaking work before it could reach its potential and the never-ending drama of her parents. Now Luke and this?

A painfully high-pitched laugh escaped her chest. "You're *not* pregnant, because you can't *get* pregnant. Why are you doing this to yourself?"

Why, indeed. But what if it wasn't a cyst or the flu? Her inner worrywart reared its ugly head and Shelby knew she wouldn't get an ounce of rest until she had a definitive answer.

She used the tub as leverage to pull herself up and hurried to the kitchen to grab her purse. Quite a change from when she'd dragged herself into the house. She'd go to the pharmacy and—

Have everyone in town talking about you?

Oh, crap. She paused on the threshold of the door. No way could she purchase a pregnancy test in Beauty. It would take an hour, tops, for word to spread all over town.

Shelby chewed her lower lip and decided her best option was to drive to the next town over. Maybe even the one on the other side of that. It was the only way of keeping the news she'd had sex and there was a *possibility,* slim though it was, that she might be pregnant quiet.

And if she got sick along the way?

More doubts flooded her brain, and she could feel the tension growing inside her, the exasperating itch of the hives that appeared whenever she stressed. What on earth would she do if she was pregnant?

You should've thought of that before you took the chance.

Shelby grumbled to herself as she locked up. "You're not pregnant. You're *not* pregnant. One night with Luke couldn't possibly—" She lifted her hand and covered her gaping mouth.

Bad enough that she'd slept with him, but if she was pregnant with his *baby?* Oh, what had she *done?*

She'd have to tell Luke. His family. Alex. And after working so hard to avoid Luke and not saying a word to Alex about that night, how could she suddenly appear with news like this?

For the second time that day Shelby collapsed into her car, the gentle *thud* of her head on the leather seat packing the force of a two-ton wrecking ball.

She wasn't pregnant, never would be, never could be. "You're getting nowhere, Shel. Save the drama for your mama and go get a test."

Then you can forget you ever slept with Luke and ruined everything.

LUKE PARKED the rental car behind Shelby's bright red BMW, amazed she still drove the sweet sixteen present from her parents. The car had been secondhand when she'd gotten it, but she'd obviously taken good care of it. Not surprising with her perfectionist nature. She and Ethan had that in common. Both were neat freaks.

A dog barked in the field to Luke's left and disappeared into the trees. He followed the dog's progress, then his gaze shifted to the huge stone building Shelby had inherited. He whistled softly, impressed that Shelby had been able to land such a prime piece of real estate.

The mill house remained from the first logging/lumber business in the state, built by an Englishman who'd come to America in search of adventure. Using stone from the creek bed flowing down the mountain, the man had built the sawmill and powered it by the same water source, then cured and housed the wood inside the warehouse-size structure.

After being handed down for generations to the firstborn son, the last heir—a local banker—had no children to inherit the legacy. Apparently, the man had fallen ill six or seven years ago and liquidated much of his wealth, surprising everyone in town by giving this property to his longtime bank manager, Shelby's grandfather.

Shelby's grandfather suffered a massive heart attack soon after taking possession, so the land passed to Shelby. In the meantime, the banker continued to battle his illness alone.

Luke made his way around to the other side of his rental, noting the similarities between the mountain valley and Mystic Magi. He'd present his brainchild to Sony in a matter of weeks, but until this moment he hadn't realized how much his work resembled his Tennessee hometown.

Two walkways led to Shelby's house. A low, stacked-stone wall welcomed visitors and indicated the way to the front entrance, flanked by sunflowers of varying shades and sizes. Several birdhouses and hummingbird feeders were quite popular with their visitors, and a dog dish and water bowl were under the carport off the shed in back. Luke chose the second path, captivated by the colorful palette surrounding Shelby's house. He would have guessed her to have had a black thumb like Alex.

Along the way Luke noted arched windows and leaded-glass double doors had been added to the mill house to fully enclose it. Was Shelby converting it to a home? Made sense. The foreman's cottage, where she lived, was pretty small.

Distracted by the beautiful building taking shape nearby, Luke stepped onto Shelby's narrow porch and paused. Beyond the plain, glass-paned door, she paced back and forth, her hands twisted together at her waist. One glance at her expression revealed her agitation and—something else.

Shelby wasn't sick now. Which meant what? The thought of seeing him had made her sick?

Luke ground his teeth, his hand fisting around the sack

he carried. He didn't bother knocking and his anger ratchetted higher when the door automatically opened beneath his fingers. What woman didn't lock her house?

Shelby whirled in a rapid about-face, her hand flying to her chest. "Luke?"

He entered her kitchen and shut the door behind him. "You should lock your door."

"I usually do but I just— What are you doing here?"

"I came to check on you. You seem to have made a remarkable recovery."

She looked away, swallowing. "I—I am feeling better. I'm sorry about today—your shoes. I'll pay to have them cleaned."

"Don't worry about it." He watched her closely, trying to figure out her mood. "You look flushed. Are you sure nothing is wrong?"

"It's the heat."

Every muscle in his body tightened a little more.

Silence filled the house and Shelby gave him a weak, nervous smile.

"Shelby, what's going on?"

"I don't know what you mean."

Her teeth sank into her lower lip, drawing his attention there. Memories of that night swept over him and he stifled a groan. Despite his irritation with her, he remembered exactly how her mouth felt, tasted. The way her pale skin gleamed in the light and the husky way she'd breathed his name when she'd sunk on top of him.

Shelby lifted a hand and tucked her hair behind her ear, her gaze not quite steady on his but she sure tried hard for it to be.

"Luke, I owe you an apology. I've handled what happened very poorly. I should've woken you, said something or left a note. But I had to get to work and—well, I'm sure you've realized by now that night was a huge mistake and never should've happened?"

He moved closer, drawn even though he knew he'd be better off to keep his distance. "It didn't feel like a mistake."

"But it was. I know you're probably angry, and you have every right to be. I should have—"

"Returned my calls?"

"Not slept with you," she countered, her tone soft but firm. "I'm sorry."

"Tell me why you think it shouldn't have happened." He could think of several reasons if he tried, but that was beside the point.

"Because I don't—" she closed her eyes briefly "—*do* that sort of thing."

Thank God. He'd hate it if that was her MO.

"Especially not with guys like you."

Guys like him? Damn. In a heartbeat he was transported back to his supergeek days in high school. He massaged the back of his neck and processed that. Knowing what she meant was one thing, but hearing it? "But you did do it. More than once." Petty, sure, but he liked being able to remind her of that.

Shelby held up her hand, regret pinching her features. "That came out wrong. I meant I shouldn't have slept with you because you're Alex's brother and it's made things…awkward. And it was wrong. I shouldn't have led you on that way."

"We had a great night together." The pulse at her throat beat visibly and he noted it picked up speed as he moved closer, near enough that he smelled the coconut scent of her hair. "Are you denying that?"

"I'm trying to apologize. That's all. Once I realized how

stupid it was to endanger our friendship and what was at stake, I felt awful. I shouldn't have behaved that way and I'm sorry I did."

Sorry…or scared that she'd lowered her defenses with him and let go? Luke stared into her summer-green eyes and tried to muster some of his twin's aloofness and cool attitude. Nick had a knack for getting to the bottom of things, an amazing feat considering his brother wasn't all that talkative. "I can think of a lot of things that night was, but a mistake isn't one of them."

Shelby shook her head, golden strands in her brown hair glittering beneath the old-fashioned lights of the kitchen. "We're practically strangers."

"We've known each other since we were children, Shelby. That hardly rates us as strangers."

Her chin lifted and she hugged her arms around her waist, closing herself off. "That makes it worse. We hadn't seen each other in years. I'd had a bad day and you… I turned to you for comfort, but it doesn't change the fact that I shouldn't have used you that way."

He set the bag of food on the closest countertop and leaned against the cabinet. "What we did was mutual. I didn't mind."

"*Luke*. Stop saying stuff like that. It shouldn't have happened."

"We'll have to agree to disagree there." He paused, studying her. "Unless there's something you're not saying? Something else you're upset about?"

Shelby blinked, swallowed. In less than a second the color drained from her face, but just as quickly it rushed back into her cheeks and scorched them with rosy intensity, highlighting the red blotches on her neck and what he could see of her upper chest. Her hives. Yeah, they were more than strangers. How else could he recognize her stress reactions? Know what they were? But was her upset about more than having to face him?

In a heartbeat he was reminded of the other reason he'd come to see Shelby. His sister-in-law Darcy's whispered comment to a newly expectant cousin at the wedding reception had cut him off at the knees. *"That's how I knew I was pregnant. One minute I was fine and the next I was sick. And my chest! Oh, my goodness, I jumped two bra sizes almost immediately."*

Shelby lifted a trembling hand to her temple and rubbed. "Luke, I don't mean to be rude, but I have a lot of stuff to do and I'm still not feeling well and—"

"Did anything else happen that night?" His gaze dropped to Shelby's chest and shot back to her face in surprise. *It's all in the details.* "Shelby…are you pregnant?"

SHELBY FOUGHT the sensation of the walls closing in on her. Seconds passed that seemed like hours. The question left her literally shaking in her shoes. She didn't know. Not for sure, because she was too afraid to take the stupid test. So how could he know?

It's a guy thing. You didn't use protection, remember?

Stupid, stupid, stupid mistake. But there wasn't supposed to have been a need for it!

Luke's tall frame took up too much of her small kitchen, his brooding demeanor not at all his typical, easygoing self. His gaze was direct, never wavering from hers, and for a guy who'd blushed every time he looked at her as a teenager, the change to quiet, confident male was disconcerting.

"Shelby?"

Denial was instant. She automatically shook her head, her attention fastening on the navy, black and silver swirling pattern printed on Luke's medium blue T-shirt. He'd looked wonderful in his tuxedo but this casual, tanned and muscular version of Luke was infinitely more appealing. He was Clark Kent but sexier.

The silver in the shirt's design gleamed at her, making her remember the silver-gilded mirror beside the hotel-room door and the way she'd watched their image in it. Heat flooded her insides and she looked down only to find herself fascinated by the shredded holes in the legs of his loose-fitting jeans. He had bony knees, strong thighs. *And a taut butt that looked great in wash-worn denim.*

Luke wasn't nearly as developed as his weight-lifting twin, but his upper arms bulged when he moved, and his chest and abs beneath the shirt were well defined. And he'd had no problem with her weight that night when things had gotten…strenuous.

"Are you sure?"

She swallowed back a moan of unease when a knot formed in her belly. "I'm not pregnant."

It was true. It *had* to be true. Being pregnant would mess up everything, just like her impending surgery would. Time, money. She had plans that would be totally screwed up if—

"Have you taken a test?"

Her focus automatically shifted to the logoed brown sack on the table. Before she could even think of taking the few steps to reach it—*hide it*—Luke had the pharmacy bag in his hand. He watched her closely as he reached inside.

"Luke, it's not what you're thinking. It's just—"

"Just what?" His jaw locked tight when he pulled the box

free and saw what it was. His dark blue gaze hardened. "I take it this means no?"

Couldn't anything go right today? Did they have to do this now? "It's not like that." Oh, yeah, that sounded convincing.

"Then how is it? You must think you are, or you're in serious doubt. You weren't going to say anything?"

"I'm *not*."

"Then why do you have this?"

Because I'm scared. Because I can't believe we did what we did. Because if I am, it's all my fault and the timing sucks and Alex will hate me. She lowered her lashes and concentrated on staying calm.

"You can't ignore what happened or wish it away, Shelby."

Oh, but she could try. She didn't acknowledge his words, but she didn't deny them either. She'd most certainly wish it away if she could. They'd played together as children, picked on each other as preteens and gone their separate ways in high school since she and Alex ran with the popular crowd while Luke had struggled to find his way in the shadow of Nick's many escapades and rebellions. But with one kiss she'd burst into flames, the chemistry intense and completely unstoppable. How did that happen? How was it possible? "The test is to set my mind at ease. Women take these all the time."

He stared at her like she'd grown two heads. "Yeah, they do—because they think they might be *pregnant*. You've been sick a lot like today? Morning sickness?"

Would he just lay off? Refusing to get into details as to all the reasons she couldn't be pregnant, she focused on facts. "The chances are slim to none. Okay? Stop worrying." Her attempt at a breezy laugh came out as a strained wheeze. "You know how I am. I live for schedules so I can stay on top of things, and I've been really stressed lately. Sometimes my periods aren't normal and combined— That's why I bought the test. See? You have absolutely nothing to worry about."

"And you sound like you're trying to convince yourself." Luke didn't move. "Fine, it's a precaution. So why don't you go take the test?"

Take the test? Now? "I'm not going to go pee on a stick with you hovering on the other side of the door." His gaze swept over her and left a trail of heat in its wake, reminding her that he'd seen her naked and made her moan with satisfaction. "I'm *not* pregnant!"

Luke looked surprised by her outburst, maybe because for the first time since he'd arrived, her words weren't calm or reassuring but instilled with a panic she couldn't disguise. Shelby crossed her arms over her chest and winced, noticing for the first time how tender her breasts were. She always got tender close to her period.

But wasn't that also a symptom of pregnancy?

Stop fretting over every little thing. You're turning into a hypochondriac.

"You obviously aren't sure." His dark head tilted to one side, his expression too shrewd. "There are things women have to limit. Caffeine and peanuts, fish."

Caffeine? Shelby lifted a hand and nibbled on her nail. So if she was pregnant, she'd have to go without caffeine? She lived on caffeine. How did anyone start the day without a jolt to get them going?

"Sweetheart, that night things were crazy and you said birth control was covered, but nothing is foolproof."

Sweetheart? The endearment sounded so natural the way Luke said it, another reminder of that night.

"A woman at work last year got sick and took a round of

antibiotics. Next thing she knew she was having kid number three. Go take the test, okay?"

It sounded so easy. Just take the test and be done with it. Simple. So why not do it?

Because he called you sweetheart. He wants more, you know that. That night, she'd rationalized the decision in the hazy, passion-dazed depths of her mind. Told herself that she and Luke could be together—just for one night—and everything would be all right. But as soon as it was over she'd known it was a huge mistake, that she'd lied to herself. Nothing that powerful was a good thing.

"Why is this happening?" she whispered softly, so low she hoped Luke didn't hear her. She stared at him, unable to believe he was in her kitchen and he held the stupid test and they were having this conversation. How could things change so fast?

"Shelby, we have to know what we're dealing with here and there's only one way to do that."

Concern, coaxing. Tenderness. Luke was such a nice guy. The most sensitive of his brothers, the most observant. Those traits were some of the many things about him that had always appealed to her. They were also the biggest reasons she should have stayed away from him.

"You know, regretting what we did has nothing to do with you," she heard herself say out of the blue. No easing into it, no pretty sugarcoating. He had to hear her, remember who she was. Remember who she wasn't. "Luke, you were wonderful. And the night was amazing. But *nothing* changes the fact that it shouldn't have happened."

"Except this," he said, holding up the box.

Her guilt grew. "It's just a precaution."

"Then stop putting it off and go take the test."

"But—"

"I'm not leaving until you do."

Luke didn't budge. Didn't blink. But at least he hadn't called her sweetheart again. Maybe he'd gotten the hint?

Shelby snatched the test from his hand.

CHAPTER FOUR

SHE MADE HIM WAIT on the porch.

Luke stared out at Shelby's backyard and breathed in the humid evening air. The stars overhead were so clear. Evenings in California were nice, but not like this. Here the sky looked like a charcoal-colored blanket sprinkled with glitter, some of the sparkles brighter than others.

Crickets and frogs created an orchestra of sound, and somewhere in the woods he heard what was probably a buck marking a tree with his antlers. Listening brought peace and comfort to his chaotic thoughts, and he made a mental note to expand and enhance the audio when Aiya travels through the forest to see the warrior prince.

A sudden tingling sensation made his neck prickle, and Luke turned to see Shelby. Wearing khaki pants and a snug brown T-shirt, she stepped onto the small porch off the kitchen, and just like that his body heated up like a nuclear plant about to blow.

How could they view what happened from such different perspectives?

Mars and Venus, buddy. "How long?"

"Two minutes." She tucked her hair behind her ear and dropped her arm to her side, the charm bracelet she wore pinging against her watch in a metallic melody.

"You still wear it."

She glanced down at her arm. "Your grandmother gives me a charm for my birthday and Christmas every year. It's special."

Since Shelby refused to make eye contact, he waited patiently, willing to keep his silence if it meant she'd stay put. She was the kind of woman who made a man take a second look, maybe a third. California was crawling with physically perfect women desperate for a break in their acting or modeling careers. But Shelby's face had a quality far more intriguing, an arresting mixture of spunk, quiet bravado and hard-as-nails gumption. One glance and a person knew Shelby wasn't a woman to be taken lightly, and the combination of beauty and brains was a killer.

Which was why the thought of her carrying his baby didn't bother him nearly as much as he knew it should, especially now that the shock had worn off. He used to wait for her to gift him with a smile, a glance, happy with whatever she'd give him. That night she'd kissed him, come on to him, and he remembered thinking that it was right, remembered thanking God that the wait was finally over.

"It won't be positive." Shelby glanced at him quickly, but looked away when she realized he watched her. "The odds are against it."

So she'd said. He got the feeling there was something more behind her words but decided not to press. It wasn't important. Figuring out how he'd convince her of the next step should the test be positive was. "Do you feel like eating? I brought soup and ginger ale to settle your stomach."

"You bought soda? That's quite a concession on your part. Thank you."

Shelby smoothed her hand over her neck and rubbed, softly at first then harder. How many times had he seen her do that?

Heard his mother and Gram fuss over her because when the hives appeared, it meant Shelby's stress level was too high.

"It's a beautiful night," he murmured, hoping to distract her long enough to get her to breathe. "The sky is different in the country. Must be the clear air and lack of lights."

His attempt worked. Shelby took a deep breath, lifted her face to the heavens and, for a moment, the rubbing stopped.

"I'll have to remember what you said about the lights. I don't want to ruin the ambience when I open the mill house."

That got his attention. "Open it? As what?"

A proud smile flashed, bright as the stars overhead. "A restaurant. *My* restaurant."

"I noticed the construction. That door is a work of art."

Her face softened. "It is beautiful, isn't it? I found it on an online auction. It used to be part of a monastery."

"When will the construction be completed?"

"In about six months. Maybe less if…everything goes as planned."

The moment the words left her mouth she apparently remembered the test. The scratching began again.

"I remember you, Alex and Gram in the kitchen, laughing and talking. I know you like to cook but I didn't know you wanted to own a restaurant."

"Neither did I until I worked at the diner. I started thinking about it because there were so many things I wanted to change but couldn't because it wasn't mine. Then my grandfather was given this land by his boss. He'd bring me out here and we'd explore. The whole place was pretty overgrown, but I'd make us a picnic and we'd just…talk about the possibilities." She laughed, the throaty sound a nice change from the panic of earlier, though threads of the emotion were still present. "I never told Alex this, but he *really* had a thing for your grandmother. He thought Rosetta was the perfect woman."

"Gram is pretty great."

Shelby smiled sadly. "Yeah, she is. Anyway, one day I mentioned wanting my own restaurant. Not long after that he passed, and he left the land to me with a note that told me to follow my dreams. I couldn't believe it."

Neither could anyone else. "Was your mom upset that he didn't give it to her?"

"Some." Her shoulder lifted in a shrug and she shot him a sheepish glance. "I don't know why he did that. I was surprised myself. Maybe Grandpa thought Mom would sell it or something."

"The memories of your picnics must have been special. He obviously wanted you to have it." And her parents had had a rough time of it. That was part of the reason Shelby had spent so much time at their house. Gram and his mother had known Shelby was better off with them than listening to her parents' marriage fall apart over and over again. How many times had they married and divorced? He'd lost track.

Shelby glanced at her watch and gulped nervously. "Luke, I didn't mean to ruin things between us, you know, our…friendship. I want you to know that."

Luke cupped her elbow in his hand and gently squeezed, feeling the chill on her skin despite the warm night air. "Nothing's been ruined. I don't regret what we did. I loved making love to you."

He shifted his stance against the porch railing and tugged Shelby closer. She didn't acknowledge the gesture, just stared out at her property, physically close but as emotionally distant as a woman could get.

Finally her eyes met his. "But things have changed. I don't want you to think that I don't *care* for you. I do, but—"

"But now we're here. And if that test is positive, we have to deal with it."

Shelby swallowed, the audible sound thick and telling, her eyes dry. The only time he'd seen her cry was at her grandfather's funeral, but even then she'd only released a tear or two before she'd squared her shoulders and taken her place following the casket, one step in front of the other like a good soldier.

She was strung so tight. He wasn't a psychologist, but he knew it wasn't healthy. Their night together was the result of her reaching a breaking point. What about the next time when he wasn't around? What would she do then? Would she repeat that night in June? Be with someone else?

The air whooshed from his lungs. He couldn't think of that now. Whatever had upset her had left her teetering on the edge of a cliff. She'd been angry, scared. Closemouthed as always about her personal business but desperate for contact, aggressive in her passion and needing to control what they did, how they did it. If there ever was a next time, if she ever reached that fierce, out-of-sync point again, he hoped she came to him. Prayed she came to him, only him.

Shelby checked her watch and his thoughts were cut short when she abruptly turned on her heel. Luke followed her into the house, wishing he didn't notice the sway of her hips and how the spot where her neck and shoulder met begged to be kissed.

She had apparently carried the little stick into the living room because she stopped by the couch and picked up the test, but she didn't look at it.

"No matter what the result is, it doesn't change anything."

They both knew better. She'd always been independent—she'd had to be from an early age—but why was she pushing so hard? Was it such a bad thing to be pregnant? The stigmas of old weren't relevant now. Women had babies out of wedlock all the time. Was there another reason she didn't want a baby?

Or was it that she didn't want the baby to be his?

His heart pumped ice through his veins. "Are you seeing someone? Is that why you've been avoiding me? Because of another guy?" Was that the cause of her upset that night? A fight with her boyfriend?

Her nostrils flared and two hot spots of color filled her cheeks. He'd insulted her and he called himself every kind of a fool for making the situation worse. Their single night together had been every man's fantasy, but he knew Shelby wasn't one of those women.

"What you must think of me," she drawled softly.

Luke grimaced at his blunder and reached out to touch her. She scooted out of range. He followed, trapping her between his body and the couch before she could go too far. He cupped her chin and lifted her head to stare directly into her eyes. "I don't think that of you, and I'm sorry for implying it. Shelby? I'm sorry. I'm a little out of sorts right now, not thinking straight. I know you wouldn't do that."

Seconds ticked by. Finally she accepted his apology with a nod, her lashes lowering protectively over her eyes. "I can't blame you. You didn't come home this weekend expecting this. It's my fault we're standing here right now."

"I wasn't exactly protesting."

Her mouth twisted into a sad smile. "I know what I told you about being safe, Luke. I thought…I was." She dug her toes into the carpet beneath their feet. "But regardless of what this says, I don't expect anything of you."

"If you're pregnant, I'm going to be a part of the baby's life."

"Because of duty? No, I don't want that."

She didn't *want* that? "I will do right by my child, Shelby."

"But—"

"Why are we arguing over this when we don't have the result? Look at the test. What does it say?"

She stared down at her hand but didn't uncover the results window.

Luke waited the two seconds he was able then took over. Her fingers were icy. Stroking gently, he held her hand cradled in his and used his thumb to push hers from atop its position over the clear plastic.

Shelby sucked in a sharp breath. "I'm…pregnant."

He stared at her bent head, at the red blotches on her skin and the pulse fluttering rapidly at her throat. He could only imagine what she was thinking, the surge of panic she probably felt at the shock of it. If his heart pounded any harder in his chest, it was going to burst through his skin.

But his brain was already working, trying to figure out a way to get her to understand he'd meant what he said. They were in this together and no way was she going to deny him his child. "No, Shelby. *We're* pregnant."

SHELBY STARED at the rectangular stick, Luke's words echoing in her head. *We're pregnant.*

It wasn't even possible. The test had to be wrong!

Luke pulled her into a one-armed hug and she let him, needing something to prop her up because her legs were shaking. *Pregnant?*

Frustration radiated from Luke and the arm around her shoulders was hard with tension. All caused by her stupid, stupid decision. But for a moment she closed her eyes, and with one inhalation the scent of his cologne and the August day seeped into her, calming her. When she opened her eyes and saw the test still gripped in her hand, reality came crashing down on her like a tidal wave. Pregnant. Single. With a screwball family and Luke— Oh, Luke. She hadn't just messed up her life, her plans, she'd messed up his, too.

"Shelby, it's going to be okay."

"Of course it is," she said, trying to instill confidence in her tone. She had to think of the positives. She had a home, a good job. Her parents might not be together and her mother might be difficult to handle on a good day, but they would help her all that they could. Of course it would be okay. She'd make it okay.

Somehow.

One trip to the doctor will prove the test wrong. It's a mistake.

Because how could she be pregnant? How could her doctor have *told* her such a thing was next to impossible if it wasn't true?

She could hear Alex ranting now about health care in small towns and— Oh, Alex was going to freak!

Shelby extracted herself from Luke's embrace and paced away from him, stopping only when she reached the window and could go no farther. She was too hot, her clothes too tight, the room too small. She had to deal with this in an adult, mature way when all she really wanted to do was scream *no, no, no* like a sleepy toddler whose balloon had blown away.

It's not true.

"Calm down before you hyperventilate."

She pressed her forehead against the glass and relished the clarity brought by the cool pane. Think. She had to think.

"I'm fine." She wouldn't be able to get in to see her doctor until Monday and that was nearly thirty-six hours away. She'd be certifiable by then. Pregnant?

Saying it over and over again isn't making it go away.

But how could it be true? "We need another test." She nodded slowly, firmly. Why hadn't she thought of that? She'd take another test and when it was false, she'd know the first one was a mistake. Doctors didn't tell women they couldn't have children unless it was true. "They had a two-pack at the store but I thought— I'm going to go get one. Two out of three, you know?"

She crossed the room to get her purse, but Luke snagged her arm.

"Everything's closed now."

She couldn't meet his eyes. Couldn't let herself see the tenderness and worry and rock-steady strength she knew she'd find, because she'd wind up turning to Luke for comfort again when that's what had gotten them to this point. "There's a twenty-four-hour pharmacy in Pierson. I'll go there." Unbidden, her gaze shot to his face. His expression was one of solemn patience, tolerance, which spiked her blood pressure even more.

"Shelby, the test was positive. According to the box, they have a *ninety-nine-point-eight-percent* accuracy rate."

The room shifted beneath her feet. She managed to stay upright, but only because Luke held on to her. The instant she knew she wouldn't fall on her face, however, she loosed her arm and turned back to the window. "How can you be so...calm?"

"You're scared enough for both of us."

"I'm *fine*." Her lashes lifted to his reflection in the window. Luke apparently thought she couldn't see him as he ran both hands over his head and down his neck where he squeezed. He was trying to keep his cool for her, but she'd bet he wished now he'd run in the opposite direction that night. She certainly did. "I'm sorry." *For coming on to you, for needing you. For messing everything up. If I would've been stronger I—*

"For what? Did you do this on purpose?"

She shook her head, her breath fogging the glass in front of her.

"Then don't apologize. It's okay."

Her laugh lacked humor, low and derisive. *Okay?*

Luke's hands settled on his hips. "Shelby, come on. It's a shock but…it's done. We've known each other practically all our lives. The next logical step isn't such a drastic one if you think about it."

Shelby scratched the top of her hand. She got the feeling her version of logical and his were two totally different things. Logical to her meant parting ways before things could get any worse.

She'd thought about the concept of marriage all her life. How could she not examine every aspect of it when her parents were so good at marrying but so lousy at making it work? No, if Luke meant the next logical step was marriage, he was in for a surprise. "Let's not get ahead of ourselves here."

Luke stiffened, his dark head lifting. "Ahead of ourselves? You're carrying my baby."

She swung to face him, searching for a way to convince him and knowing there was only one. With Luke she couldn't be soft, couldn't be kind. Bluntness was the only way to get him to see what she already knew. "A baby who is an *accident*." Her voice roughened, lowered, when she saw him flinch just slightly. *Oh, Luke.* "I don't mean to be cruel, but the truth is we're talking about the product of a one-night stand, not a love child." Her voice cracked, but she didn't pause. "I'm the one who told you not to worry about protection. This is my fault and I take full responsibility for what's happened. There is no next step."

Luke paced across the room, back again, his long strides sharp and heavy on the tile floor. "There were two of us in that room that night. I could've ignored what you said and gone downstairs and bought what we needed but I didn't. We're both responsible for this." His jaw locked, Luke quickly glanced at the clock on her wall and glowered.

"Do you have plans with your family?" She could only hope. Maybe then he'd leave and she could go get another test and—

"No. I was checking the time because I have a red-eye to California." Swearing softly, he took a step toward her, his hands lifted, palms out. "Shelby, come with me."

Shock flooded her. "What? Where?"

"To California," he said, moving slowly until he stood before her. "We need to talk this out and make plans before our families get involved. You know we do. I'd spend a few days here but I can't. The company I work for is in the final stages of perfecting a new game for Sony. It's a huge deal and I have meetings this week that I can't miss."

"Then go." He stared at her, incredulous and angry and losing patience fast, but she didn't care. Go with him? She was reeling as it was. How did he expect her to cope any better with him hounding her and talking about the *next logical step?* She felt the pressure, the expectation. But everything she worked for, everything she'd tried to achieve, was at stake.

He lifted his hand and touched her hair, smoothed it away from her face. "I can't leave you like this."

Her chin lifted. "The world doesn't stop spinning when these things happen." And neither could hers. She wasn't the type to collapse into a heap of tears at the first sign of trouble. Hives, maybe, but not tears. Tears were her mother's way of coping, getting attention, help—the more the better.

But not Shelby. She had plans, things that had to be done. Regardless of what the test said, of whether it was positive or not, those plans hadn't changed. If anything, it meant she had to work harder to prepare for what was to come. Work harder, so that when the gossip started maybe somebody out there would say something positive instead of bringing up her family history.

Besides, pregnancy was a physical process. Carry the baby for nine months then give birth. She had time. The restaurant would open as scheduled. She'd get it up and running and—

You expect to work eighteen-hour days pregnant?

She'd find a way.

"I know it doesn't stop, but we can make it slow down for a few days while we come to terms." Luke tilted his head to one side. "Shelby, be reasonable. If you come with me, you can hang out at my place, swim in the pool. Relax and sleep in."

His eyes lowered to the hives on her neck and chest, and she fought the urge not to tug her collar higher, not to scratch.

"Wouldn't it be nice to take a few days to figure things out without having to deal with everyone here? Who saw you buy that test? Saw you getting sick today or maybe saw us going to my room that night…" He edged closer, as if approaching an animal ready to bolt. "Shelby? *Shelby?*"

"What?"

"Stop scratching."

The skin of her collarbone burned from the scrape of her nails. She'd given in and hadn't even realized it. Shelby dropped her hand to her side.

"What can I say to convince you to come with me?"

"Nothing. I'm not going anywhere." Running away wasn't an option, no matter how appealing.

Luke's dark eyebrows pulled low. "I know it's a surprise to both of us, but the natural order of things is for us to—"

"*Not* do anything else we regret," she stated before he could say something crazy. "Luke, I can't go with you. I have a job, a house and responsibilities. What about my parents? They'd want to know where I was going."

"So tell them."

Absolutely not. The last thing she wanted was her mother involved. Oh, what had she done? One moment of weakness, one *night*— "No, not when we're not even sure it's true." She forced herself to focus on one detail at a time, ignoring Luke's glower. Why hadn't she bought the two-pack? "But even if it is, I don't have any expectations from you. I'm a big girl and I realize perfectly well that what happened that night was nothing more than two people sharing a bed."

He met her stare dead-on. "Is that right?"

"Yes, that's right."

Luke's dark blue gaze narrowed even more. "What if I have expectations?"

Then he wouldn't be like the majority of guys out there who played the field never to be heard from again. *He also wouldn't be Luke.* "We had a great night," she said softly. "But that's all it was. We don't have a relationship, Luke. You want me to come with you? See where you live? *Why?* Wait, let me guess." She held up her hand when he opened his mouth to speak. "It's because *you* expect *me* to give up my home, my family, my *dream*—" she turned her hand to indicate the window and the mill house beyond it "—and move to California?"

"I make a good living there, Shelby."

"And because you're the man, that's how things will be? No, I don't think so." She couldn't be so powerless, refused to be. What would happen when Luke realized what a mistake this was? When he walked out? She'd have given up everything and for what?

"Shelby..." Luke's tone lowered to one of coaxing tolerance. "I realize there are a lot of things we need to work out. But that's just it—*we* need to work them out before other people are involved. I know it's sudden and I'm not trying to insult your intelligence or your abilities. I know single women raise their children alone, but the thing is you don't have to. I want to take responsibility and do what's right for all of us."

Her mind focused on the inane fact that she'd never heard Luke say so much at any one time. A few words here and there, a shy, sexy smile that curled her toes, that blue-eyed stare of his that made her think he pictured her naked but—

Now's not the time to zone out, Shel. She couldn't help it though. As far as she was concerned the argument was over. She wasn't going anywhere, wasn't getting married. Wasn't pregnant. Period.

"You meant for it to be one night, I get that. I was even willing to accept that."

"Oh? Is that why you kept calling me even though I didn't call you back?" Her words made him sound like a loser. A flash of embarrassment crossed his face and her guilt grew. She didn't want to hurt him, she just wanted him to leave. Wanted him to realize he was better off if he did.

"The point is," he continued, softer now, "everything has changed. What about the baby's future? *Our* future? Is this really how you want it to be? The two of us fighting with each other? What kind of life is that for a kid?"

The kind she'd had. A hot, sickly flush crawled up her body, roasting her from the inside out. This was her childhood all over again. "This isn't how I want things." Her shirt stuck to her back and the itching got worse, but she forced herself not to scratch. If she'd learned nothing else over the years, it was how to control her feelings, her emotions. How to separate herself to keep from getting hurt or being disappointed. "Luke, this is…a lot to take in. I just want time to think things through before an *accident* becomes something worse."

"Something worse?" A self-deprecating smile stole over his features. "Meaning life with me?"

CHAPTER FIVE

SHELBY CLOSED her eyes and released the air in her lungs. "Don't read into what I'm saying. I just need time to think, time *by myself.*"

"How can I not read into things when you won't give me anything to work with here? I can't come back until next weekend, Friday evening at the earliest. If you come home with me we can—"

"No."

"Dammit, Shelby, you can't do this!"

She blinked, surprised by his language and the show of temper. Typically he was the last of the brothers to show any sign of anger and the sight and sound of his triggered her own. "I'm trying hard to keep *both of us* from making a bad situation worse. That's why I refuse to go to California with you and I refuse to talk about this more tonight. Go home to California, Luke. Please, do not let me keep you."

To prove her point, she walked over to the door and yanked it open.

Luke approached slowly, his expression tight. "Getting rid of me isn't the answer."

She didn't respond, just held the door and waited for him to get the point.

After a long moment of silence, Luke ran his hand

through his hair once more. "I'm not leaving until you promise me something."

Shelby braced for the impact of his deep blue eyes and wound up lost in their depths. Lined by thick, sooty lashes she saw the same fire and passion and intensity in Luke's gaze that she'd seen that night. The same awareness of her, despite what was taking place between them. It wasn't a good feeling. "What?" she managed to ask, her voice a dry, too-revealing rasp though Luke didn't seem to notice.

"Promise me you won't do anything, anything at all," he stressed pointedly, "without talking to me first."

The expression on his face, his tone, and the threads of worry and unease she heard, gave her pause. The rectangular panes of the door pressed into her back like a brand. If only he knew. But he didn't and wasn't that the point? That they weren't close? Practically strangers? "I'm not going to have an abortion, Luke." She caught the flash of relief on his features before she gave in to the urge to look away. Bad as things might seem, as bad as they *were,* she knew without a doubt she couldn't take that step. "If I'm pregnant—and regardless of what the test says, I have my doubts—it's not the baby's fault I screwed up."

Her words spurred him to action and his hand nudged her face upward until her gaze met his once more.

"Who's to say it's a screwup? There are worse things than two people like us bringing a child into the world."

Maybe there were but at the moment she couldn't think of any of them. Not a single one.

"Do I really need to remind you of what Gram would say?" He smoothed his knuckles over her cheek, tucked her hair behind her ear. "She'd say everything—"

"Happens for a reason," Shelby murmured simultaneously. How many times had she heard Luke's grandmother utter those words? Remind them that they had to have faith?

"So you shouldn't be saying our baby is a mistake. It's here, it's growing inside you and we have to take care of it."

He was right. She knew he was right. Even if she regretted that night—and she did—she shouldn't say it. What kind of woman said she didn't want to be pregnant when she didn't take the responsibility to keep it from happening?

A shallow one.

Instead of moving away and walking out the door, Luke lifted his other hand and cradled her face in his palms, one thumb stroking over her cheek in a lazy caress that belied the tension of the moment.

"Marry me."

Knowing Luke, his family, she'd realized a proposal was coming. But nothing had prepared her to hear the words on his lips. "Luke— No."

"Don't say no."

"No."

"Think about it. There are so many reasons why it would work."

She tried to pull away but couldn't with her back to the door and Luke in front of her. A rock and a hard place. "But there are so many more reasons why it wouldn't. Marriage isn't the answer. We'll have to figure something else out."

"It's the right thing to do and you know it," he countered. "We're not two kids too young to deal with this. We've known each other a long time, and we shared an amazing night. We can build on that. Give me a chance to convince you."

"I can't."

"Can't? Or won't?"

"It doesn't really matter, does it? The answer is the same."

Luke released a heavy sigh before he leaned in close and brushed his lips across her forehead. She stiffened, shocked at the boldness of it when Luke was usually so…reserved. She waited to see if he'd kiss her mouth next. What would she do if he tried?

His jaw was locked tight when he straightened, but other than holding her gaze with his beautiful eyes, staring at her like he wanted to probe the depths of her soul, Luke didn't attempt to kiss her again. He turned and stepped over the threshold voluntarily.

"I'll be back on Friday to settle this."

"I have to work Friday."

He hesitated on her porch, shooting her a look over his shoulder that was rife with anger and frustration, determination and promise. "I'll still be here."

SHELBY HAD KICKED HIM out of her house. Maybe not physically, but the whole opening the door and giving him the death glare had indicated she wanted him gone and wasn't going to take no for an answer. Since Luke didn't want her riled up any more than she already was, he'd left without argument. Mainly because he'd needed some breathing room himself since he felt ready to implode. A father. He was going to be a *father*.

His thoughts shifted to Nick. How had his brother done this on his own for the past nine years? Just the thought of being responsible for a baby scared him to death.

Luke stared into the amber depths of the drink he nursed at the Old Coyote and tried to come to terms with the fact that the woman going to give birth to his child in about seven months considered him and the baby a full-fledged disaster. Talk about hard on the ego.

"What's up with you?"

His older brother hiked himself up onto the stool beside him. Luke watched Ethan give the bar a cursory sweep for potential female interest and felt the same old surge of inadequacy that he'd felt as a gawky teen trying to follow in his cool brothers' footsteps. Ethan and Garret had both been wildly popular with girls. Nick, too. One look, one hello, and they were good to go. But him?

He dated in California, but every time he came home he fell right back into his old persona of being the nerdy brainiac. What was up with that? "Guess you never outgrow being a geek," he murmured to himself.

"What was that?" Ethan raised his voice to be heard in the din around them.

"Just hanging out." Luke took a sip and swallowed. "I'm crashing in Nick's old apartment until it's time for my flight. What are you doing here? I thought you were going to tell the parents tonight."

Ethan ordered a soda and shook his head. "I decided to wait until tomorrow morning, first thing. Mom's exhausted from the wedding rush. She needs a good night's sleep, not to have my antics dumped on her." He leaned back to peer into the billiard room. "Come on, I see an open table."

Luke shoved himself off the stool and followed. "It would've helped if you would've chosen somewhere peaceful."

"Niger is where I'm needed." Ethan shifted closer to Nick to not be overheard as they made their way to the billiard room in back. "Don't worry about me. I'll have a translator and an armed escort. I know what I'm getting into."

"I seriously doubt that, but I'm glad one of us thinks so."

Ethan's eyebrows rose high on his forehead. "That's cryptic." He grabbed a cue stick. "Come to think of it, you don't look so hot. Where'd you disappear to after the reception?"

"I needed to get out of the tux."

"Ah. Shelby still not giving you the time of day?"

Luke stiffened at the mention of Shelby, glad the two guys at the second table had finished their game and left the area before Ethan blasted that out for all to hear. What was it about family that gave them such clairvoyant power? "What do you mean?"

His brother slid him an all-knowing glance and continued to rack the balls. "Anyone with eyes could see you searching the crowd for someone today. And I noticed Shelby took off every time you got close."

Luke shrugged stiffly and grabbed the chalk to give his hands something to do.

"Was she really sick or just avoiding you after you hooked up last time?"

"How'd you know we hooked up?"

Another smirk. "Didn't."

Crap.

"Give me the chalk and break already."

Frustrated with himself because of his slip, Luke did as ordered and sent the balls scattering with a sharp crack. Two solids dropped.

"Aww, man."

This time Luke was the one smirking. Perfect. Ethan was anal in that he always wanted to play solids.

Luke rounded the table to position himself for the next shot.

"Just so you know, I won't say anything about how you'd better watch yourself because Shelby is Alex's best friend and practically a member of the family."

"You won't, eh?"

"Nope. I've been tempted myself."

Prepared to make his move, Luke barely stopped himself in time to save the shot. "How tempted?"

"Don't we sound possessive."

"How tempted?" he asked again, hating the hot rush of temper he could feel crawling up his neck.

"Calm down, lover boy. Not tempted enough to have Alex coming after me." Ethan chuckled, shaking his head as though in sympathy even though he was clearly cracking up at the thought of Alex walloping Luke.

He should've known better, yeah, but what guy would have turned Shelby down?

Ethan was right about one thing, the whole family had known Shelby since Alexandra's first day of kindergarten. Even then Shelby had been opinionated and bold. She was visibly off her game today due to the shock she'd received, but, man, she had pluck. Something Luke had always admired.

"Ain't got all day, Granny."

Luke jerked back to the present and ignored the taunt, lined up his shot and let a second or two of silence pass before he gave in to the temptation buzzing about his head. If anyone would be blunt with him, it was Ethan. "You think we'd be a mistake?"

"Now there's a loaded question." Ethan's gaze narrowed as he gave it some thought. "Depends. Let's look at your history—"

"You're not performing surgery on me. Just answer the question."

"I've learned histories are important," Ethan drawled with a too-serious doctor face.

Why hadn't he kept his mouth shut? Luke sent the cue ball flying and earned another turn.

"Let's look at this logically. You typically ask a woman out on a date, but only after you've gotten to know her fairly well and it's a given she'll say yes. If the evening is decent, you immediately go into a hot and heavy one-on-one. After a while, you break up, have a dry spell three times as long as the relationship, meet another woman and do it all over again."

Were all older brothers jackasses? Luke shook his head at himself and fudged the next shot just so it would give Ethan something to do rather than run his mouth. "Maybe I like quality over quantity and don't feel the need to spread myself around—unlike some people I know."

"Scientific studies show sex reduces stress." Ethan took his shot and missed. "Gotta be the stripes."

Luke laughed at his brother's declaration. "I thought I was bad. You've got issues way worse than me."

Ethan popped a handful of peanuts into his mouth and chewed, grinning unrepentantly. "Nah. My only problem is that no woman has ever met all my requirements."

"Requirements? As in a list? You actually have one of those?" It reminded him of Shelby. She made lists, too. One time she'd come to spend the weekend with Alex and had a list a mile long, marked out hour by hour on what she thought they should do. After she'd left, he'd made fun of Shelby for doing it and Alex had told him Shelby made lists whenever she got nervous. Turned out that was the weekend Shelby's parents had split up for the fourth time. The list had been her way of coping. Which meant she was probably at home right now writing out all the pros and cons of getting it on with him. He wished he could read it. Maybe then he could come up with rebuttals and know how to deal with her.

"Why not? A guy's gotta have standards. So, what'd you do? Ask Shelby to go steady?"

Luke made a face, unamused. No more throwing the game after that comment. He scowled and bent over the table. Some of Galaxy Games's staff meetings took place around a pool table in the break room. It was how they unwound and stirred stalled creative juices. And since he spent more time in those meetings than anyone else, he'd gotten pretty good over the years.

"Come on, I'm just giving you a hard time. What's going on?" Ethan grabbed another handful of nuts.

Luke sighed and took his pick between two shots. How sad was it that the only person he could talk to was the brother who hadn't had a serious relationship in his life? He should have gone to Garret's. "Shelby's pregnant."

Crack!

The balls smacking together and entering the pocket with force drowned out the sounds of Ethan choking. By the time Luke straightened and noticed, his brother was coughing and wheezing and drawing the attention of everyone around them. A bruiser of a guy moved in their direction as though to help, but Ethan lifted his hand and waved the guy off. He downed half of his drink and coughed some more, and since he was obviously breathing, the customers went back to what they'd been doing.

"Did you say *pregnant?*"

Luke glanced around to see if anyone had heard. "Keep your voice down."

Ethan continued to cough irregularly, his expression one of utter horror. The idiot. Luke should have known better than to tell a guy who couldn't keep track of his pants. Luke almost hoped Ethan would wheeze his way unconscious. At least then he'd stay quiet.

His brother finally hacked up a lung and cleared his throat.

"There's, uh, no good way to ask this but—" Ethan sent him a questioning stare "—is it yours? Ah, man, where are you going? Come on, give me a break, okay? I nearly died from the shock while you just stood there." Ethan closed the distance between them. "I'm only saying…maybe it's not?"

"The baby's mine."

"You mean you actually asked?" Ethan blinked a couple of times. "And you're still able to stand upright?"

"Knock it off."

He held up his hands in surrender. "Sorry. I'm impressed as hell. What'd she do when you popped that one on her?"

Shelby's face flashed in front of Luke's eyes and his gut knotted. "She looked…hurt, which made me feel like a jerk. I apologized, blamed the shock and then we started arguing about what to do now."

Ethan whistled softly. "Pregnant. It's like trying to imagine Alex with a kid." A slow smile spread over his face. A chuckle erupted next and before long Ethan was leaning on his pool stick and wiping away tears, laughing so hard everyone was staring again.

"What's so funny?"

"Don't tell me you don't remember? Come on, when the girls had to take the Life Sciences class and bring home those battery-operated babies? The things cried and peed at all hours of the day and night. You don't have nightmares about that?"

Now he remembered. But he also wished Ethan hadn't brought it up. Luke grabbed the chalk and nearly broke the thing in two when he shoved it over the tip.

"And then—" Ethan gasped for breath "—Shelby took hers back and *asked* for an F." That sent Ethan into another round of guffaws. "She stomped around all weekend thoroughly pissed because they had to drag the car seats and babies to the big dance."

The weight on Luke's shoulders increased. "It wet on her dress and ruined it."

"She didn't diaper it right."

"Like you'd know how?"

Ethan shrugged. "All I know is that teacher had a wicked sense of humor. Those babies kept us from having to kill one of those asses the girls chose as their dates for prom."

Luke squeezed the back of his neck and fought the sinking sensation swallowing him up. He'd forgotten about the Life Sciences class. Was that why Shelby had reacted so strongly to the news? Surely she'd spent time around babies—real babies—since then? Didn't most women want to have kids?

"Have to say, of all of us, I didn't think you had it in you."

Luke bit back the response that leaped to mind. He wasn't going to fall for Ethan's typical older brother baiting. He aimed and— *Aww, crap.* He'd missed by a mile. "Had what in me?"

Ethan snickered. "Thanks for the setup. Now don't take this the wrong way," he drawled, bending and squinting his eyes to focus in just so, "but out of all the brothers, you've always been the good one."

Oh, for the love of—

"That's not an insult."

Yeah, right. "You think?"

"Hey, you were the one who never got into trouble, unless it was to take up for Nick when *he* got in trouble."

"I wasn't a Goody Two-shoes."

"No, but face it, any test you bombed, any class you skipped, anything you did, was usually so Nick wouldn't be the only one in hot water. You, my brother, were the official golden child with all your good deeds and heroic acts of stupidity. Now this shocking turn of events of getting a woman—" Ethan lowered his voice "—with child? You bloomin' late or what?"

"It's not a joking matter, Eth."

Ethan took a long look at him and gave in with a sag of his shoulders. "Okay, okay, we'll get serious. She's in the family way. So the question is—what are you going to do about it?"

CHAPTER SIX

"I WANT TO MARRY HER. It's what any one of us would do." The noise of the restaurant faded into the background.

Ethan's eyebrows rose high on his forehead. "Shelby's agreed to pack up and move to California?"

Wanting to marry her so that they could raise their child together was one thing, but the reality was quite another and that hit home with Ethan's question. Shelby had made her feelings clear and wasn't going to step foot on California soil. So what to do now? Did she honestly believe the pregnancy changed nothing?

"She's turning the mill house into a restaurant."

Ethan looked surprised. "Good for her. That's a great spot for one. Not far from the highway, adjacent to the golf course. But that means she's wanting to stay here, am I right?"

How could he do the right thing when she'd never agree to move? "We postponed the decision making until Friday. I told her I'll fly home again and we'd decide then."

"You're coming home two weekends in a row after years of once-a-year visits? That's going to raise suspicions."

That it would. He studied his options on the table and bent when he made his choice. "When do you leave?"

"Eleven days."

"Then the official reason is that I'm flying back to attend your going-away party."

"*Niiice*. Glad to be of service. Make sure it's a good one."

Luke laughed wryly, amazed he could find anything funny at the moment. "Will do."

Ethan scored his next shot and moved near Luke.

"Shelby thinks it was a huge mistake. I was one of those pathetic losers that got left behind in the hotel room the morning after." The words came out of nowhere. Why had he just admitted that? And to Ethan?

Ethan stilled, but other than the telltale reaction to the humiliating moment, his eldest brother acted like it wasn't a big deal. "She steal your wallet? No? Ahh, see? Then you're one up on me. Having a great night in the sack and getting left behind after your wallet's gone, *that's* the ultimate in Loserville."

"That never happened to you."

"No, but that is the ultimate." Ethan turned his attention to the table. "Why does she think it was a mistake? Other than the surprising result, I mean."

Luke shook his head, wishing he knew the answer. The real answer, not the one she'd given him. "I know she's scared. I could tell."

"Can you blame her?"

"No. We took things too fast but it's too late to change things now. Now we just have to do what's right."

"She's got to be worried about Alex and the family, too. Shelby knows we love her, but that had to be weird, waking up next to her best friend's brother, you know?" Ethan spared Luke another glance. "Things were…good?"

Luke tensed. He might not have his older brother's vast experience but he knew a good thing when he and the woman he was with experienced it. Shelby had enjoyed herself. "Things were better than good."

"That's my boy. Can't say it's surprising after all those years you lusted after her. It's a wonder you didn't self-combust."

"It wasn't just me. She enjoyed herself, too." Her upset had changed with that kiss and Shelby had gotten so worked up, she'd taken over. Kissed him, stripped him and climbed aboard while he focused on bringing her pleasure. No way could her moans of satiation have been faked.

"Look, don't overthink her leaving. That morning had to have been awkward. You've liked her all these years but Shelby was probably feeling strange about it. She woke up, got embarrassed and bailed. You did the whole next-day-call thing women expect, right?"

"She wouldn't answer her cell so I left messages. I thought if nothing else we could dance at the wedding, talk, you know? But then she avoided me. After the accident happened with Matt, everything got shoved aside."

"Wait a minute. Are you saying that until tonight, you haven't talked to her since the day before Garret and Darcy's wedding? Didn't you try to call her again once you were back in California?"

Did Ethan really think he hadn't tried? "Of course I did," Luke muttered the words, careful to keep his voice low even though no one was around to hear. "I left a couple of messages but when she wouldn't call me back, I stopped calling."

"That's cool then. You tried. Sounds to me like you did your duty. It's her loss."

Luke pinched the bridge of his nose. "Not considering she's pregnant now, it's not. You're not helping."

Ethan tugged at his ear. "Sorry, little brother. Women are complicated creatures and I can't pretend to understand them. But I gotta tell you, this thing with Shelby doesn't sound good."

He'd spilled his guts to have that as a diagnosis? Luke pointed to the corner pocket.

"You know, it might help if you moved back here."

He'd just lined up and begun the hit when Ethan said that. As a result, Luke missed his shot by a good three inches. Move back? No way. Beauty was great to visit and would always be his hometown, but until he moved to California and began working in the industry he loved, he'd felt like he was being suffocated. It had been hard growing up as Nick's twin, never able to be himself because to do so made Nick's inability to do well in school and sports look worse. People, even his family, didn't understand the bond twins shared. When people compared them and Nick came up lacking in grades or whatever, Luke also felt the pain, and he'd always felt partially to blame. Who wouldn't, considering as kids Nick had told Luke he hated looking at him? That's why he'd started keeping his mouth shut in class, not doing his homework or doing it wrong.

Nick was finally happy and slowly rejoining the family fold. It was good, all good. But Luke wasn't going to inflict more pain on him by suddenly returning now. He'd found a home in California, a place where anonymity had given him strength and the courage to try new things. People, his peers, took him at face value because they didn't know his geek-ridden past, his family or his twin, and because of that, they didn't make comparisons. In California, he was his own man. He wore his hair longer, surfed, and donned shorts for work, something his father considered play and didn't take seriously. "I couldn't give up my job."

Shelby's accusations came to mind and guilt stirred. He wouldn't give up his life but he wanted her to give up hers? That was fair? Could he really expect her to relinquish her dream when he wasn't willing to do the same? "You'll keep this quiet, right?"

"Yeah." Ethan grabbed his soda for another drink. "Man, it's going to be tough, though. Things are going to get really interesting around here. Too bad I won't be here to see it all go down."

SHELBY PULLED DOWN the car visor and glanced at her appearance in the mirror. The noonday sun was especially harsh in detailing her faults. She'd tried to disguise the ravages of her sleepless night, but no way would her mother—a woman who believed concealer was second only to lipstick—not notice the bags under her eyes. It was inevitable. But if she canceled their standing Sunday lunch date, her mother was sure to come after her to find out why. She'd learned a long time ago she'd rather face the guillotine than the Drama Queen.

What would her mother think about the pregnancy? About her decision to remain single? Shelby snorted. Yeah, like she didn't know the answer to that.

She loved her mother with all her heart. Through the years Pat Taylor—also known as Pat Taylor-Brookes depending upon the current state of her relationship with her ex-husband—had made Shelby laugh, tended her scraped knees and done all the things mothers do.

From an early age Shelby had learned that love wasn't black and white but full of many, many shades of gray. She hated some of the decisions her mother made, the things her mother did, hated the way she dressed ninety percent of the time, but she loved her anyway.

Shelby got out of her car and slowly made her way to the door only to pause on the top step. Why were the blinds drawn? Her mother usually pulled the blinds first thing in the morning.

Unless it was a bad morning.

She dropped her head back on her neck and moaned. "Please don't let them be at it again." She couldn't handle that, not today. Maybe she should leave and deal with the fallout later? But if they *were* at it again, maybe the baby news would help?

"You can't tell her." Not if the blinds were any indication of her mother's mood. And not until she'd settled things with Luke. Besides, if she did tell her, her mother would likely declare a makeover emergency and vow death to the first person to call her *grandma* instead of offering up viable solutions to Shelby's problems with Luke.

She turned to leave but stopped. Who was she kidding? Luke was bound and determined to return to Beauty on Friday and she didn't doubt he'd tell his family first thing. They were close like that. He'd get them on his side and enlist their help in convincing her to do things his way. And that *so* wasn't going to happen. She'd have to figure out how to turn their old-fashioned thinking around. But still, the only thing that would make this awful situation worse was if Marilyn Tulane found out about the pregnancy before her mother. Her Drama Mama, a nickname coined by Alex, really would lose it then.

Three out of three tests aren't wrong. The doctor said so when you called the emergency line. It's time to face the music. Just blurt it out and be done. Maybe Mom can help.

Screaming from the rooftops would *not* help.

Shelby took a deep breath and used her key to open the door. The dining room and living room were empty. The kitchen wasn't. Her mother sat at the breakfast nook, staring at the newspaper spread out over the table in front of her.

"Hey, Mom, what's up? Why haven't you pulled the blinds?" That's it, tackle the subject right off the bat.

"Shelby!" Pat jumped in her seat. "It's lunchtime already?" She wiped at her eyes, her black mascara smearing across the tops of hot-pink acrylic nails.

She was crying? Oh, not good. "Yeah. Are we still on? I, um, kind of need to talk to you."

As the owner of Pat's Hair and Nails, her mother took her appearance very seriously. She never let anyone see her unless she was perfectly put together and clothed in the latest style. Which made the fact she still sat at the table in her robe and pink fuzzy heeled slippers all the more frightening.

"Whatever it is, it needs to wait."

Shelby braced for the flood. "What happened?"

Fresh tears appeared. "Oh, Shelby. Oh, baby… You're going to think I'm a horrible person."

Shelby dropped her purse onto the varnished oak table and pulled some tissues from a nearby box. Her mother released a pitiful wail and Shelby hesitated, then grabbed the whole container. The moment Shelby pressed tissues into her mother's hand, she latched on, her many rings biting into Shelby's skin.

It was going to be a long afternoon. "Are you and Dad fighting again? You didn't call him up and give him a hard time about my window unit, did you? I told you he was away on a job. He said he'd fix it as soon as he came home."

Her mother shook her head and dabbed at her face, but the tears continued to flow. Shelby grew more nervous with each passing second.

"It's not that. Oh, why didn't I just tell you and be done with it?"

Shelby snagged a couple tissues herself and pitched in on the cleanup effort, trying hard not to smile because her mother's runny makeup reminded her of Beetlejuice on crack.

Stop it. Her mother was…animated, flamboyant, always had been. There was nothing wrong with that. Shallow people did not stay up until 2:00 a.m. baking cupcakes for school bake sales, nor did they take part in walkathons for charity.

They also don't have to tell everyone under the sun that they've done those things.

Yeah, well, back to that whole drama queen thing. Her mother liked attention. Of all the vices to have, hers could be worse. At least good things were accomplished in the process.

"Shelby, I swear to you, I did what I thought was best. But now I'm not sure I did. I should've told you, despite what he said. But I didn't want you to be hurt. You don't tell a child something like that."

Now that really made her nervous. "Something like what? Mom, what's going on?"

"Shelby, please. You have to forgive me. Please say you forgive me."

Oh, here we go. Her mother asked for forgiveness from people the way others placed fast-food orders. It wasn't really a request but a demand, an expectation, one made for show because her mother was too self-involved to truly get that she might have done something wrong and hurt someone in the process. "I'm sure whatever it is, it'll work out."

Her mother broke down and sobbed. A new set of tissues was in order.

Shelby sat on the edge of the chair and fell into the old routine. She rubbed her mother's back in slow, soothing circles, and stared at the clock on the wall. Every time her mother and father had had one of their *I want a divorce* fights and her dad had walked out, this happened. The tears, the breakdown, the regrets and apologies. But once the flood had passed, her mother sprang into action and told everyone who'd listen how she was the wronged party. The saving grace here was that her mother was technologically challenged and couldn't make a recording for YouTube. *Thank you, God.*

But watching her, the door to Shelby's past swung wide and in a split second she was a little girl again. How many times had she hid under her bed or in her closet because no matter how quiet they tried to be, Shelby heard them?

"Oh, Shelby. I love you."

"I love you, too, Mom."

"You don't mean that."

And the pity party begins. Shelby patted her back. She loved her mother, she just didn't always like her. How could two people have the same blood type yet be so different? "Of course I do. You're my mom. Stop crying and tell me what happened."

Her mother lifted her head and met Shelby's gaze. "It was a long time ago."

"Then why are you worrying about it now?"

"Because you have to know. You can't live the rest of your life not knowing."

Shelby sat back in the chair, startled by her mother's words. What on earth?

"Shelby, when I was twenty, I met a man."

Jerry Springer footage flashed in her mind. Her mother had married her father at eighteen. "You cheated on Dad?"

"*No.* No, baby, Jerry and I were divorced. I never cheated on him. Not once. Your father has accused me of that, but I never did. The man, though—" she lowered her head "—he was married."

Shelby blinked, her sleep-exhausted mind sluggish and much too slow to process what her mother wasn't saying.

Her mother and father held the record at the county courthouse for the most marriages—to the same person. They'd married each other and divorced *five* times over the past thirty years. After several years apart, things would settle down between them and they'd get back together again. But the result had been a hellish childhood wrought with one melodramatic episode after another. "Mom, why are you telling me this?"

Her mother plucked at the tear-soaked tissues in her hand, shredding them. "Because your father—your *real* father—is dead. He died on Thursday." She pointed a wavering finger toward the Sunday paper. "His obituary is printed there."

The words didn't penetrate. A part of Shelby was shocked speechless, but more than anything she felt…numb. Detached. Like she had last night after seeing the results of the pregnancy test. Not even the increasing itch of her hives could break through the shell. "Are you saying Dad isn't my…biological father?"

Her mother's lips trembled. "No, Jerry is not your father."

Shelby didn't remember standing. Didn't remember walking to the sink. She'd come wanting advice and assurances that no matter what happened between her and Luke she'd have her mother's support.

How do you trust someone with such a thing when they've lied to you your entire life? "You kept this secret for twenty-eight *years?*"

"Shelby… Baby, come sit down. Please, let me explain. I was so young. I'd married Jerry right out of high school but neither of us knew what we were doing."

"You still don't."

Her mother didn't deny the statement.

"We divorced the first time before you were born. You

know that. But things weren't over. I still loved him but...we had so many problems and obstacles to overcome. It isn't easy being young and dirt-poor with big expectations."

Shelby understood expectations. She understood having a dream that seemed to cost more than the moon but—

"Zacharias was older, dashing, but so sad. We knew it was wrong but at the time, we were exactly what the other was looking for."

She couldn't breathe. This kept getting worse and worse. "Zacharias?" She wheezed the name. *"Zacharias Bennington?"*

Her mother nodded. "He'd just taken over the bank from his father. I worked at the diner as a waitress while I went to cosmetology school, and every day I'd take the deposit to the bank and bring my dad a piece of pie to eat on his lunch break. One day Zacharias was there and we...talked."

"Grandpa's *boss?* The one who gave him the— Oh, my *word*," she said, collapsing against the countertop and feeling the sharp corner bite into her hip. "He did have an heir to pass the land on to—me?"

Her mother nodded. "He left it to your grandpa and hoped that would keep the gossip down because they were friends."

"And now he's dead?"

"According to the paper, he died on Thursday evening. Shelby, please understand. I was young."

"He was *married*. And he was Grandpa's *age*. How could you?"

Pat's face was bright pink, nearly the pink of her ridiculous slippers. It was the first time Shelby ever remembered her mother blushing. Embarrassment wasn't her thing.

"He was in his forties at the time, hardly an old man. And

there were extenuating circumstances. His wife couldn't be a wife to him. She—"

"Oh, please. Do *not* make it worse by making excuses." Shelby snatched her purse off the table and turned toward the hallway. Of all the— How had this happened? How could she not have known?

"Shelby, don't go. Please, let me explain!"

"I don't want to hear any more. All my life you've been out of control. It was just one dramatic scene after another. There were no boundaries. You'd do it, say it, live it and worm your way out of the consequences later. But now you're telling me *I* was a consequence—and you lied about it? You can't explain away a twenty-eight-year-old *lie!*"

"Baby, *please*."

Shelby yanked open the door but paused before stepping outside. "Who knows about this? Tell me, and whatever you do, don't lie now." Out of her peripheral vision she saw that her mother stood at the end of the hall, her arms wrapped around herself as she sobbed.

Shelby hardened her heart at the sight. "Does Dad know or did you lie to him all of these years, too?"

"He knows."

The words stabbed deep. Everyone knew mothers and daughters didn't always get along, but her father... No matter what had been going on between him and her mother, Jerry Brookes had always been there for her. Always. He'd never taken his anger or upset out on her. But all the while he'd known? Kept the secret?

"You might as well hear the rest, Shelby. I'd rather you hear it from me."

A raw laugh erupted from her chest. "How commendable of you." She leaned her head against the wood panel and stared at the cloud-darkened sky. A late-summer thunder-storm darkened the distance and rumbled over the mountains, perfect for her mood.

"I lied about the pregnancy. Not only to my father, but to Jerry. I was so embarrassed, especially when I told Zack and he said he wouldn't annul his marriage to his wife and marry me. The woman had been in an accident. She was in a long-term care facility. The marriage was on paper, nothing else, but he said he couldn't leave her even though he loved me."

Every married man's story. "So since the wife was technically out of the picture, the two of you decided it was okay to cheat on her. Nice, Mom, do you kick puppies, too?" Shelby stared at her mother. Had she ever known her at all? Her mother had always been a bit shallow and self-centered but…how could she do that? Shelby would never have guessed her mother would go so far. How deceitful could a person get? "*Why* are you telling me this now? Why the sudden urge to come clean?"

"I wanted to tell you in case you wanted to go to the funeral and—and say goodbye to your father."

Unbelievable. Say goodbye to a total stranger? He wasn't her father. She felt absolutely nothing for Zacharias Bennington except contempt. The man her mother had divorced time and again, *he* was her father. Her dad had known all of these years but he'd still loved them. And look what he'd gotten in return.

Shelby stepped over the threshold, her heart aching, ripped open once more by her mother's actions. Why now? Why today when she needed her mother so badly? "It's no wonder Dad left you. What I can't believe is that he ever bothered to come back."

CHAPTER SEVEN

SHELBY WASN'T SURE of the time. She wasn't sure of much of anything, except that hours had passed. The rumbling engine and the crunch of gravel in her driveway sounded horribly familiar, and as she sat on the cool floor inside the mill house she debated if she could stomach another confrontation in such a short amount of time. What did you say to the man you thought was your father but now wasn't?

A door slammed and the sound of Jerry Brookes's booted feet drifted toward her house. She didn't move. Maybe he'd go away.

Several knocks sounded, the echo bouncing off the rock-strewn mountains surrounding the valley where she lived. Her name was called. The screen door squeaked open as her dad let himself into her house. But no matter how hard she tried to make herself get up and face him, she couldn't do it. *Please just leave.*

"Shelby Lynn?"

She hadn't heard him approach the mill house. The newly installed wood and leaded glass door swung open and the last of the sun's rays highlighted the dust motes floating in the air. Her father—Jerry—stood silhouetted in the doorway, looking broad and formidable, a man's man. One she'd always known to be a big old teddy bear but who'd probably been devastated by his wife's betrayal.

"That's more than a storeful of baked goods you got made up in there."

She'd gone a little overboard. Brownies. Cookies. Muffins and her special apple turnovers. She'd have to scramble to get them delivered to the grocery and hardware stores tomorrow morning before she went to work, but the managers liked her products and she'd see a little profit from her baking frenzy.

If she could get the turnovers into the country club's kitchen and to the chef before Mr. Long appeared, Betty might even feature them on the menu like the seasonal fruit tarts Shelby had made over the summer.

Jerry lowered himself onto the polished plank floor beside her, his brown steel-toed boots black in places from dirt and grease.

Shelby sighed. "She shouldn't have called you."

Jerry settled his shoulders against the stone wall and nudged her gently. "No, she shouldn't have. You should've called me."

Shelby closed her eyes in an attempt to combat the fatigue dragging at her. She'd eaten a banana while making the brownies but hadn't had anything else and her body was protesting.

You have to eat. It's not just for you anymore.

How could she forget? But on the other hand, how could she eat when her stomach was knotted up like a hangman's noose? "I was divorce number two, wasn't I?"

It wasn't really a question. She hadn't been able to distract herself completely this afternoon, and her mind had wandered down turbulent paths and revisited memories with X-ray eyes and an adult's perspective. "You got back together and remarried because you thought I was yours. She told you I was yours. Then you found out I wasn't and divorced the second time. I'm right, aren't I?"

She rolled her head against the wall to look at him. With only one of the double doors partially open, it was fairly dark inside the stone building, but she was able to make out his bearded face and the glint of sorrow in his soft brown eyes. She looked nothing like Jerry, or her mother, for that matter. Why hadn't she ever noticed?

"You weren't the cause of anything," he told her. "You were the prize, not the problem."

"But that's when you found out?"

Visibly reluctant, he nodded slowly. "That's when I found out. We'd moved into the little house where your mama lives now. I was putting some boxes away and dropped one of them. Inside were all the notes and letters he'd given her, Polaroid pictures of them together."

Shelby let that sink in before she let her mind go to the next question. How must he have felt to find his wife—even an ex-wife at the time—had kept mementos from her lover? "But after a few years you came back. Remarried." A laugh left her chest, rough and scathing. "The third time was supposed to be the charm, wasn't it? Then I got sick and you left again. What did she do?"

"Shelby—"

"I need to know the truth. I need—" her voice cracked with strain "—for someone to be honest with me instead of lying to me."

Seconds passed. Jerry exhaled and the gush disturbed the sunlit dust. The particles jumped and whirled.

"I was laid off. Your cold turned into pneumonia and your fever went sky-high. We had to give you ice baths to bring it down. But the damn doctor didn't want to treat you because he knew we couldn't afford to pay and we didn't have any insurance."

"What did she do?"

"She…went to him."

Of course. "And knowing Mom, she probably rubbed it in your face."

"She didn't have to. I was ashamed I couldn't provide for my family. Your mother was scared out of her mind because her baby was sick and there was nothing I could do. Then she disappeared. I figured she'd gone to get Alex's daddy, but when she came back she walked into the house carrying a wad of cash like nothing I've ever seen." He snorted, shook his head. "Thousands of dollars. Just like that. I wanted to give you everything and couldn't, and here was a man who wouldn't acknowledge you publicly, but he'd toss his money around so long as no one knew."

"I was his dirty little secret."

"You were a beautiful little girl he missed out on raising because of his own stupidity." He growled the words, making it clear he didn't like her reference. "But seeing her with that money… I'd never contemplated murder before but I did that night." Beneath the scrub on his face, his jaw firmed. "I even accused her of sleeping with him to get the cash, called her a whore. I know it wasn't true. Your mama has her faults but she's not like that."

A sound came out of her throat, derisive.

"She's not, Shelby-girl. Your mama is… She's like a child. She's bright and colorful and wants a lot of attention, demands it and finds a way to get it if she thinks she isn't getting enough. But if you look below the show you see she's got a good heart and, most of the time, she means well. She's just…needy."

Immature and self-centered were better descriptives. "You're making excuses for her."

"I'm tryin' to get you to see that people are who they are. You can't change them." He inhaled and sighed again. "Shelby, the point is that many a man has gone to prison over stupid things done in anger. I was this close to going after that son of a—" He broke off and wiped a hand over his mouth like he wiped away the curse. "He wasn't worth the dirt on my shoes, but I was that mad about it. Your mother and I— We could've conquered the world together, but when we fought we rubbed each other raw and bleeding. And after I knew the truth our fights always revolved around Bennington. Maybe we were divorced during the time you were conceived but she was *my* wife. It's a wonder someone didn't get hurt."

Someone had gotten hurt. Her.

Shelby rubbed her hand on her jeans, able to feel the grime on her fingers from where she'd swept and cleaned the mill house floor like a madwoman until sliding down the wall to rest.

"Once I cooled off and calmed down I wondered what kind of man would've chosen pride over your health? I admitted that she'd done the right thing. You needed help and that was all that was important, not my pride. Your mother took me back."

"But you left *again*. You didn't stay long and you got divorced the third time. *Why?*"

"That third time was because…accepting money to get you the medicine and help you needed was one thing, but I wasn't going to let that man support us."

"Support you? How?" Shelby searched her mind for events, comments, but so much of her childhood had been spent outside to get away from the tension. When she wasn't riding her bike or hiding in her room, she'd practically lived at the Tulanes. Anywhere but home.

"She wanted me to take money from him. The man was a banker. He could arrange things and be discreet but I couldn't tolerate a handout. Especially not from him. Pride is a dangerous thing. You and Alex were friends and all, but I didn't want her daddy or anyone else thinking I couldn't take care of you, and no matter what your mama said, I knew there would be talk."

"So you left again."

A tired smile crossed his face and he nodded. "After we split up that third time, I got a job clear-cutting a place outside town." He grunted. "That damn tree took me down quicker than a blink. Your mother heard and came to see me. She brought me food. Cleaned the place up. She fussed over me something fierce, and I'd be lying through my teeth if I said I didn't like it. I missed her. Missed you both.

"I'd had some time to calm down and I realized she'd made some good points about the money in regard to you. He owed you. Not me or your mother, but you. Every father bears a responsibility to his child and there isn't a man out there that should be getting by with shirkin' on it." He scratched his chest, his callused skin rasping against the fabric. "Anyway, I set down some rules about if and when we'd ever take money from Bennington again, that it had to only be for you when you needed something or got sick. Your mother agreed. We got back together and had a stretch of a few good years."

"Until—" She shifted sideways and stared at him in horror. "My car?"

Jerry's smile was grim. "Among other things. You weren't sick. And there was nothing wrong with you not having a car like that at sixteen. It's dangerous putting a know-it-all behind the wheel of something that drove that fast. A BMW," he muttered, shaking his head. "But Pat said Bennington wanted you to have it." He swore softly. "Then she turned around and got it early saying you needed to practice in it and I knew your mother wanted the thing for herself. She drove it the first six months until you got a job and needed it."

"She chose a car over your marriage? I wish she would've told him where to stick it." She shoved herself to her feet and stalked across the floor, thankful it was getting darker inside the building because she wobbled drunkenly.

"You weren't sayin' that at the time. Shelby, sit down before you fall down."

"I'm fine. I just…got up too fast." When her head stopped spinning, she went to the door and stared out. A deer stood at the corner of her yard, and three more jumped from the woods across the road and made their way to the apple tree by her mailbox. She'd have to buy a case of soap again, otherwise her fruit trees would be history. It looked silly to have soap hanging from strings in the limbs but the scent seemed to keep the deer away.

"Those were divorces three and four. Do I even need to guess why you divorced last time?" Her words sent the deer running, out of the yard, across the creek and into the field beyond. "Even though he never acknowledged me, I'm Zacharias's heir. That's why I got this place, isn't it? Why Grandpa left it to me instead of her. *That's* why you left once and for all."

Her fault. So many of their marital problems could only be blamed on her, because she existed. More proof that she and Luke had to do right by the baby and not repeat her parents' mistakes.

"No. He gave this place to your grandpa to pass on to you two years before I left. You just didn't know about it. I divorced your mother that last time because Bennington's wife finally passed and I got this fool idea in my head that since she was gone, maybe he'd finally do right by you both. I wasn't going to stand in the way. The name Bennington held more clout than Brookes."

Shelby turned back to face him, anger filling her. That didn't make sense. "You fought all those years and then just gave up? I don't want his *name*. Why would I when he wasn't here for me?"

"I did what I thought was best. With his wife gone, he could man up and give you the life you deserved."

"All I ever wanted was for you and Mom to get along!" She thought of the hours she'd endured her mother's drama, the tears, the way her mother had torn the house apart each and every time Jerry left. All the years, the ups and downs. Things had finally settled down, then the rug had been pulled out from under her again. And all because Jerry wanted to be *noble?*

She'd barely finished college and gotten her business degree because it had been everything she could do to work her regular job, go to school and keep her mother's salon running until her mother had managed to drag herself out of her funk. And for what? Zacharias hadn't married her mother or acknowledged Shelby. It was all for nothing.

"I don't expect you to understand my decision."

"Good. Because I don't. I can't fathom why—" Her head spun and she reached out to balance herself.

"Shelby?" Her father hurried to her side and took her arm. "Did you eat today?"

"I'm fine, I—"

He wrapped his arm around her waist and pushed her

gently over the threshold, across the stone porch and yard to her house. "Look at you. Damn hives are back. Why do you do this to yourself? It's all right to get mad. It's not your fault your mama and I couldn't get along. We screwed up, not you. I should've been a bigger man but—"

"A bigger man?" She stumbled on the second step leading to her back door but her father's grip kept her on her feet. "You did everything you could to make her happy but she never was. *Why* did you keep coming back? Why not just forget about my lying, cheating mother and her Daddy Warbucks and live your own life instead of acting like a revolving door?"

Inside the kitchen, he yanked a chair from beneath the table. "Sit down." Her father grabbed a turnover from the cooling rack and shoved it into her hands. "Eat that and listen to me. I did what I did because I loved you like the daughter I thought you were the first five years of your life. It doesn't make sense, I know that. I've said that to myself time and again, but I loved your mother. Simple as that. She was always high-strung, that's just her way, but I knew that when I married her the first time. I couldn't even blame her for shackin' up with Bennington because if she hadn't, you wouldn't be sitting here right now."

Shelby swallowed the small bite she'd shoved into her mouth and battled the queasiness. "No one is worth what you went through."

His shoulders sagged at her words, and he sat back in his chair. "You were both worth it. Don't you believe love is worth fighting for?"

"Love? If she'd *loved* you, none of that would've happened. *Nothing* is worth setting yourself up for that much grief and upset." She shook her head. "It just proves that love is one of those things people dream about but never get, much less keep. It's just…a moment in time that doesn't last."

Jerry pushed himself to his feet. "I hope you realize you're wrong before it's too late. And you are wrong, Shelby Lynn. True love is worth every moment of pain you might feel as a result." Her father bent and gave her a kiss on the cheek. "I've got to be on the job at four o'clock tomorrow morning and I need to head back, but I want you to call me, day or night, if you need me or anything else happens. You hear me?"

She nodded. "Thanks for coming all that way."

"I wouldn't have wanted to be anywhere else. I had to come see for myself that you're okay."

Shelby smiled. *Okay* was far-fetched. Still on her feet was more apt, but only because she'd had so much practice over the years. *Weebles wobble but they don't fall down.* The silly jingle from her childhood sounded in her head. She was definitely part of the Weeble toy club. "Be careful driving back. Watch out for deer."

"Always do." He walked to the door and paused. "Shelby…you said you didn't want his name. I'd be mighty honored if you'd keep mine."

Her thoughts immediately shifted to Luke and his proposal. What would Jerry say if she told him? "Don't worry. I have no intention of changing it."

CHAPTER EIGHT

"Where were you this weekend?"

Anne-Marie followed Luke into his office like she always did. The habit had started after her separation from her ex when she'd come in with coffee, prop her feet up and try to distract herself by brainstorming with Luke.

"I dropped by your place Saturday night but you weren't home."

"Another of my brothers got married this weekend. I flew home for the ceremony."

He glanced up in time to see Anne-Marie inhale, her recently enhanced chest lifting beneath the black, slinky top she wore. Paired with white pants and no sign of a bra, she made California casual the hottest thing since Blu-ray. Too bad she'd gone more than a little overboard since her divorce.

Once voted the up-and-coming female entrepreneur to watch, Anne-Marie's midlife crisis had occurred at the age of thirty-four and included the boob job, revealing clothes and a sad bent toward sleeping with losers, a result of being blindsided by her now ex-husband's affair. Even so, she possessed a great brain for business—if she'd lay off on the vanity clothes and get back to why she'd hired them all.

"You should've said something. I haven't been to a wedding in ages. We could've danced again."

The first and only time they'd danced was right after her separation. She'd had a few too many drinks and practically mauled him during the four-minute song. "I guess I thought Tennessee would be too boring for you."

Luke lowered his messenger bag to the desk and removed his laptop and the notes he'd taken on the flight to Tennessee. The return trip to California had been a wash because he wasn't able to concentrate on anything but Shelby and the baby, the way she'd looked when he'd left her house. Shell-shocked. Confused. Determined to do things her way. And while he'd come to the realization that he'd settled for a one-night stand with her because he'd thought it was all he'd ever be able to have, he was tired of settling for less than what he wanted. Especially with this new development. He still couldn't wrap his mind around the thought of being a father, but he was also excited about it. He loved kids.

"Did you get the notes I e-mailed for Mystic Magi?"

He'd gotten them all right. "Yeah. Someone's been busy."

Anne-Marie shrugged her bare shoulders and braced her hands on the desk, the move pushing her breasts together in an impressive display revealed by the hole in her blouse where the straps of her top crisscrossed in front and wound around her neck. "That's why I stopped by. I wanted to go over them with you in person." She leaned forward and smiled. "What did you think?"

He thought they needed to have a talk, friend to friend. "Anne-Marie—"

"You didn't like them? Luke—" her tone turned chiding "—it's just a few suggestions."

Horrible suggestions that would lower the high quality of the game. He dropped his gaze, found himself staring at a hefty amount of cleavage and jerked his eyes back to her face. She smiled a slow, teasing smile, aware of where his eyes had gone. What had happened to the woman with the plan to set Galaxy Games at the top of the charts? Where had she gone? If something didn't change soon, if she didn't get her head in the gaming world and stop coming on to every guy there, he worried for the health of the company. And for her.

"Look, when I was reviewing the progress slides I could tell you've been stressed lately. What was the deal with adding that old mill to the castle keep? And why did you change Aiya's hair color back to that mousy brown? I liked the new look we were working toward."

If he was stressed, it was because he was doing her job and his own with very little to show for it. He smiled grimly, once again reminded of how much Mystic Magi was based on Beauty—and Shelby's home. *Not to mention Shelby herself?* He'd changed the heroine's hair and added the mill after that night with Shelby. "The colors throughout are jewel tones, and her hair is golden-brown, not mousy. She looked too Goth with hair that black."

Anne-Marie flicked her hair over her shoulder. "I don't know. Now she looks very…masculine."

"Think of her as low maintenance." This time his teasing smile was genuine. "Something I doubt you know a lot about."

She arched an eyebrow high, but a grin curled her red lips at the corners. "Well, I see you've returned in a mood. But I'll admit, I've learned to like my feminine comforts."

The old Anne-Marie was tough as nails and ballsy. She didn't care about feminine comforts. A slightly polished-up Goth kid herself, she'd worn combat boots, spiked jewelry and cami miniskirts when he'd first come to work here. And he'd liked her that way. She'd shot straight from the hip. But now?

Her husband's betrayal with a softer, more feminine-looking woman had cut Anne-Marie's confidence to the core. And even though Luke understood Anne-Marie's initial response and commiserated with the pain of her marriage ending, he thought her dive into self-pity and surgical enhancement, her grand makeover scheme, should've ended before now. It was time to get back to business. "We're going for the best imagery possible, right? That means you can't put a heroine in the jungle with three-inch nails and long hair and expect a gamer to consider her realistic."

"Yeah, yeah, fine," she said, seating herself on the edge of his desk. "I'll trust your judgment. For now. Guess I'm getting nervous. We can't afford to let this chance slip through our fingers, Luke. We have to keep our momentum going. So, maybe the two of us should make plans to get together this weekend and brainstorm how we'll approach the purchasing team. My place or yours?"

He paused in the act of emptying his messenger bag, his instincts kicking up in awareness. He respected Anne-Marie as his employer, but his deference to her authority was taking a nosedive. Hadn't she learned her lesson the last time she'd mixed business and her personal life? "Uh…this weekend isn't good for me. I have plans."

"For the entire weekend?"

"My brother is leaving the country on a humanitarian medical mission to Niger and we're having a party to see him off."

"Ethan?" Her eyes widened in surprise.

Luke could practically see the cranks turning in her mind as she cycled through the many conversations they'd had about their families.

"Wow. From what you've said about him, he's never struck me as the humanitarian type."

"I think it's his way of taking a break and getting out of town for a while." He didn't go into detail about how Ethan had been overlooked and the big promotion to chief of surgery that he'd wanted was given to someone else.

"Well, I wouldn't want you to miss his send-off. But we do need to figure out our strategy."

"We can add that to the list this week."

Anne-Marie crossed her arms over her chest and tilted her head to one side, her oversize earrings dangling nearly to her shoulder. "Or I could go with you," she suggested. "I've never been to Tennessee. What do you say? We could make it a working weekend. It would be nice to put faces with the names I've heard."

Luke hesitated, unsure of what to say. First she wanted to come to his apartment, now to Tennessee with him? She wasn't suggesting they spend the weekend together, was she? "Uh, no need to do that. I've been working on the presentation. We're good. Besides, you need to be here. Unless there is something else going on?"

Anne-Marie paused for a slight moment, then she smiled at him and shrugged. "Nothing major. It, um, would've been our anniversary but—"

"I'm sorry."

"Hey, not a problem." Standing, she tugged the lacy bottom edge of her top and revealed more of her breasts in the process. "Have fun. But don't even think about extending your time there. I expect you to be in that chair first thing Monday morning."

"No problem."

"And my notes?"

Those he definitely had a problem with. "I'll go through them and take a closer look."

"That's my boy. Pay close attention to the story suggestions. I think they'll make the scenes really pop."

"The story is perfect. We're at the tweaking stage, not rewriting."

A funny look stole over her features. "Careful, Luke. Your ego is showing." She reached up and patted his cheek. "It's perfect when I say it's perfect."

SHELBY SPENT Monday and Tuesday trying to distance herself from her thoughts and avoiding Luke's phone calls. He'd left several messages asking her to call him back and check in, just to let him know she was feeling okay, but she'd ignored his requests and erased the messages. Listening to him sounding so concerned and masculine, his voice rough with an edge that made her shiver, threatened her resolve so she'd done what she'd felt was necessary.

She'd talked to Alex briefly when her friend had called to check on her and Shelby found herself battling guilt. Things were going to be so awkward when Alex found out. She should've come clean from the beginning, but how does that come up in idle conversation? *Yeah, we need to do lunch, and, oh, by the way, I did your brother.* Shelby used work as her excuse to keep the call brief and ended the misery.

She would've liked to have disclosed to her best friend the news about her mother's confession, but she still couldn't wrap her mind around her paternity. How could she expect other people to understand when she didn't?

Basically it all led Shelby back to her life-learned conclusion that keeping things in perspective was the only way to control uncontrollable situations. Focus on a single problem, a minute detail, fix what was able to be fixed, and just *deal*.

Yes, she was pregnant. But pregnancy was a process, one that took months and would require her to do no more than eat and rest properly. Women worked right up until their delivery these days and with her father promising to spend as much time as he could helping her finish the interior of the mill house, she had seven months to get things done. The question was whether to time the opening before or after she delivered?

In seven short months.

"Ms. Brookes? You have a phone call. It's Rosetta Tulane. I don't know what's going on, but I could hear someone screaming in the background."

Her heart jumped into her throat. Luke's *grandmother?* Oh, no. Had Luke told them? "Ah, thank you, Michelle." She took the portable phone and held it to her ear, walking away from the hostess's podium so as to not be overheard. Thankfully the hallway leading to the meeting rooms was clear. "Hello? Rosetta?"

"Hello, dear. Can you hear me?"

Shelby pressed her finger to her ear. Someone was indeed screaming. "Yes, I can. What's going on?"

"I'm sorry for bothering you at work but it's an emergency. You need to come right away."

"Come where?" Wait a minute. She recognized that screech. "Is that my *mother?*"

"Yes, dear. We're at Mason Cemetery, attending the burial of Zacharias Bennington."

The burial? Oh, Lord, no. Please, no!

"Your mother is here and she's quite upset." Rosetta's voice dropped. "Shelby, you need to come quickly."

She didn't want to. She hadn't talked to her mother since

her big confession and she didn't want to talk to her now.
"I—"

"She threw herself on top of the casket—"

"What?" Shelby pressed a hand to her mouth when her
stomach threatened to heave.

"—and had to be removed. She keeps babbling something
about… Well, I'll fill you in when you get here."

Rosetta knew. Shelby could tell by the tone of the older
woman's voice. Alex's grandmother *knew* all about her
mother's affair with a married man, how Shelby was the unfortunate by-product. All because the Drama Queen had
made a spectacle of herself—*again*. "I'll be right there."

It was a busy day and Mr. Long wasn't pleased that she
had to leave due to a family emergency, but he handled the
news with frowning concern and told her to drive safe. She
was going to have to give the man more credit. In the right
moments, he appeared quite nice, nearly human, and less
like the guy on *Hell's Kitchen*.

It took her twenty-two minutes to get to the cemetery, and
during every one of them she pictured her mother telling
Zacharias's mourners every lurid detail of their secret affair.
Finally Shelby topped the rise where the road leveled off and
slowed to a stop. The funeral was obviously over but, from
appearances, the attendees had lingered to see the encore.
All of the guests stared at her mother, who'd apparently
thrown herself full tilt into mourning her former lover by
dressing in widow's black and…a veiled *hat?* Where on
earth had she gotten that?

"This can't be happening." It was like a scene out of a
movie where the best friend/mistress showed up with her
face veiled so the wife couldn't recognize her. The only
problem was that her mother had lifted the veil and draped

it so that it flapped in the breeze, and at this moment she was holding court beside the casket surrounded by Luke and Alexandra's parents, the matriarch of the Tulane family, Rosetta, and quite a few of the country club's patrons. "Oh, crap. Oh, crap, oh, crap, oh, *crap*."

All her life Shelby had fought to keep her chin up, to ignore the talk and speculation about her parents and their on-again, off-again marriage, to rise above the drama her mother so loved and to create the persona of a professional, *normal* person.

But in a matter of minutes her mother had ruined everything.

Shelby got out of the car, her entire body on fire as humiliation and degradation coursed through her veins. This was what her father meant when he said he'd had to separate himself from her mother. The time had come. As soon as she got her mother away from the casket, she'd have to keep her distance—or go to prison for strangling her.

Prison just might be worth it.

Maybe you could run the kitchen.

Every eye was on Shelby as she made her way to the burial plot. She'd removed her crested uniform jacket on her way to the car due to the heat, but her lavender-colored blouse and white linen pants stuck to her skin and the hives that had *almost* gone away returned with a vengeance. She felt them but she kept going, one foot in front of the other instead of what she really wanted to do, which was turn tail and run the other way. How could her mother *do* this? Hadn't she done enough to embarrass them?

Her mother was sitting dead center in the front row, and Shelby tried hard to think of the positives. First, there truly weren't that many mourners at the burial. Apparently, her biological father didn't have many friends or else he'd outlived them. Second, her mother was no longer *atop* the casket. And third and best of all, the casket was closed.

She couldn't imagine viewing her biological father's face for the very first time since finding out he actually *was* her father at a moment like this.

"What are you doing?" she growled as she stopped just shy of stepping on her mother's feet. Stilettos. What woman wore four-inch, open-toed stilettos to a funeral?

The same kind who dressed like Zsa Zsa Gabor.

"Shelby! Oh, baby, I'm so glad you decided to come. I know he treated you wrong, but turn around, honey, and at least say goodbye to your fath—"

"Will you please, for once in your life, *shut up and not make a scene?*" Shelby forced herself to glance at the people around them, unable to make direct eye contact until her gaze met that of Rosetta Tulane's. Shelby faltered, wondering why she hadn't realized before that Luke inherited his eyes from his grandmother. "I am so sorry."

Rosetta tilted her head to the side, her expression one of sympathy and love. Compassion. In an instant Shelby saw Luke, because Rosetta wore the same expression as Luke after she'd taken the test.

Shelby blinked and tore her attention away from Rosetta, well able to imagine what Luke's family thought of the spectacle, and addressed the portly minister holding his Bible in front of his belly and frowning at them with hell and brimstone disapproval. "Please forgive the intrusion. As you can see my mother is...not right."

"I'm right as rain, Shelby Lynn. Why, you make it sound like I'm—"

"Mother, let's go." Shelby bent and tried to pull her mother from the seat.

"Shelby, dear, why don't you and Pat come with us?" Rosetta placed her hand on Shelby's shoulder. "You're both upset. Let us drive you home."

"I'm *fine*." She could only imagine how she looked. Her blouse covered her arms, but bright red splotches the size of quarters now covered the tops of her hands. She felt them on her neck, her scalp, didn't doubt they were beginning to form on her face, which only happened under the most extreme of stressful circumstances for which this apparently qualified. Bennington's Spotted Illegitimate Daughter. There was a caption and photo for the newspaper. "I just want to go. Mother, *get up*."

"You're angry with me again." Big tears flooded her mother's eyes and trickled past her fake eyelashes. "I can't ever do anything right with you."

Shelby managed to keep from rolling her eyes, somehow. *Here we go again*. "We'll talk about this in the car."

Her mother didn't move. "I'm sorry, Shelby. I'm so sorry I didn't tell you sooner. I should have but I knew you'd be hurt and upset and you are, because that man—"

"Isn't able to defend himself. Can we please discuss this in private?"

"I tried but you won't return my calls. I had to do something to set the record straight."

"Shelby, perhaps—"

Shelby held up her hand when Marilyn Tulane spoke. "Thank you, but I'm fine. We're fine, aren't we, Mom?" She bent closer to her mother in the hopes her voice wouldn't carry. "Do you have *any* shame whatso*ever?* Get. *Up*." She grasped her mother's other arm and pulled, trying to find purchase even though her heels kept sinking into the grass. Seeing what she was doing, Luke's father, Alan, stepped forward and together they managed to get her mother to her feet. Without a word, they headed toward the parking area. Rosetta and Marilyn followed behind them.

And so did the whispers. The snickers. The stares and the shaking of heads. Her entire childhood repeated itself in an instant. Teachers at school, classmates and their parents. PTA meetings, the Grand March at prom. Scene after scene.

Shelby did her best to ignore them all but she was aware of every word being said. With Alan's help, she shoved her mother into the passenger side of her Beemer and managed a strangled thanks to the Tulanes. Rosetta tried to stop her once more, but Shelby put her head down and marched around the car to the driver's side. She had to get out of here before she committed a crime with witnesses around who'd testify against her later.

She started the engine and pulled away with a jerk of the wheel, acutely aware of her mother lifting her hand to those watching and executing a textbook-perfect pageant wave.

CHAPTER NINE

"DID YOU GET what you wanted?" Shelby demanded quietly on the way down the mountain toward Beauty. The scenery would have been breathtaking if she'd had any attention to spare it. The slightest touches of orange, yellow and red could be seen in the trees, but distracted as she was by her mother's abominable behavior, it took everything in Shelby to keep the car under control on the curvy road.

"I don't know what you mean."

"That was a man's *funeral*."

"That was your father's *funeral* and I had to have my say."

"You made it a sideshow." Shelby squirmed in the seat, attempting to scratch the itch on her back. When that only created more itches, she glanced over at her mother. Her stomach coiled like a snake ready to strike. *Please don't throw up now.* The last thing she needed was more drama if her mother found out about the pregnancy. "Take off that stupid hat. You look ridiculous."

"It's designer and it's beautiful."

Only a drama queen. Of all the mothers in the world, why did she have to be hers? *I won't do that to you, kid. I promise. Grandma, on the other hand...* "Why, Mom? Why did you do it? You don't think you caused enough pain this week? You *had* to cause more? Rosetta said you threw yourself *on top of the casket*."

"I was angry. It just…hit me. All these wasted years."

"There wouldn't have been *any* wasted years if you had stopped acting like a child and taken responsibility for your life."

Her mother sniffled. "That's easy for people to say, but they haven't walked in my shoes."

No one could.

"Shelby, don't you see? I had to have my say. I had to see for myself that he was gone."

"Dead usually means dead."

"I also wanted to give those stuffed shirts a piece of my mind. It's their fault he was so uptight about our affair."

"He was a *married man*. Those people had nothing to do with him being embarrassed over what happened. Anyone would be. It's called morals." That, and the fact he was probably embarrassed by her mother's antics. If *she* was embarrassed by her mother, a straitlaced, married banker would most certainly be embarrassed given all he had to lose. And with her mother's flight-of-fancy mood swings, he'd probably realized pretty quickly that anything was possible.

"But they're the reason he wouldn't divorce his wife. He said it would look bad on him and on me."

She didn't want to think about the man who'd refused to acknowledge her, but her mother's comment made her believe that Zacharias had tried to spare Pat's feelings by blaming the situation, not her flamboyant personality. "And it would have. Don't you remember the part about in sickness and in health? You've said it enough times you should have it memorized by now even if you've never kept your vows."

Pat shook her head stubbornly, her earrings clinking together. "But if they'd supported him and left him alone, he could have acknowledged you. That's the important thing. You would've been able to grow up as a Bennington, gotten to know him."

"*Why* would I want to know a man who was ashamed of my existence?"

"I know you don't understand my behavior but…he could be kind. Zacharias was deathly afraid of scandal, and he said his father would have him removed from the bank if anyone ever found out."

Shelby glanced across the interior of the car, knowing there had to be still more to the sad, pathetic story she told. But did she really want to know?

Curiosity killed the cat.

She jerked her attention back to driving and slowed as she approached a curve. Her mother's words repeated in her head, bringing more questions. "Dad said you wanted him to take money from Zacharias. Is that what you did?" A thought struck and she swore softly. "Is that how you bought the salon?" Shelby glanced at her again, and released her breath in a huff when she saw the truth on her mother's face.

"Shelby…now, it's not what you're thinking."

Shelby gripped the wheel tighter. Oh, but it was, wasn't it?

"Jerry got upset about it, too, but like I told him, I had to be able to support you. I'm glad I took that money. After Jerry walked out, things were tight and—"

"You sponged money off him." Her tires squealed as she entered the S-shaped curve. "You were mad that he wouldn't acknowledge me *or* you, so you made him *buy* your silence. Dad blamed Zacharias, but what he was really doing was protecting you because of what you did. You extorted money from the man."

"I did no such thing. I accepted money from him, yes, but it was to help you. You were best friends with Alexandra Tulane, of all people. Zack might not have acknowledged you, but do you think he wanted his daughter to not have the things Alex had? How do you think I bought those pageant dresses?"

Her ears popped as they descended and the ground began to level out. Beauty was ahead. None too soon, either. She'd *despised* her mother forcing her into those pageants for everyone to ogle and talk about her. Had her mother hoped someone would figure it out? Wonder where the money came from for the gowns and the lessons?

"It was the same as child support."

Child support? "Dad *paid* child support when you split up. I remember seeing the checks. Did you give his money back?"

"Shelby Lynn, don't give me sass over things you do not understand. Since Zacharias wouldn't acknowledge you, Jerry made sure no one thought you weren't his."

Jerry Brookes had been her father in every way that mattered most. But he was a working man, one who could have used the money he'd sent her mother. Shelby shook her head, simply unable to comprehend her mother's gall. How greedy. How utterly, utterly greedy! "So you asked both of them for money and they gave it to you?"

"Jerry knew people would talk if he didn't. He wasn't going to be a deadbeat dad."

"He wasn't, my biological father was." Shelby squeezed the wheel. "Dad said the first time you went to Zacharias was because I was sick but afterward you went back for more. What did he say when you kept coming back?"

Her mother fussed with the beads and sequins on her black silk purse. "Shelby…he'd told me he *loved* me. He made me promises and we had a *baby* together. That should've counted for something. That man was taking care of his wife and had her in a home treating her like a queen when she didn't know him from Adam, but *I* had given him a daughter. It was up to him to take care of us, too."

"And now that he's dead, you're shouting it from the rooftops because he's not around to give you any hush money and—" she laughed, the sound dark "—probably didn't mention you in the will. I've already received my inheritance from him, roundabout though it came, but you... Nice, Mom. That's it, isn't it? Even though he bought you the salon, you want more. And since it's doubtful you'll get it, you went out and ruined his name."

You could have avoided all this if you'd gone to California with Luke.

Shelby rubbed her aching head. Running away wouldn't have solved anything, and if Rosetta had called her cell phone and discovered she was in California even more questions would have been raised. It would have been the icing on top of the lopsided and burned cake.

"First you were mad because I kept the secret, now you're mad because I felt passionate enough to be honest and tell people how he treated us?"

"You've humiliated us—me and Dad *and* yourself, not to mention Zacharias Bennington. At least it was private before, but now? What happened, Mom? Couldn't you find enough entertainment on your soap operas?"

Her mother turned sideways in the seat. "Shame on you for not appreciating the pain and upset I went through to give *you* a good life. Jerry left me because he couldn't stand the fact that your father *wanted* to help us."

"You might have put a pretty spin on it, Mom, but you virtually blackmailed the man. Had Dad gone along with it, it would've made him an accomplice." Shelby pressed her foot harder on the gas as they passed the Welcome To Beauty sign. "I would've respected you more if you'd have taken up for the man you loved and screwed over, rather than the one you cheated with." She turned down the street with a jerk of the wheel, her mother's house up ahead on the right. She used to ride her bike down the street, used to climb the neighborhood trees, used to believe the things her mother told her. "Now that Zacharias is dead you're scared, aren't you?" Her mind was full of memories, anger. Fear. Did her paternity change things? Who she was? "Not only is your sugar daddy gone, but the man who *really loved you* and gave you chance after chance that you *blew* is gone, too. Which leaves me— the daughter no longer talking to you until someone has to *call me* to come get you. You are unbelievable."

"Why? Because I wanted people to know how horribly he treated you? Now when they read his will and you're not in it, they'll know what kind of man he really was for denying his only child."

"I got the mill house. It's more than enough from a man I never knew."

Her mother released a loud harrumph. "That broken-down pile of rocks and land is nothing compared to what he should've given you."

Maybe she ought to feel more like her mother but she didn't. Zacharias Bennington was simply a name to her, a man who'd given her something she hadn't even realized she'd wanted at the time. "It's my home and my future."

The hat wobbled on her mother's head. "And what about me? You think the salon keeps me warm? It'll never be enough, not after I lost Jerry because of him. I love you. I'm not sorry I did what I did, because I had you, but Zacharias can never repay the pain he caused me."

Shelby glanced at her mother and saw a sad, embittered woman. Too flamboyant, too loud, too everything—because she tried too hard. Shelby sat back, amazed she hadn't realized it before now. Her mother behaved so over-the-top because she was desperate to be accepted by people, because she wanted respect. She didn't realize that by acting this way, she lost more and more of the very things she wanted. "Then maybe you need to think about that. Maybe you need to work on building friendships and relationships that aren't based on using people for what they can do for you. Mom, stop being so shallow and *grow up*."

She glared at her mother and tried to remember the good times they'd shared. She was screwed up, yes. But not bad. And while Pat created the messes she always found herself in, it didn't mean Shelby loved her any less. The saying was true, you could pick your friends but you couldn't pick your family. "Look, think of it this way. Everyone in town will hear about today and clamor to the salon to get the gossip. You're still going to be the center of attention and can tell your side. I hope throwing yourself on a coffin was worth it." She pulled to a stop outside her mother's house. "Goodbye, Mom."

Her mother lifted her chin to a haughty angle but didn't move.

Shelby glanced at her watch. "I have to get back to work."

"I did us both a favor, Shelby Lynn. The news is out there, honey, and he's to blame, not you."

"I would've preferred my privacy."

"You're so ungrateful. Jerry *left me* because of all the things I did for you."

"Dad left you because you rubbed your indiscretion in his face time and time again, demanding money from someone who made a mistake and just wanted to be left alone." Was that how Luke would feel? Were she and the baby his mistake, one he felt honor-bound to marry and raise? *You think?*

"Why shouldn't I use the opportunity to make our lives better? Any other man would've made a list of the things he wanted to buy with the money Zacharias owed us, but not Jerry." Her mother's mouth trembled and twisted, and fresh tears sparkled on her false eyelashes.

Shelby felt old, like her mother's parent instead of the child.

"He worked so hard and I *hated* it. He was never home, and always so tired when he was. Why should Jerry have had to get up at the crack of dawn while Zacharias sat there in his daddy's fancy office? He was willing to give Jerry the money to start a trucking company like he wanted."

"Do you hear yourself at all? Dad didn't want a handout. He wanted to do things for himself."

"Yes, well, we've seen how well that's worked out for him, haven't we?"

"Dad's not the one with the problem, you are." Shelby scratched her arm and turned the air conditioner up a notch to cool her burning skin. "I love Dad for exactly who he is, not what he does."

"So do I—I'm not ashamed of what Jerry does for a living, but is that why you spent more time at the Tulanes in their fancy house on top of the mountain than with us? Is that why you wanted Alan or Marilyn Tulane to drive you and Alex *everywhere* in their Mercedes and fancy cars instead of your own parents? You and Alex *walked* to the movies instead of letting me take you."

"Because you always made a *scene*. Because you flirted

with the boys *our* age. I stayed at their house because you and Dad were always fighting or getting a divorce or you were crying and freaking out."

Her mother huffed and made a show of grabbing her purse. "Well, I'm so sorry my life embarrassed you when all I was doing was trying to make it better for us." Pat grabbed the door handle and slid out of the car onto her stilettos. "I might make a scene or two every now and again but you know what? At least I haven't turned to stone. I live my life, I *confront* my problems. I don't hide from it or pretend it'll go away or shut down like you. That's something you get from your father—your *real* father!"

CHAPTER TEN

SHELBY WAS RUNNING on nothing but grit and adrenaline by the time Friday rolled around. She'd spent the past week making mistake after mistake and paid the price for them each time. First she'd seated Mrs. Randolph by Ellen Spencer, Mr. Randolph's recently discovered mistress. Mrs. Randolph was not pleased.

After that, she'd forgotten to schedule enough waitstaff to cover a business meeting taking place in the conference room and had to pitch in and help serve—leaving the food order for the wholesaler on her desk unapproved, which caused a serious lack of produce for the menu. Each time she thought she had things together, another wall would topple. All because Luke's return was foremost in her mind. That, and the chat she'd had with Mr. Long as a result of her many fumbles.

The club's manager had called her into his private office last evening and, in no uncertain terms, he let her know that the club's staff were expected to conduct themselves with professionalism and integrity both on the grounds and off. Then the man had surprised her by saying the phone calls he'd received about the incident that took place at the cemetery had been favorable in how she'd handled an obviously trying situation. She was distracted, yes, but in all the time she'd worked there she'd never made a mistake, which was why he was overlooking the past week and reminding her that sometimes work could be a blessing in that by concentrating on it she could leave her problems behind for a while.

Sitting there like a bug under a microscope, Shelby had known Luke's parents, possibly even his grandmother and her friends, had been hard at work, making sure she kept her job. The Tulanes had even added a party booking to the mix, and declared they wanted Shelby to handle all the details for Ethan's farewell gathering on Friday evening.

You should be grateful, not angry. But she was both. She was grateful that they watched out for her, but angry that they'd stepped in when she could have handled things herself, angry that her mother had caused a scene in the first place. She didn't need their so-called help—or Luke's. What was it with all their do-gooding ideas? Growing up around the Tulanes, she'd thought their acts of kindness had seemed larger than life, romantic or even heroic. But now? It was interference, pure and simple, and by requesting she handle the party, on top of their phone calls to Mr. Long, she felt indebted to them—and leery that she was going to have to face Luke at such a public event.

Shelby became obsessed with checking the time as evening approached. There was no sense in turning a bad situation into a nightmare. Why make everything worse by marrying? What could she say to get him to see that?

She stifled a yawn despite the turmoil of her thoughts. She could barely keep anything down because of the morning sickness, couldn't sleep because of worrying about what her mother might do next, and dreaded Luke's return. All she wanted was to get in her car and drive away.

You can't go far on $2,786.23.

Yeah, well, if she were her mother's daughter, she'd shock everyone by following in Pat's footsteps and cause another scandal by withdrawing the loan money earmarked for her restaurant and skip town. But she was not her mom and every single penny would go to finish the mill house.

"I heard you've had a bad week," a voice said behind her when she was on her way to the main dining room via the conference hallway.

Shelby gasped and turned. As though conjured by her thoughts, Luke stood in the doorway of the smallest meeting room. He looked rumpled after his long flight. His black hair was pushed back from his forehead, the length of it curled at his nape, and he wore a navy suit jacket that matched his eyes. Tired eyes, she noted. She wasn't the only one who'd missed out on sleep this week. A niggle of guilt surfaced. Should she have called him back? "I didn't expect you until later."

"I pulled a couple all-nighters and bugged out early." He snagged her hand and pulled her into the unoccupied conference room.

"Luke, what are you doing?"

"Checking to make sure you've taken care of yourself this week."

"I'm fine."

"You don't look it. I can see how exhausted you are."

"Gee, thanks for sparing my feelings." Shelby dug in her heels in an effort to avoid the conversation.

Luke firmed his hold and lifted his other hand to her cheek. "You're always beautiful, but you look ready to collapse."

"So do you."

"Nothing some sleep won't fix. How do you feel?"

The tenderness in his expression tugged at her heart. "It's been a long week."

"Have you been sick the whole time?"

She heard someone approaching and bit back a gasp. "Move." Surprising Luke, she put her hands on his chest and shoved him into the conference room far enough to close the door. She pressed her head to the wood panel and listened until the footsteps faded away.

Luke's hands settled on her shoulders and turned her to face him. The lights were off but the late-afternoon sunlight streamed in the windows. Shelby's stomach coiled tighter and tighter, and the weight on her chest made it difficult to breathe. Luke stood too close and things were such a mess and why did he have to smell so good? "I have to get back to work."

"Not yet."

"I've got a ton of things to do for Ethan's party."

"They'll wait."

"Mr. Long wasn't happy with the stunt my mother pulled this week or my involvement in it when I had to go pick her up." She left out the part about her screwups. Luke didn't need to know everything.

"He won't say a word."

Because of her connection to the Tulanes? Who wanted to go through life like that? She wanted to stand on her own.

"Stop worrying. Long was out on the driving range overseeing a problem when I drove in. Looked like he'd be there a while."

"Oh."

"Shelby, we need to talk. I gave you space. I didn't even grumble too much when you didn't call me back all week. With everything that happened with your mother I tried to back off, but it's time we deal with this."

"We have nothing to say that hasn't already been said. I'm not having this discussion now, especially not *here*."

Luke placed a palm against the door by her head and leaned in close. "We have to give our baby the best life we can."

"Exactly. Which is why it would be a mistake for us to get married and make each other miserable." Why was he in her face? When had he become this…assertive? A part of her—that flutter inside her stomach she tried to ignore—would admit to liking this masculine, alpha side of him. But the woman in her who had to be in control was more than a little freaked.

"Like your parents?"

Unable to breathe, she sidestepped him and paced to the windows. On the patio below, the waitstaff set up the buffet tables while several of the ground crew wiped down chairs and cranked shade umbrellas to their fullest width. "Leave my family out of this. We want different things, Luke. It was only one night. Marriage would be a mistake and end in divorce. I wouldn't want that."

"I don't, either. But I also know the perfect way to prove to you that we're more compatible than you think."

The husky timbre of his voice made that little flutter go haywire. Her heart thudded in her chest and she was transported to that wonderful, horrible night. The words he'd growled into her ear while he held her close, the heat of his mouth and breath on her skin.

Luke stepped forward, his gaze sweeping her body from head to toe. Watching him look at her warmed her insides and made her want to believe him. Made her want to think she wasn't a product of her upbringing and she could have the kind of life the Tulanes had. But how could she when she carried a boatload of emotional baggage from her screwed-up parents?

Shelby moved away, around the conference table, so that

every step he took toward her matched one that would get her closer to the now unguarded door. "Stop. We're not playing some stupid game of boss and secretary. Just stay there."

His lips quirked up at the corners. "What are you so afraid of? That I'm wrong? Or that I'm right?"

She should have known Luke would behave this way. Maybe he'd always been the shy one, but they'd spent too much time together playing in the attic. She knew how stubborn he could be, how determined. "Luke, I'll deal with this, okay? I don't expect anything from you. Not marriage, not money—nothing." Steel laced her words and a bitterness crept in that she couldn't hold back. She didn't want Luke tossing cash around like Zacharias Bennington and turning her into her mother.

"People are going to find out. What then?"

It would be a disaster and horrible. What adult woman accidentally got pregnant in this day and age? She'd probably be fired for cavorting with guests. Management frowned on that. But in her time off circling the want ads, maybe she could lie low and it would blow over? Shelby shook her head firmly back and forth. "What about it?"

"What kind of man would I be to walk away from you?"

A smart one? "I don't care what other people think." *Liar.*

"I don't either. But I'm not walking away from my child or its mother. All you have to do is trust me. I'll do my best to make you happy, to be a good husband. All you have to do is say yes."

"No."

Steam practically came out of his ears. "Why are you being so difficult? What about the baby? Do you care that it's going to wonder why we're not together? Why he or she wasn't more important than our petty differences?"

Why their parents had married in the first place? "I'll explain."

A disgruntled rumble sounded in his chest. "How? What are you going to say to make life better? You had a single parent off and on for years. How'd it feel?"

Scary. Out of control. Didn't he get it? Maybe she did owe him an explanation as to why she wouldn't marry him, but she couldn't tell him the truth. If she did, if she told him how scared and frightened and freaked-out marriage made her, if she told him she wanted to be loved but didn't want to put herself out there and wind up a needy, clinging woman like her mother, he'd pour on the charm. And she'd fall for it, hook, line and sinker, even though she knew—*she knew*—they would all be better off if he just left her and the baby alone.

She could control what she did, but she'd never be able to control him or his actions. How could she protect a child against that when she couldn't protect herself? "Marriage won't solve our problems, Luke. If anything, it would magnify them."

"Shelby, two months ago you couldn't get close enough to me. Why can't we go back to that?"

She felt her cheeks heat with an embarrassing glow. "I made a *mistake*."

"Everything happens for a reason."

"Not always. You want to know the real reason I slept with you?" *Don't say it, don't tell him. What if he—* "I slept with you because I was told I needed surgery. I—"

He straightened. "What kind of surgery?"

Her smile was wry. "The kind that ends all possibility of ever having children. The point is I needed someone and you were there. But make no mistake, Luke, it was just sex."

"It made a baby," he insisted softly. "Shelby, I'm going to tell my parents the news this weekend. I'd like it if—"

"What? *Why?*" She stared up at him in horror, too shocked to move when he slowly closed the distance between them once more.

This weekend? Couldn't they wait a few weeks?

"My mother isn't handling Ethan's departure well. This will give her something positive to focus on. She'll be thrilled."

She snorted. "I seriously doubt that."

"She will be. The longer we wait, the more likely it is that they're going to find out another way."

That was true, but didn't he realize how crazy everyone was going to get once they knew? And her mother… Drama queens lived for stuff like this and there would be no avoiding her mother once she found out. Shelby needed more time, more space, more breathing room to come up with a plan. "If I don't want to tell anyone about my baby—"

"*Your* baby? Where do I fit into this picture?"

Nowhere! "I don't mean to hurt you."

"You're hurting yourself. You're hurting the baby. Are you that afraid of having a real relationship?"

"I'm not afraid of anything."

His hands fisted at his sides and a muscle ticked just beneath his left eye and in that second he looked formidable and so sexy her toes threatened to curl. Who knew Luke's alpha side would turn her on?

"That's a crock. Your parents really did a number on you, didn't they?"

Just walk out and leave. What can he do? "As mad and upset with me as you are now, it will be worse when you wake up and realize I'm right. You think you'd be nice during a divorce? That we'd be civil? No one is. I'm doing us both a favor, Luke."

"No, you're shortchanging us both. You expect me to do

the *same thing* to my baby that was done to you. You want me to go on with my life and not acknowledge its existence like Zacharias did?"

She hadn't thought of it that way. But wasn't that what she was asking? Shelby raised her head and glared at Luke, but instead of intimidating him, Luke stood his ground and stared into her soul, made her feel vulnerable and angry.

Her sense of foreboding expanded, and when she couldn't take Luke's stare any longer, she nodded slowly. That was what she wanted. If he didn't acknowledge the baby, they could go on with their lives. She could raise the baby and—

Turn it into your dirty little secret?

Disappointment changed to fury, resignation, and drew his mouth into a tight line. "I'm sorry you feel that way. I'll call Garret and get the ball rolling."

She blinked. His brother, Garret, was one of the best attorneys in the state. "With what?"

"Getting custody of my child."

Her breath froze in her chest and it took her several seconds to shake off the shock. "What?"

"You don't leave me any choice."

"You'd take the baby from me?"

Luke scrubbed both hands over his face briskly. "I don't want to, but if you won't marry me and give us a shot, then, yes, I'll do what I have to do. I'm going to be an active father, Shelby, not one missing in action."

The queasiness became full-fledged nausea and she swallowed repeatedly.

"I won't argue visitation. You can come to California to see us whenever you like."

Come to— "You can't do this. How would you take care of a child and work?"

"The same way you would."

The scent of his cologne teased her nostrils. She'd been so sensitive to scents lately. Food, flowers. But Luke's smell sent a shiver over her spine and the queasiness abated, just a tad. But that didn't make sense.

"Shelby, I don't want it to be this way. I want us to come to terms, for both of us to be involved in our baby's life. Marriage was—*is* the way to do that." Luke moved toward the door but jerked his thumb toward the window. "I left something for you in your car."

"What is it?"

Luke hesitated, his hand on the knob. "I doubt you'll like it but I thought—" A wry smile pulled at his lips. "I don't know what I thought. I'd hoped you'd come around. I went to see a friend and was walking by a store when I remembered how much you hate to shop. It was in the window and…I could see you in it." A dull hue rose in his face. "I knew you wouldn't find anything like it around here, and you used to like surprises."

She still did—when they were good surprises. But in an instant she knew what the gift was and, like the baby, it wasn't a good surprise. "You bought me a *wedding* dress?" How arrogant. Every woman wanted to pick out her own dress. Yet the gesture was also sweet because Luke was right about the shopping thing. She hated it, having spent too many hours trapped in the car with her mother driving to the mall for marathon retail expeditions.

"Maybe you can sell it online or something."

"Luke, please, don't do this. We wouldn't stand a chance. My life is here. Yours is there. Whoever compromises loses."

"Only if you choose to look at it that way." He opened the door but paused again. "Shelby, we don't have any more obstacles between us than every other couple out there. Garret and Darcy, Nick and Jenn. They're still settling in and getting used to one another, but we've known each other forever. We even like each other, despite all this. Geographically, we'd have to figure something out, but that night? I'm smart enough to know that type of experience doesn't come along every day."

Memories swept over her, through her. "It was the moment, nothing else."

"It wasn't the moment, it was *us*. The two of us together. The child you carry was made by you and me and it should be raised the same way, together. Sweetheart, I'm going to ask one last time. Will you marry me?"

Shelby shook her head, shocked. "Those are the only two options you'll consider? Marriage or court?"

"If we both set our minds to it—"

"*Set our minds to it,*" she repeated with a rough laugh, her hand over her stomach, like the baby wasn't hearing every word, like she could protect it from their harsh tones. "Think about what you just said. Doesn't that tell you something? We shouldn't have to set our minds to it. We should *want* to get married."

"I do."

Shelby turned back to the window. "Well, I don't. I *won't* marry you."

CHAPTER ELEVEN

HOW DO YOU WIN an argument when the other side holds all the cards?

Two hours later Luke leaned against the railing beside the table where his family sat and pushed his food around on his plate, his appetite gone. After being angry enough that he had called Garret for legal advice, he'd gone for a walk around the grounds to cool off and avoid his family and the guests attending Ethan's party.

What was he going to do? How could he convince Shelby to take a chance? And if she didn't, how would he raise a baby in California alone? He'd have to hire a nanny, but did he want someone else raising his son or daughter? Maybe he could arrange to work from home part of the time so he'd be there for the baby. His job was important to him but it wasn't as important as family. But how did he make the compromise between work and his personal life? Was this what Shelby meant in that whoever compromised, lost?

He almost wished for the good old days when he could guarantee a shotgun wedding by informing their parents. It still wasn't out of the question. One word to Shelby's mother and Luke knew the woman would be all over the idea of being related to the Tulane name via marriage. But since he doubted Shelby was speaking to her mother at the moment,

Pat's reaction would only serve to make Shelby more determined *not* to marry him.

"Take it down a notch, little brother. Gram's picking up on your frustration with Shelby."

Luke stiffened and turned his attention to Ethan. His brother stood beside him while the rest of the guests mingled in the cloud-dappled sunlight beneath the tabled umbrellas and awnings.

When Ethan's comment registered, Luke shifted his attention to Gram and found her gazing at him with her ever-knowing blue eyes. "How long has she been watching me?"

"Long enough. You doing it on purpose? You haven't taken your eyes off Shelby since she stepped outside. Gram's got to be wondering why."

He wasn't doing anything on purpose but how could he not stare at Shelby? Pale before their discussion in the conference room, the mother of his child now looked ghostly. Despite her makeup, dark circles detracted from the beauty of her green eyes and her face was nearly the color of the clouds above their heads, her hair lacking its usual bouncy shine. Add the red hives visible on her neck above the high collar she wore, and the overall image was something to be worried about.

Shelby was a basket case of nerves, and stress wasn't good for her or the baby. She was angry with him over his decree that he'd sue for custody and he wasn't too pleased with himself for blurting that out. But her cold reaction to him had made him too angry to guard his words.

It wasn't a new trait on her part. He'd seen her shut down many times over the years. Shelby would argue up to a point, then simply shift to silence like a flipped switch. She internalized her upset. He knew, because the hives would appear, and she'd start doing this thing where she'd pause and take a deep breath, like she was so overwhelmed she couldn't breathe. He'd seen her do it in the conference room, again when she'd stepped out the patio doors. He didn't want to be the one to do that to her, make her feel that way. He wanted the baby, but he wanted her happiness, too. Wanted her, a life, sex and fun and all the things Gram and Grandad had had during their long marriage together. Pressuring her wasn't the answer. He had to find another way, change his approach.

"Look who I found."

Luke turned at Alexandra's statement, his whole body going on high alert. As one, all of the male members of his family seated at the table stood. He and Ethan straightened from their slouched positions.

Shelby waved a hand that trembled. "Please, sit down. I just came by to say hello and to wish Ethan a safe journey," she murmured, her gaze skittering away in a hurry when it landed on him.

Ethan pulled Shelby into a hug. "Thanks, sweetheart. Why don't you join us?" He sent Luke a taunting smirk that told him to eat his heart out.

"Sorry, I'm working. Thank you, though."

"Mr. Long is a reasonable fellow," his father said, holding Alex's chair for her to be seated. "I'm sure he wouldn't mind if you took a short break and joined us."

"Shelby, please do. You look a little pale, dear." Gram smiled. "Ethan, get Shelby a chair."

"I'm fine. I—"

Ethan snagged a chair from a nearby table and practically shoved Shelby's legs out from under her. Luke didn't argue the treatment, especially since the move placed Shelby closest to him where he leaned against the railing.

Shelby's eyes widened to the size of silver dollars when she saw the lobster on the table in front of her. Luke saw her swallow several times and what little color she had in her cheeks faded. He stiffened, wondering what he should do but unsure how to get her out of there without attracting too much attention.

"I'm, uh, sure Mr. Long is looking for me. I'd really better…go." Shelby shoved the chair back with a surge of movement that knocked it against the railing with a sharp *clang.* "Oh, I'm sorry. I—"

Luke snagged her arm when she practically wove a circle on her feet. "Are you all right?"

Panic crossed her features and for the first time that day, he saw a crack in her protective shell. She actually looked at him as though asking for help, her eyes expressing everything she couldn't. And in that moment he vowed to do whatever he had to make her believe in him. His job, his life, nothing would be worthwhile unless Shelby and their baby were at his side.

"Shelby, are you sick again?" Alex asked. "She was sick last week, too. That's why she didn't stay for the wedding."

"Shelby, sit down. Alan, why don't you—"

"I'm fine." Air wheezed out of her lungs and a white line circled her mouth. "Really."

"You don't look it." Alex scooted her chair back and moved around the table to where Shelby stood in his hold. "You look like you're ready to hurl. Sit down." Alex pressed Shelby back into the chair, not taking no for an answer.

"Her blood sugar might be low. Maybe she should eat something," Ethan said.

His brother's suggestion appeared perfectly innocent, but the look Ethan gave Luke was anything but.

"No, I—"

Alex grabbed a plate of food and shoved it under Shelby's nose. "He's right. You know how you get when you don't eat. The lobster is divine, and you should try some of— *Shelby?*"

Luke grimaced when Shelby clamped a hand over her mouth and shoved Alex and the plate of food out of the way just in time to stumble to her feet and bend over the railing.

The entire female population of his family scrambled out of their chairs, patting Shelby on the back, bringing water and napkins, tissues. Even his father stood at the ready in case she collapsed. Everyone but him, Ethan and...Gram. Luke avoided eye contact.

"The last time I got sick that quickly was when I was preg— *Oh.*" Darcy's words trailed off into stunned silence. His sister-in-law pasted a weak smile to her face and bounced the baby in her arms, glaring up at her husband. "You could've told me *why* Luke wanted custody advice."

Darcy's whisper carried and all eyes turned to him. Luke chose to keep his silence.

"What's going on?" Alex demanded. "What legal advice? Something for Shelby?"

"We should take this inside," Luke suggested quietly. "Away from the guests."

Alex's gaze locked on Shelby's face and her mouth dropped as she apparently formed her own conclusion.

Shelby opened her mouth but no words came, not even a denial.

Before Luke could be too pleased with the pregnancy news being forced out in the open, his gut twisted because Shelby squared her shoulders and lifted her chin high, battle-ready despite her sickness.

"Let's go inside," he said, grasping Shelby's arm. "Will someone make our excuses?"

"I will." Darcy made a face. "Shelby, I'm sorry. I should've kept my mouth shut. I know how gossip gets started and I hope you'll forgive my blunder."

Shelby managed a smile before he ushered her inside the country club, glad to see the dining room virtually empty. His immediate family congregated in a corner and all eyes turned to Shelby. He sought Alex's gaze and nodded toward the hall exit. Lucky for him, his sister got the hint.

"Um, Shel? Let's go to the ladies' room so you can freshen up."

Without a word, Shelby and Alex walked away and he watched as Shelby did that struggle-to-take-a-breath thing again.

"Luke?" his father prodded.

"I'm the father." He forced himself to meet his father's disapproving stare. "I called Garret to ask about getting custody of the baby because Shelby has refused to marry me."

A roar of outrage and exclamations met his words as everyone began talking at once. Luke listened with half an ear, his attention tuned to Shelby's every movement. She hadn't made it to the bathroom yet and at the sound of everyone's protest she faltered, paused, then took off like a shot.

"YOU SAID *NO?* Why?" Alex demanded of Shelby as they continued to the ladies' room.

Alex would have to have had superhero-like hearing to catch Luke's quiet announcement to the rest of the family.

Shelby had a hard time pulling her gaze from the windows. Outside, busybody Mrs. Forbes yakked away to an equally nosy Mrs. Thomason. Both women alternately nodded and shook their heads and she could only imagine what was being said. Had they seen her getting sick? Did they know why most of Luke's family had left their guests to come inside?

"Shelby? *Why* won't you marry Luke?" Alex demanded impatiently.

Shelby forced herself to focus, wishing she was anywhere but there. "Because I don't think it's the answer." She pinched the crease of her forearm in an effort to stop the itching. "And it was an accident," she murmured, avoiding Alex's ever-watchful eyes. "Two wrongs won't make the situation better."

"But it will," Alex argued. "You know it will."

Shelby shoved her hair off her face. "I need to get back to work before I get fired."

"Dad will handle Mr. Long. Come on," Alex ordered, grabbing Shelby's hand and tugging. Shelby reluctantly let Alex pull her toward a side exit and out into the late-afternoon sunshine, but only because doing so got her away from everyone. What a nightmare. Luke's parents knew, her mother still didn't know, and she'd never hear the end of that.

Amazingly, Alex remained quiet until they reached the pool house. Replete with a bathroom, changing closets and a lounge area, the pool house had been the spot for a lot of their girl chats growing up, basically because the boys weren't allowed inside. Luckily it was empty, but the moment the door closed, Alex planted her hands on her hips and glared.

"Luke?"

"I'm sorry." Shelby moved to the sink and turned on the tap, cupping her hand and pooling the water to rinse her mouth.

"Why didn't you tell me?" Alex demanded. "You're really pregnant?"

Shelby nodded, eyes closed.

"If you're having symptoms now, it obviously happened a while ago. When? And why won't you marry him?"

Shelby met Alex's gaze in the mirror and noted her friend looked hurt and angry and on the verge of tears. Everything she was afraid Alex would be. Only friends had the power to hurt each other this way. "I didn't tell you because he's your brother and it shouldn't have happened." She turned off the faucet and grabbed some paper towels. "As to why?" She groaned. "Where do I start?"

"Then why sleep with him?"

"I wasn't *planning* on it. Neither was Luke. It just happened."

"And yet you took the risk of getting pregnant? That doesn't sound like either of you. You're two of the most responsible people I know."

Normally, yes. Not that she had a lot of experience, but she'd always protected herself the few times sex had been an issue. Avoiding eye contact, Shelby explained about her doctor visit. "I was upset and angry and totally freaked-out. I know it's no excuse but I needed someone. That's all I can say. I totally lost it because thinking you don't want kids because of a horrific childhood is one thing, but being told you *can't* have them? I was heading home after a lousy day and there he was and—I don't know. We started talking and then we were kissing and then…it happened."

Alex stepped in front of her. "From what you just said, it sounds like you picked Luke for a reason."

Picked him? "No. It was an accident. He was there."

"So were a lot of other guys, but you chose Luke. And you took a risk you've never taken before. There has to be a reason for that."

What did Alex want her to say? Her reaction wasn't what Shelby was expecting at all. "I thought I couldn't *get* pregnant." She ran her hands through her hair and shoved it off her face. "It was a *moment*. I—I felt like I'd been slammed against the wall and I couldn't breathe and—"

"*And* we're back to the fact you chose Luke when any guy there could've given you sex. But you didn't want that, did you?"

"I don't know what you mean."

Alexandra's violet eyes narrowed shrewdly. "Yes, you do. Oh, Shel, you could've picked up anyone, but you *didn't*. And you can't stand there and tell me there wasn't more to your decision than the fact Luke was *there*. The doctor said you couldn't have kids. Do you think maybe you wondered if something were to happen, of all the men to choose Luke would be—"

"What? *No*." She shook her head firmly back and forth. "I didn't plan it at all!"

"I doubt you did. But subconsciously maybe you hoped something *would* happen because you chose him." Tears flooded Alex's eyes. "*How* can you deny Luke his child? How can you be that cruel?"

Alex's accusations hit like physical blows. "Does it have to mean marriage?"

"Why not marry him? We're talking about Luke. Luke, who has *always* had a thing for you. Don't stand there and pretend you weren't aware of it. You've always liked him, too. Make this easy on me and marry him. Put me out of misery because if you don't, I'm going to have to smack you around."

A rough laugh left her chest and they both smiled, the tears, the tension, a little lighter due to Alex's joking threat.

"Alex, I like him. Okay? And I care for him, but *like* and caring do not make a marriage."

"Friendship does. And you said yourself you turned to him when you needed someone and he was there for you. Wow, what a horrible trait in a husband."

"You're making this personal."

"It *is* personal! You slept with *my* brother. You made a baby with him and now you're blowing him and all the rest of us off?"

It sounded so awful but it was true. All true. The tension inside her grew, winding tighter and tighter. "It's complicated."

Alex muttered under her breath and brushed her knuckles over her lashes. "Shel, if you'd chosen Ethan that night, okay, I'd get why you'd be worried about marriage, because he's still a horn-dog. But I can't stress enough that Luke isn't Ethan." Alex dropped her hands to her side and huffed. "How can you *not* want Luke involved in the baby's life when he's such a good guy?"

"I know that. It has nothing to do with him not being a wonderful man. He's…he's great."

"Then marry him, for pity's sake."

And then what? Divorce him five times? After watching her parents love each other, who could tell if she knew how to love? What she'd told Jerry was true. Love was a moment. "Have you heard nothing I've said? It would never work. Even if he lived here, it probably still wouldn't work. But how would we ever get along when he wants me to move to California? Alex, he wants me to give up everything."

Alex frowned at her words, deflating. "Really? We'd definitely have to change his mind about living here, but if that weren't a problem?"

Okay, so maybe she'd stretched the truth a bit about that

since Luke *technically* hadn't asked her to move to California because she hadn't given him a chance to. But self-preservation was instinctive. She didn't want Alex to hate her. "It wouldn't work."

"You keep saying that, but I get the impression you're thinking with your brain and your memories, not your heart." She stepped close and put her hands on Shelby's shoulders, shook her gently. "Shel, a *baby*."

Shelby closed her eyes when her stomach protested the thought with a nauseating twist. She groaned. "Alex, what am I going to do? I've never even babysat."

Luke's sister laughed, the sound teary. "I know. And I know you're scared. I would be, too. But you don't have to do this alone."

"That's what Luke said."

Alex's expression hardened, her dark hair and red lipstick very dramatic paired with her red strapless dress. "Because it's true. You've got Luke and me and all of our family to help you. But you can't shut us out of the baby's life. And if you do, Luke has every right to sic Garret on you. I'm sorry, but that's how I feel. The baby belongs to both of you. Where is the fairness in you keeping the baby from him?"

Alex's statement hurt. But everyone knew blood was thicker than water. What else did she expect? "I didn't want anything more from Luke than *one night*. Now suddenly everyone is talking marriage and— It's crazy."

"The best laid plans change." Alex winced. "Bad pun, but you get my drift. Look, it's done, right? So why not turn everything around?" She pulled Shelby close for a hug. "You two have had a thing for each other for years. Admit it."

Shelby closed her eyes and struggled to come up with the right answer. "Childhood crushes don't count. We didn't even have a crush on each other at the same time. I liked him before I even knew what a French kiss really was and he liked me after—"

"He saw your red bra at a sleepover. Doesn't matter, though. Shel, it's way more than a crush when you go to bed together."

Shelby pulled away. "You're trying to make it romantic when it was just sex."

"Let's not get too detailed, please. That's my brother you're talking about, remember?" Alex tugged Shelby over to the rattan love seat and made her sit. "What if…just go with me here for a minute, okay?"

"Do I have to?"

"Yes. What if this wasn't an accident?"

Shelby lowered her head and stared at her hands. "Rosetta's saying?"

"Yup. You know Gram's usually right. So think about it. That night? When you needed someone so badly and Luke was there? When the two of you connected in a way that wasn't supposed to be possible? That's a pretty big coincidence, don't you think?"

"It was sex."

"Sex that made a baby when you'd just been told you couldn't have one. Are you seriously telling me that doesn't strike you as significant?" Alex grabbed her arm and shook her gently. "What if subconsciously, you turned to him because you know your feelings for Luke have always run deeper than friendship? And maybe, just maybe, you thought if there was the slightest chance the doctor was wrong, Luke was it?"

Shelby shook her head that it wasn't true but…was it?

"Shelby, I know you didn't do this on purpose. But it happened and you have to do what's right."

She buried her face in her hands and moaned. "Now you

really sound like Luke. I'm more objective, I think. I know what the best thing is."

"Refusing him?" Alex got to her feet and stalked away. "Luke will make an amazing father. He's patient and kind, and you're not being fair. That's my niece or nephew you're carrying."

"I know! But you know what else? When we divorce, I'll lose you all. You don't know what divorce does to people. Nice people, people who've always gotten along and loved each other turn nasty and hateful. Nothing would ever be the same. But if we could work something else out, we could still be—"

"A family? Shel—"

A thud hit the outside of the pool house, startling them both, and Shelby used it as an excuse to move to the window. Outside Nick and Matt passed a football back and forth. The ball was on the ground more than in the air, but Nick constantly encouraged Matt in his throws.

Just like Luke would.

Was Alex right? Why had she chosen Luke that night? Had she subconsciously hoped that the doctor was wrong and something *would* happen?

If she were brutally honest, if she dug deep to that spot within her she'd learned to guard…maybe. Given all Luke's wonderful qualities, his friendship, the way he'd looked that night, like he understood what it was like to feel out of place.

Alex moved to stand behind her. "They're cute together, aren't they?"

Shelby didn't respond.

Alex wrapped her arms around her and put her chin on Shelby's shoulder. "Whatever happens, we'll make it okay. We have to because we're sisters at heart. You've gotta stop running, Shel. You need to face the craziness of your parents and deal with it."

"I have."

"Nice try, but you haven't. Not even close. Every marriage doesn't end in divorce. Look at Mom and Dad, and Gram and Granddad. What if you and Luke could have that? Would you really throw away your chance because your parents couldn't get their act together?"

An overwhelming sense of longing caught her by surprise, but it was followed by despair. She wanted her chance, but Alex didn't understand. "You don't know what it was like. You were never there during the worst of it. I made sure of that."

Alex hugged her again. "I know. But I could still tell. Shel, you're not your mother and you're not Zacharias Bennington, either. You're you, and you're a good person. Can you really deny Luke the chance to be a father? Keep us from the absolute pleasure of watching the baby grow up? It was bad enough only seeing Matt a couple times a year."

Shelby closed her eyes. "I don't want anyone to get hurt. That's what I'm trying so hard to avoid."

"Denying us hurts worse, Shel. My family, most especially Luke, has given you friendship and love. We wouldn't take it back for anything, but if you do this, you're taking it back."

"That's low. Alex, I *can't*—"

"You can if you want to. The question isn't whether or not it's the right thing to do, but whether or not you want what you can have. Are you going to throw it all away?"

Outside, Nick chased Matt in an attempt to get the ball and she smiled sadly when Nick caught his son and swooped him up in the air. Matt's laughter ran out, loud and innocent.

She could so see Luke doing that. Playing. Laughing.

Doing the things fathers did, and deep down, she knew she couldn't deny him. Not because of what Alex said, but because she was Jerry Brookes's daughter and Luke had the right to know his child. Who could be that cruel when Luke's interest was so genuine in a world filled with men who walked away and never came back? Men who never acknowledged their child's existence.

She felt physically ill at the thought of Luke suing her for custody, so how could she turn around and expect him to play the role of distant parent? What about his rights? It wasn't fair. None of this was fair, but how could she ask him to make a sacrifice she wasn't willing to make herself?

CHAPTER TWELVE

"STOP WORRYING," Garret ordered, careful to keep his voice low. "She'll come around before we ever get close to filing with the court."

Garret had gone out to check on things outside, then returned with a status report. The gossips had seen Shelby hurling over the balcony and had drawn their own conclusions—correct ones. According to Garret, everyone now wondered when the wedding date would be, doubling the pressure Luke felt if Shelby continued to refuse him.

"She's too damn stubborn."

"She'll do what's best for the baby. She might not do it for herself, but Shelby doesn't strike me as the kind of person to accept half measures. Once she gets used to the idea of being pregnant and having a child, she'll come around. It's barely been a week, right? Just give her time."

Luke sighed at the thought of a court battle. Could he really put her through that? He'd have to if she expected to keep him away. "What's taking Alex and Shelby so long?"

"Maybe Alex is making progress."

Maybe. If anyone could convince Shelby to see his side of things, Alex could. But was that what he wanted? For Shelby to have to be talked into marrying him?

"Are you sure about this if Shelby *does* agree?" Garret

glanced around. "Luke, I know how Mom and Dad feel about things, but if Shelby's dead set against marriage, maybe you should try to work something else out."

The side door opened, the one Alex had dragged Shelby out of, and one by one the remaining members of his family turned to watch Shelby head straight for him. Alex was two steps behind her and looked a little nervous, like she didn't know what Shelby was about to do. Not good.

Without a word to Garret, Luke separated himself and met Shelby halfway, aware that all conversation amongst his family had stopped.

"I'll do it," Shelby muttered without preamble, her gaze on his chin. "I'll m-marry you, but *only* with conditions."

The rest of his family slowly gathered round. Shelby's face reddened and Luke couldn't blame her. He would have liked some privacy for this conversation, but he knew better than to attempt to get it. At least he wouldn't have to repeat everything a multitude of times since they were all hearing it firsthand. "Ignore them. It's not like they'd listen if we asked them to go away. What conditions?"

Shelby glanced around, her face reddening even more. Then she squared her shoulders and met his stare. "I'm not moving to California. Regardless of what you do with your job, I'm staying here, *living* here, and so is the baby."

She'd marry him but not live with him? Of all the—"Shelby, I can't move back to Tennessee. I can't leave my job."

"That's my condition. I'm not giving up my home or my plans for the mill house. Period."

"Luke, you don't want to whisk her off to California away from everything and everyone she's ever known, do you? You expect her to have the baby *there?*"

The way his mother said *there* made California sound like a foreign country.

"Of course not," Gram added. "Luke knows how important it is that a pregnant woman be surrounded by family during such an exhausting time. She needs support and help. And if he's always working, the right thing to do is let her stay home."

Wouldn't her home be with him? Why were they taking *her* side? This was his life, too. His baby and, if she said yes, his wife. He'd support her. Help her. Shouldn't that be enough? Heat crept up his neck and into his face. His own family supported her instead of backing him up. Then again, it wasn't a surprise, not considering how they felt about his life so far from home. "I *can't* move back to Tennessee."

"Then don't." Shelby's lower lip trembled, but she acted like it didn't. "If you want to live and work there, fine. But I'm not moving and when the baby comes, it stays here with me and our families. You can…come home on weekends."

The last of her statement was ingenious on her part, guaranteed to keep his family happy and make him look like the bad guy. And it worked. As one, his relatives nodded in agreement, sliding him looks that were a combination of chiding, coaxing and amusement.

Stock-still, he glared into Shelby's set features. She actually expected him to agree to her being his weekend wife? No freaking way.

Garret stepped close to his side, turning so that his back was to Shelby and the majority of the crowd. "Shut up and listen before you say something you regret. Shelby's counting on you to say no," he pointed out. "If you want her, you're going to have to jump through the hoop and deal with the fallout later. You wanted marriage and you're getting it this way. Say yes."

Luke ran a hand over his shaggy head and noted his father's gaze followed the movement. Alan's expression reeked of disapproval. His hair, his occupation. Living in big, bad California and playing video games wasn't a job according to his physician father, but designing them so others could waste their time? That was even worse. Toss in Shelby's pregnancy and he was a great big wad of disappointment. No wonder Nick hadn't spoken to the family for so many years.

"Say yes," Garret ordered. "Now."

Why did Shelby have to make everything so difficult? "Yes," he snapped. "I accept."

"There, see?" Gram sent him a wink.

Shelby gaped at him, her mouth falling open in surprise. Garret was right. She really had expected him to back off and not agree to her stubborn stipulation.

"That'll do. For now," Gram murmured, flashing Luke the same smile his grandfather had once claimed had the power to knock a man on his ass and leave him senseless.

But he wasn't his grandfather. His family had been after him for years to move back, at least live within a few hours' driving distance. But California was the hub for what he did and he had to stay there. Could they see that? No, they expected him to drop a lucrative career to move back and do what?

It took him a moment to realize Shelby still looked thunderstruck by his agreement. He decided to take advantage of her silence, before she could change her mind or think of something else to add to her list of conditions. Pulling the velvet box from his jacket pocket, he dug the ring from the folds.

"What— *Now?*"

Luke ignored Shelby's hushed question. He snagged her hand and slipped the ring on her finger, waiting for her reaction. But all she did was curl her fingers into a fist and stare at the pear-shaped emerald surrounded by two layers of diamonds. He'd never considered her a diamond solitaire kind of woman and had bought the ring the moment he'd laid eyes on it. Had he made a mistake? Did she want something more traditional?

"It's…beautiful."

"It matches your eyes."

"Is Uncle Luke going to kiss her?" Matt asked from the sidelines.

Luke hadn't realized Nick and his son had entered the dining room, but Luke smiled at his nephew's suggestion. Not a bad idea. At least in that he and Shelby got along.

Luke lowered his head for a kiss only to find his lips brushing the corner of Shelby's mouth when she turned her head. In response, he slipped his fingers into her hair and held her gently, brushing another kiss along her cheek then across her lips. She trembled and that, more than anything, cut through the haze of turmoil attacking his overloaded brain. Shelby was scared. Anyone in her right mind would be scared, and Shelby had more reason than most. He'd have to remember that. Adjust and make allowances. "We'll make this work."

"You're delusional if you really believe that."

Luke held back a husky laugh. There was his happy bride.

"So, we making the announcement tonight?" Ethan asked.

Luke stared at Shelby's averted face and knew he couldn't give her too much time to gather her flagging emotions. He searched his mind for a suitable date and then had a brainstorm of his own. "Yeah. And I'd like you to be here for the ceremony."

"But…Luke, your brother leaves in a few days." His mother

exchanged a look of concern with Gram. She no doubt worried at the suddenness of it—and the planning. But his mother was good, the ultimate charity event organizer, and he knew she could pull something together in the time allotted, blindfolded and with her hands tied behind her back. "I suppose we could go to Pigeon Forge tomorrow," he suggested, knowing full well his family wouldn't go for that.

"Not on Labor Day weekend, you can't. Those chapels book months and even years in advance," Alex said.

Shelby shut her eyes and took a deep breath. "Do we have to do it so...soon? I'm sure Ethan would understand."

Luke glared at Ethan to keep him quiet.

"Sorry, sweetheart. If it's all the same to you, I would like to be here," Ethan said, lifting the glass in his hand. "It's not every day one of my brothers gets married."

Everyone laughed at that. Luke doubted many families had three weddings in a year.

Luke slipped his hand beneath Shelby's chin and nudged her face back to his. "Everyone is here now. And Judge Chambers is a guest. He can issue a special license." He smiled, knowing without a doubt that his father's old friend would agree to the request.

"Um, couldn't we just go to the courthouse before Ethan leaves? Have a small, private ceremony? With everything that's happened this week," she whispered, "don't you think that would be...best?"

"Nonsense, Shelby."

His mother pulled Shelby into a hug, a blatant sign of motherly support. Then again, why wouldn't she love this turn of events? Shelby had gotten him to agree to come home more often—something Marilyn and her prayer circle hadn't managed to accomplish.

"I say we do this right. Rosetta and I are getting to be old hands at planning weddings. When do you return to California, Luke?"

"Sunday afternoon. I won't be able to return again until after Ethan's left for Niger."

"Well," his mother murmured, sliding Shelby a sympathetic but firm glance, "it looks as though tomorrow is your wedding day."

CHAPTER THIRTEEN

MR. LONG GAVE Shelby the rest of the weekend off and actually seemed okay about the turn of events. Then again, in the face of making the Tulanes happy, she figured he didn't have many options but to go with the flow.

Two hours after agreeing to marry Luke, Shelby found herself seated at a table with Marilyn, Rosetta, Alex, Darcy, Jenn and a whole slew of Luke's aunts and female cousins.

"What about a dress?" Alex asked. "Do you know what style you'd like? We could try to run to Nashville tonight." She checked her watch with a frown. "If we spent the night and got started first thing in the morning, we could be home by evening. Maybe sneak in a mani-pedi?"

Shelby opened her mouth to respond, but someone put heavy hands on her shoulders and leaned over her. In an instant she recognized Luke's touch. How scary was that?

"Shelby has a dress."

"You do?" Alex frowned.

"I bought her one as a gift. If it fits, I'd like her to wear it." All of the women stared at her, waiting for her to comment.

"She hasn't had a chance to see it yet," Luke explained.

His hands gently squeezed and, like it or not, she felt a measure of comfort from his touch, his scent. Was she making the right decision? Doing the right thing for the baby? "I'm sure it's beautiful. It'll be fine. If not…I'll find something."

The talk continued around her as women chimed in with their opinions on the hows and must-haves.

"What about flowers? Do you like roses? Or calla lilies?"

"Yoo-hoo! Shelby!"

Shelby's heart stopped. *Oh, no. Please, no.* She turned toward the dining room's entrance and moaned when she saw her mother blocked by the hostess.

"Shelby! There, see? There's my daughter. Shelby, come tell this nice woman who I am."

Shelby shoved away from the table. It was bad enough to sit there with Luke's family but to have her mother join in? "I have to go."

"Sit down, Shelby." Rosetta curled her hand over Shelby's and held her in the chair. "Breathe, child. You're going to be sick again if you don't."

Everyone watched as Ethan spoke with the hostess and Pat beamed at the handsome doctor for coming to her rescue. She curled her arm over his and played the simpering debutante as Ethan escorted her down the balcony steps and across the dining room toward them. And with every step the knot in Shelby's stomach grew larger.

Please don't make a scene, please don't make a scene, please don't—

"Oh, I just can't believe it! My baby is getting married and having a *ba-bee!* Shelby, come give your mama a hug."

Rosetta squeezed her hand again before releasing it. Shelby reluctantly stood and her mother nearly toppled her with a perfume-laden bear hug that shoved hairspray-laden hair into Shelby's face.

"Oh, honey, why didn't you tell me? Is that what you

wanted to talk about on Sunday? After everything that's happened this week—"

"Mom, please, just sit down."

"No, baby, I can't. We have to settle this once and for all." Large tears filled her mother's eyes and trickled out over her eyelashes, real ones this time. "Please, tell me you forgive me."

Like she could refuse in front of Luke's entire family, with the members of the club and everyone else watching? Her gaze shifted to find Luke and she saw him eyeing her with concern. "It's fine, Mom."

"Really? Do you mean it?"

She knew her mother wouldn't stop until she agreed. Shelby felt her face heat even more. "Yes. Please, sit down." *And behave.*

Jennifer scooted back her chair and stood. "Ms. Taylor, we're glad you could join us. Take my seat by Shelby."

"Oh, thank you, sweetie. Look at me, I'm shaking like a leaf! It isn't every day you find out your only daughter is having a baby. Can you see me as a grandmother?" she asked those at the table as she seated herself. "I've already scheduled a facial and full-body mud wrap." She shook her head and her oversize earrings wagged back and forth like pendulums. "I wish you had at least called me, Shelby. A mother wants to hear these things from her daughter. But I suppose," she said with a drawn-out sigh, "that doesn't matter now. Why, I couldn't believe it when Martha Bumgarner called the shop to tell me what was going on here." Pat pressed her fingers to her mouth and let the tears flow. "To think your father died when he could've—"

"He wasn't my father." Despite nearly whispering the four words, Shelby's voice carried to the others, and she felt their pitying stares.

Her mother dabbed at her eyes. "Of course you feel that way, Shelby. Why would you feel differently when he never did right by you?"

Shelby eyed the closest door. She could make it in about ten steps.

"Where were we?" Rosetta asked, effectively halting the subject and steering them back on course. The older woman took Shelby's hand once more, her grip casual but firm. "What kind of flowers would you like, dear? Roses?"

"Oh, yes. Roses are so elegant," her mother drawled. "Shelby, you must have roses. Bunches and bunches of them."

Shelby attempted to smile but couldn't muster the energy. "It doesn't matter."

The table fell silent and Shelby knew she'd screwed up again. Of all things to say. Most brides cared about flowers and dresses. Most brides wanted to marry their grooms. Most brides were in love. *Hello? You're not most brides.* "I meant, whatever you think is best. I'm not good with flowers."

Her attempt to smooth over her blunder must have worked. The ladies began suggesting their favorites and conversation resumed.

"Would you like a drink, Ms. Taylor?" Darcy asked from across the table.

"I believe I would. Thank you. I had to park a mile away and I'm parched."

Just what she needed, her mother dehydrated and drunk. "Mom, maybe—"

"A diet, please. Shelby, really, how could you wait so long to tell me about you and Luke? I could've been dieting all this time. Oh, I'll never find a dress this late. I can't just pull any old thing out of the closet. What will I wear?"

"Here." Ethan held out a drink. "In lieu of a bachelor party, this will have to do."

Luke accepted the glass and found himself surrounded by his brothers, father, cousins and uncles.

"To marriage," his father said, raising his glass. "May your marriage to Shelby be long and lasting, full of happy times and love."

"And lots of sex," Ethan added, drawing chuckles from the others.

Luke took a drink but couldn't pull his focus from Shelby. She sat on the other side of the dining room with the women, scratching one of the blotches covering her every time her mother spoke, which was pretty much nonstop except when his mother or Rosetta cut the woman off.

"You sure about this?"

He looked at Garret and nodded. "Yeah. Stop asking me that."

"Shelby is great, don't get me wrong. But she doesn't exactly look like a happy bride-to-be."

Garret was astute as always. "She doesn't think we can make it."

His brother stiffened. "Then maybe you should wait until Ethan gets back from his trip. Luke, you and Shelby have to *both* want this to make it work."

"We'll be fine."

Garret wrapped his arm around Luke's shoulders and drew him away from the others. "The whole thing about you not being able to move back…what was up with that?"

Luke felt the intensity of his brother's stare. "What do you mean?"

"Come on. I know there were some issues between you and Nick growing up. All that stupid stuff with him always getting into trouble and you backing him up when you should have steered clear."

It's what brothers, twins, were supposed to do. "I like California."

"I know you do. But how's a marriage going to work with you gone five days a week?"

Not easily. "I'm hoping she'll come around. All I know is that I want to be a father."

"And Shelby's husband."

He didn't deny it. "Is it so obvious?"

"Only to those who know you've always liked her. Just make sure you know what you're getting into and remember pregnant women are moody, irritable and cry at the drop of a hat. Rational behavior takes a hike when those kinds of hormones are involved."

Luke accepted the advice without comment. Garret knew what he was talking about because when his brother had met Darcy she'd been very pregnant with another man's baby. The thing was, Shelby was moody and irritable on a good day. But unlike most guys, he'd give anything for Shelby to cry and shout and make a fuss, anything instead of pushing him away.

SHELBY STARED at her reflection in her bedroom mirror and tried to calm her racing heart. Her wedding night. If someone had said last week that she'd be married right now, she'd have called him crazy. But crazy was just how this felt. She knew of people who'd run off to Vegas, Gatlinburg or Pigeon Forge after knowing each other a short amount of time, but even though she'd known Luke over twenty years, it still seemed absurdly sudden. Freakishly, frighteningly sudden.

The ceremony had been held in the backyard of Marilyn

and Alan's mountaintop home, the occasion even more beautiful than planned due to Luke's interference in the arrangements his family and her mother had made. Last night when the women had sat around the table, she'd let them decide everything. The music, the flowers. But Luke had vetoed their decisions—and proved just how well he knew her.

Instead of roses, her bouquet was made of a mixture of miniature sunflowers, roses, mums and ivy with the sweet scent of honeysuckle tucked into the mix. Instead of classical music, Luke had requested his band-member cousin—a country music wannabe living in Nashville—sing Joe Cocker's "You Are So Beautiful" and dedicate it to her. From within the house she'd watched the crowd wipe away tears while she and Jerry—dressed in his one and only suit that he hated but had worn just for her—waited in the living room by the back door for their cue.

The initial music had begun and she'd been sick to her stomach because her mother wasn't there yet—a sign Shelby instinctively knew meant trouble. Seeing her glance over her shoulder toward the front entrance, her father had given her a hug, told her he loved her, then said he wouldn't hold what she'd said about keeping his name against her and, if she'd changed her mind, his truck was waiting outside.

The temptation to take him up on the offer had been so strong. Then she'd looked out the window and seen Luke taking his position at the end of the aisle and she knew she couldn't do that to him. The music began and it was time and there they went, toward Luke. She and her father had just stepped outside when her mother made her entrance wearing a white suit, white sparkly heels and yet another hat with a veil. Her mother had wrapped her arm around Jerry's free one, posed for the photographer, and then they were on their way again, the guests' whispers loud in Shelby's ears.

Everyone had been shocked. Shelby was momentarily, too, but she'd also expected her mother to do *something* to draw attention to herself and she had. Jerry was right. In life two constants were death and taxes. The third was her mother making a spectacle of herself in order to be the center of attention. But Shelby also had a feeling there was more to her mother's bride attire than simply fodder for gossip. She'd felt like a third wheel standing by her parents. The way they'd looked at each other. A part of her knew her mother well enough to suspect her mother was hoping her father saw Pat as a bride again. His bride.

Now the wedding was over. The cake had been cut, the bouquet thrown and she and Luke were back at her house for the night since he had to go back to California tomorrow. She was supposed to be changing, but all she could do was stare at the beautiful gown Luke had given her, amazed all the way down to her toes because it was so very perfect, exactly what she would have chosen for herself.

Strapless, the bodice was heavily beaded at the top and over her breasts, the number of beads and sequins lessening at her ribs and finally ending in trickling sparkles at her waist where her skirt was lightly gathered on the left. The rest of the white material cascaded to the floor, straight and simple and very elegant.

When she'd got up that morning her hives were still visible, not exactly something a bride wants on her wedding day. Luckily the small dose of allergy medicine her doctor said was safe had helped them disappear.

"Shelby?" Her bedroom door opened, startling her.

"I'm not ready yet."

Her comment brought a smile to Luke's lips. "I'll help you with your dress." He crossed the room and, before she could argue, his hands tugged at the zipper.

"So you expect sex, just like that?"

LUKE STILLED momentarily at Shelby's query, then smoothed his hands up to her shoulders and began a slow massage. She was tighter than the bow Aiya carried in Mystic Magi.

"I suppose you want laundry services, too?"

He hadn't graduated top in his class for nothing. Shelby was trying to pick a fight, trying to keep him at arm's length and get him angry. Angry enough to wig out on their wedding night and let her sleep alone? Not happening. He knew why she pushed, knew he had to push back. His gaze met hers in the mirror. "I don't expect you to wait on me hand and foot," he told her, dropping his head to kiss her temple.

"Good thing."

He trailed his lips to the crook of her neck and the tender skin below her ear. She might not like the situation but she responded to him. Her lashes lowered, her breath hitched in her throat, and she tried to hide the shiver that coursed through her at his touch. He felt it, though.

"It'll never last."

They were back to that again? He debated the merits of kissing her senseless to shut her up. But just yesterday he'd wanted her to rant. Not argue and bicker with him over the inevitable, but to truly blow up—explode until she released all the tension and the hives went away on their own. He grazed his knuckles down the length of her spine revealed by the dress, liking the wave of goose bumps that followed his stroke.

"You want sex now but what about when I'm huge and

you're in California with inflatable blondes? What then?" she demanded, turning so that she faced him, her arms crossed over her chest to hold up the dress. "Who's to say you won't get grossed out by a big, fat pregnant belly and find some entertainment on the side?"

Luke stared into her green eyes, able to see the fear she tried to mask with bravado and spunk. She wasn't a crier, not his Shelby. She was a fighter, one backed in a corner and swinging with all her might. "If you're so worried about it, why not join me in California?"

Her mouth flattened into a sharp line.

Luke lifted his hands and cradled her face, leaned lower and nuzzled her nose with his. Her mouth parted, close. Close enough that he heard the nearly soundless moan she gave before she touched her tongue to her lips. "The thought of you carrying my baby turns me on," he told her bluntly. "You are so beautiful, Shelby."

"Luke…"

"I expect fidelity from you for the next fifty years or so." He bent his knees to be at eye level with her and had to smother a sigh when she set her jaw and glared at him. "If I can't honor my vows and promise fidelity to you, how can I expect it in return?"

"Fifty years?"

"Wanna make it sixty?" He dipped his head and kissed the corner of her mouth, the other corner, brushed his lips over her soft cheek and slid back to her mouth again. "Shelby…" Her stiff arms dug into his stomach because she still held the dress. "I'm in this for the long haul. You have to stop thinking of us in the short-term and get used to the fact that I'm now your husband and I'm going to be your husband for a long, long time."

A rough laugh left her chest. "Guys say anything when they want sex."

"I want it all."

She shook her head, her expression heartbreaking. "No one can have everything. Luke, seriously, you're delusional if you—"

He covered her mouth with his, delving, tasting. Sometimes, there was only one way to shut a woman up.

CHAPTER FOURTEEN

LUKE'S LIPS COVERED hers and Shelby found herself giving over to the sensation. His tongue swept inside and stroked, deeper, and the kisses blended one to another. His mouth nibbled and sucked at her lips and her mind shut down, her body melting into Luke's as he pulled her closer with single-minded intent.

Then it hit her. She could do this, have this, if she did things her way. Why hadn't she thought of that before?

Her arms curled around his neck, her fingers plunged into his hair and held tight while Luke's hands slipped inside the loose front of the beautiful gown. He cupped her breasts and squeezed and she forced herself to bite back a moan. The dress pooled at her feet.

Luke swung her up in his arms and in seconds he'd lowered her onto the sheets, removed her hose and the slinky underwear—a gift from Alex—and continued his wedding night seduction by kissing the skin revealed. She stared up at the ceiling and floated on a cloud of questionable desire, needing him but not wanting him that way.

How could it be like this? How could he make her feel so much? Want the things she knew better than to believe in?

"Stay with me, sweetheart."

The order was whispered against her skin as Luke made

his way up her body. Shelby closed her eyes, kept them closed, and let him kiss her, touch her as he wanted, careful to remember this was nothing more than sex.

Luke dropped kiss after kiss onto her body, each one threatening to be the one that made her heart skid out of control. She let her hands roam. Over the taut muscles of his shoulders, the velvety soft skin of his ribs, down to his belt and the front of his suit pants. She hesitated there, then pulled, unbuckling, unsnapping and unzipping, and drawing more than one frustrated chuckle from Luke when her actions turned a wee bit rough in her effort to rid him of the clothing.

He had a light dusting of jet-black hair on his chest that trailed down his stomach, and she ran her fingers through it, then lower over the enviously flat plane of his stomach.

"I can't wait to be inside you again."

Luke brushed her hands aside and lowered himself onto her. She didn't like it. Didn't like his weight, didn't like feeling so submissive or the way he didn't kiss her hard enough.

She strained off the bed, pushing against his shoulders until he lifted his head in question. Without a word, she pushed at him again, until Luke rolled and settled onto his back. Wanting more, wanting to feel and experience the power she'd felt that night, she pushed at his clothing until he freed himself of it and tossed it aside.

"Now what, sweetheart?"

Luke's smile flashed bright in the room lit by a lamp and the light from the hall. His hair fell over his forehead and should have looked boyish, but he was all man, reminding her of a sexier Orlando Bloom after he'd gone pirate. With a heated glance that had her stomach coiling in an entirely sensual way, Luke very deliberately drew her down, until she had to place one of her hands on his chest to stay balanced, over him.

Luke was lanky and hard and tanned, his skin paler on his hips and thighs, a funny strip of light skin surrounding one of his ankles. It took her a moment to think of what caused it and then remembered he liked to surf—something he couldn't do in Tennessee. Another reason for him to stay in California.

"What are you thinking?"

She wouldn't look at him, couldn't. Because if she did she was afraid he'd see her thoughts and know she'd never be able to give him what he wanted. Not everything. To give everything left her with nothing when he got tired of flying back and forth, tired of her moods and mountains of emotional baggage.

"Who wants to think?" She shifted and settled her leg firmly over his hips, smiled when she saw him tense and move his hands to grip her thighs. Shelby heard the rasp of his breath when she lowered her head to kiss him, closed her eyes and nudged her lower body in perfect position to take him within her.

"Look at me."

The husky order couldn't be ignored. Shelby lifted her heavy lids and found herself snared by Luke's dark blue gaze. Her breath froze in her lungs until she glanced away, distracting herself and him by moving on him until she found rhythm.

His hands tried to slow her fast pace and she pulled them away, curling her fingers through his and pressing them to the bed. To do so meant hovering over Luke even more and she tilted her head back when his mouth found her breast. He teased her with the promise of what awaited them, sharpening her awareness of where they joined and how it felt to be Luke's wife. But then the panic came, washed over her like a wave and sucked her out to sea.

Shelby pulled away and shoved herself upright, the act drawing a groan of pleasure from Luke when the angle and her weight drove him deeper.

"Shelby…sweetheart, come here."

Shelby shook her head and kept up the pace, not giving in to the temptation. This was what they could have and she didn't want to want more.

Over and over again she plunged her hips down on him, feeling the tension within her grow and expand, knowing he watched her, hearing the words he murmured, but still unable to give him everything in return. She could feel him, touch him, taste him. She just couldn't love him. The tension crested sharply within her and she bit her lip hard to stifle the cry of pleasure ripping from her throat. So good, *so* good.

Luke's hands gripped her hips to keep up the pace, grinding her against him until she had another miniclimax and he found release. Gasping, her body covered in a light sheen of sweat, she collapsed onto his chest, then rolled to the bed beside him. She'd stand by her decision to marry Luke for the baby's sake. She'd give him this.

Luke would soon learn that it would have to be enough.

"YOU GOT *MARRIED?*"

Luke unpacked his messenger bag on Monday morning and wished there was a way to avoid the conversation ahead. Lousy didn't begin to describe his mood. "Over the weekend."

"You can't be serious. *Luke?*" Anne-Marie slammed her palms down on his desk, her multiple bracelets jingling. "What the hell? You went home to see your brother off on a medical mission. You said nothing about getting married."

"What's to say? We wanted to keep things private. I got married on Saturday." And left on Sunday afternoon. That had been the hardest thing to do. After a shower he and Shelby had made love again that night, slept late the next morning, then he'd scrambled to grab his computer and bag to make the airport on time. He was going to have to buy more clothes, that way he wouldn't have to pack anything.

"*Why?* Who is she? Why haven't I once heard you mention dating someone recently?"

He resigned himself to a long day. "She's no one you know."

"Do *you* know her?"

"Yeah. Shelby's a longtime family friend."

Anne-Marie stared at him, her expression one of incredulity and upset. "But now suddenly you're married?"

"It's okay. Everything is fine. I'm fine," he said, borrowing one of Shelby's favorite lines.

"Were you drunk?"

He sighed. "No."

"Well? What were you thinking? You know how it is when we go before the purchasing and marketing teams. The long hours, the weekends. Does your new little wifey-poo know you'll practically be living here? This project is due in less than a month. You can't be in newlywed land right now."

But she could come on to and flirt with everything in pants? That wasn't distracting? "It'll be ready. The project is on schedule."

"*Was* on schedule. Production ran into a glitch this weekend while you weren't here. I, um, gave them the programming changes I wanted made."

"What? All program—"

"Is supposed to be okayed by you, I know. But you weren't here."

He ran a hand over his head. "I'll go down there now."

"Not until we're finished," she said in her best employer

tone. "Luke, *talk* to me. Obviously you didn't think this through. You couldn't have. If you had, you would've waited until this deal was done." Anne-Marie straightened and planted her hands on her hips, her forehead furrowed in a tight frown. "Why marry her now unless—" She exhaled in a rush. "She's pregnant?"

Luke continued unpacking his computer and searched for the jump drive he carried with him everywhere.

"She is, isn't she?" Anne-Marie wet her lips and shook her head, dazed. "Wow. Do you even know for sure if it's yours?"

"It's mine." He growled the words, sick of being questioned about it. Not everyone had the morals of an alley cat.

"Because she told you? Please, that's the oldest trick in the book. She probably slept with some guy who dropped her like a hot rock once he got off."

He counted to ten before he lifted his head and glared at her, trying hard to remember Anne-Marie had had a rough marriage and been treated like a hot rock herself. "Don't talk about my wife that way."

Anne-Marie glared right back. "Then don't be a *fool*."

"Shelby doesn't play games like that."

"Oh, Luke…" Her tone softened to one of pity. She speared her fingers through her hair and raked it back from her face. "There isn't a woman out there who hasn't played a game with a guy at some point in time. It's the Eve-factor. You're a handsome guy. And brains? Give you a computer and you're great. But let's be blunt. You're the kind of guy who sits and watches the party, you're not the guy on the dance floor with the hot girl."

Like his brothers. The comparison was stupid and utterly juvenile, but he'd always compared himself to them. And while Nick had lacked the ability to make good grades, his bad boy image had taken on a life of its own, leaving Luke to feel like the ultimate geek because he'd been tongue-tied around the opposite sex for so many years. He knew he gained female attention but Anne-Marie was right.

He set the messenger bag aside and opened the lid of his laptop. A press of the button had the screen lighting up. She wasn't saying anything he hadn't figured out in puberty.

She sighed again, shaking her head slowly back and forth and regarding him with yet another expression he couldn't decipher. "Luke, I need you here, okay? I'm being totally selfish but you've got to realize why I'm so concerned. As your friend, I'm trying to help you understand this isn't a good thing for you."

"I'm not in kindergarten. I know who I am and what I'm doing."

"Okay, stop. Luke, stop." She put a hand on his arm. "Let me be a friend, and say what needs said. Let's say the baby is yours. Okay, mistakes happen. But *no one* marries because of a pregnancy anymore. And this woman? You probably told her about this deal with Sony, didn't you? I'll bet she has big plans for that cash. Did you at least make her sign a prenup?"

He didn't answer.

"You didn't, did you? How could you *do* this? You know what your portion stands to be if this goes big." She dropped her hand and paced away from him, back again. "I know what we can do. You can call my attorney and arrange for some kind of settlement or give her some money for an abortion. At least you'd be done with it before this goes any further."

His hand fisted over the tiny jump drive. Friend or not, employer or not, that was hitting below the belt. Anne-Marie meant well and she'd been burned by marriage. He knew that, but she was talking about his baby. "My child isn't something to be thrown in the trash because it wasn't expected."

Why was Anne-Marie so upset? Was she that afraid he'd move back to Tennessee?

"My point is there's no reason to be tied to this woman. How long were you together? I'm going to take a wild guess and say it had something to do with the first wedding a few months back. Love was in the air, you'd had a few drinks, and she probably took one look at you and decided you were her ticket out of Hooterville. She's probably already redecorating your condo and— What?"

Something in his expression must have given him away. "Nothing." Luke tossed the drive onto his desk.

"No, I hit a nerve with that," she murmured shrewdly. "I know you. We've worked together too long for us not to know each other's triggers. What was that look about?"

Luke rounded his desk and shut his office door, wishing he'd noticed sooner that it was wide open. "Anne-Marie, I appreciate your concern and your friendship, but my private life is none of your business."

Her mouth flattened and she drew back, looking thoroughly insulted. "I'm only looking out for you."

"And I appreciate that, but I don't need you to look out for me. The project will be fine. I'm not moving back to Tennessee, or leaving the company. When I fly there on the weekends, I'll still be accessible and—"

"She's still there? You *married* her and she stayed *there?*"

Luke swore under his breath and released the doorknob before he broke it. "With the baby coming and me working the hours I do, we thought it best."

"Who decided?"

He scrubbed his hands over his face. "Why bring her here if I'm never home?"

"Why fly to Tennessee when she could fly here?" she countered.

A flicker of something he couldn't identify flashed in her eyes. Hurt? Betrayal? It looked like more, way more than the friendship she claimed—but that had to be wrong. Then in a split second he saw the truth. The early morning coffee chats, the teasing…Anne-Marie had been looking for more from him. "I'm sorry." He was embarrassed that he hadn't realized she'd been serious. *Really observant there, Luke.* "Anne-Marie—"

"You're not interested. I know." A brief smile flirted at her full lips. "I thought we were getting closer, you and me."

"That's why you stopped by last weekend?"

She exhaled in a rush. "Look," she said, her tone firming, "I was mistaken. Surprise, surprise. Story of my life lately. Let's move on, shall we? I pay you and everyone else here very well to work weekends when it's necessary. And right now? It's necessary, Luke. I need you here. You can't disappear then pop back in at your convenience during the most critical time in this project. Newlywed or not, we need you."

The company? Or her? The jump between subjects made his brain hurt. He'd never understand women. "I can pick up a phone and read e-mail in Tennessee, just like I can here. We're in the final stages. Mostly making tweaks. The project will be fine, *if* you let me do my job. You made me Lead Creative Director for a reason. You shouldn't have given those changes to programming without getting my input first."

"They were in regard to issues that needed to be addressed. You weren't here to address them, so I did."

Luke stared at Anne-Marie and wondered how much of her meddling in the project was out of boredom. Lately she'd gotten in the bad habit of sticking her nose in areas of development she wasn't qualified to take on. "You're getting a hundred percent from me."

"I need a hundred-fifty. How many times have we talked about this game being our big break? The preliminaries are out of the way and Sony is *hooked,* but we can't present this as a showstopper if you're obsessed or worried about that woman."

Back to Shelby. His instincts were screaming again. Anne-Marie was jealous. And this guilt trip was all about her feelings and the two of them. Of course, there wasn't anything between them. Sure, he'd flirted his share with her, but he'd never crossed the line. He'd learned to not make the same mistake that his predecessor, Anne-Marie's ex-husband, Saul, had made. He'd never get involved with his boss, never endanger his job and reputation.

"This company is small and personal. We've all grown close, right? Especially us."

He nodded once. Everyone at Galaxy Games knew everyone else's spouses' names. They knew their kids, pet peeves. Played practical jokes and shared the ups and downs of life. It was a close-knit group.

"Luke, I wish you had come to me." Anne-Marie's voice dropped and she moved close. "I know you've been lonely. It isn't easy spending so many hours on a computer instead of with people. But we could've turned to each other instead of you winding up in this mess." She lifted a hand and stroked it up his arm, petting him. "How can your marriage work when she doesn't respect you or care for you enough to move here to be with you?"

Luke didn't answer. Anne-Marie's words struck home,

struck deep. He'd thought of little else since taking his vows. How could they make it work when Shelby was so determined to fight him? Keep half the country between them?

Shelby's image flashed in his mind, the way she'd looked when they'd made love. She'd climaxed, he knew that, but she'd held a part of herself back. She didn't trust or believe in him, in them, and she didn't plan on trying. Could he change her mind? Was it possible? The distance between Tennessee and California was nothing compared to the emotional distance separating them at the moment. What would the future bring? More of the same?

"I don't mean to hurt you, Luke." Anne-Marie curled her hand around his arm. "Talk to an attorney. Get some options. And remember that I'm here for you."

Luke stiffened and pulled away from her, reminding himself that Anne-Marie wasn't a bad person. She was reeling from a nasty divorce, and not in a mind-set to see most marriages weren't made in Hollywood where vows were made to be broken.

Anne-Marie followed, trying to get into his personal space. "You're such a great guy, Luke. Don't let yourself be—"

"I'm not calling the attorney." Luke moved to establish some distance. "Shelby and I will make our marriage work for our baby's sake."

That wasn't what Anne-Marie wanted to hear. Like a shift in the wind, her eyes hardened and anger filled every line and muscle of her body. She drew herself up to her full height and plastered a smile on her face, showcasing her too-white teeth and too-red lips, but her eyes remained cold and angry.

It's all in the details.

"I wish you well, then. But we need to be clear on something."

He matched her tone. "What's that?"

"Your work is my livelihood, and if you can't get your head in the game, if I feel you're ruining our chance because you're pulling a disappearing act when we need you here, I'll find someone who can play with the big boys."

A threat? "Mystic Magi is my game. I've overseen every aspect of it from the beginning."

Apparently satisfied that she'd gotten through to him, Anne-Marie smirked. "Your contract states that anything created while under my employ is a product of Galaxy Games, including your precious Mystic Magi. If I think for a second you're not giving this company your absolute best, I'll have to take action. It's what anyone in my position would do."

He'd met plenty of playground bullies as a kid, but he'd never come up against a female version before. All because he hadn't accepted her offer? Seriously? "You can't afford to lose me."

Anne-Marie arched an eyebrow and shook her head, releasing a caustic laugh on her way to the door. "Oh, Luke. *Sweetheart*," she drawled, copying his Southern twang, "I've always liked you and I wouldn't *want* to lose you. Never. No, I have no intention of ever firing you. But I will replace you as Lead Creative Director so fast your chair won't have time to spin. Use that genius brain of yours and think about that before you waste my time flying home to your pregnant little hick."

CHAPTER FIFTEEN

LUKE WAS COMING HOME today.

Shelby smoothed her hand over her hair and knew she needed a trim. The problem was her stylist was her mother and things were still…awkward.

You can't be angry forever. She is your mother.

True. And despite the lies and the stunts, she still loved her mother. Knowing Zacharias hadn't wanted to acknowledge her existence, could she blame her mother for lying to protect her?

She lied to protect herself. You were an added bonus.

Sighing, Shelby rubbed her forehead. She'd call later. Make an appointment for next week and deal with it then. Time was supposed to heal wounds, right?

Shelby pulled into her driveway, the flash of her headlights sending a rabbit scurrying for cover. She saw Luke's rented sedan and the nerves she'd fought all day returned.

Don't be stupid. You've talked to him every day this week, sometimes two or three times a day.

Their conversations had covered what she'd eaten and how many times she'd been sick, their favorite television shows, stupid stuff that happened at the country club, the game Luke worked so hard to perfect and everything in between.

She liked his nighttime calls the best. In the dark of the

bedroom, she snuggled beneath her cool sheets and pictured Luke in his lonely office, the computer light glaring, his desk overloaded and a mess, those goofy, black-rimmed glasses he wore to read perched on his nose. She realized with a sick twist in her stomach that in a freakishly short amount of time she'd begun looking forward to hearing his husky voice, counting on those calls and on him the way she'd promised herself she wouldn't.

But it was so easy to lie in the dark and talk to him.

Shelby parked beside Luke's car, her heart pounding in her ears when she saw his tall form step from her back porch. Just the thought of him being there had her body warming. A deep-rooted quivering began inside her, because she knew what they'd do and she didn't want to want him that much.

But you do.

Her car door opened with a squeak of the hinge. "Hey, sweetheart. Welcome home."

She inhaled and grabbed her purse and the restaurant supply catalogs she'd taken to work with her. The moment she stepped out of the car, Luke pulled her to him and buried his nose in her hair.

"Mmm, you smell good. I've missed you."

He was warm and solid, lean but strong. She closed her eyes, not happy to feel some of her tension drain away, just like that night in June.

"Come on. It's getting chilly. Let's go inside."

Shelby glanced up at him, caught her breath at the heat and desire she saw in his gaze. Would it always be this way?

Luke dipped his head and brushed a kiss over her mouth, lingering, pressing for more when her lips parted and he could slide inside. Within seconds they were both breathing heavily and Luke hustled her toward the back door.

"Where's your key?"

She gave it to him, hoping he didn't notice the way her hand shook. The moment the door shut behind them, Luke lifted her up until her toes barely touched the floor and snuggled her hips against his.

"I don't know if I can wait long enough to get to the bed. I've missed you so much, Shelby."

His expression backed up his words. The tired lines around his eyes and the corner of his mouth told of a long week, and his muscles were hard and taut.

A surge of emotion she dared not name sparked to life and shook her to her core. Luke was smart, kind, handsome and actually moral. He wanted her, the baby, mistake or not. She could so easily fall for him.

But how did she know he wouldn't change his mind?

Shelby shoved her thoughts aside and pulled away, far enough that she could yank his shirt over his head. Luke's smile flashed in the dim house and he reached for the light switch, but she caught his hand and carried it to her ribs instead. Luke's hand firmed, then shifted to her breast. He cupped her and squeezed, releasing a low, strangled sound of lust.

Without a word, they tore at each other's clothes. She unbuckled his belt and tried to open his jeans, but he yanked her crested jacket down her arms and tossed it aside. She tried again, succeeding in undoing both the snap and zipper while he unbuttoned her blouse and opened her front-snap bra, shoved her pants and underwear down her legs until they fell to her feet, and she stepped out of them.

Luke followed her step for step toward the kitchen table but she stopped just shy of reaching it. Shelby settled her hands at his waist and pushed his jeans and underwear low, letting Luke take care of removing them. Head down, distracted, Luke didn't see her bite her lip as she shoved him gently backward onto the side chair positioned with its back to the wall.

"Hey—"

She followed quickly, pressing her mouth to his and smothering his protest while straddling his legs and settling herself on his lap.

Luke's hands gripped her waist, pressed her against the bulge of him until her breath locked in her chest. She closed her eyes and squirmed closer, reveling in the groan he released. He lifted her higher and took his dear sweet time nuzzling his way around the loosened bra cups.

"I want you." He wrapped one arm around her and held her in position while using his free hand to cup her and tease with his lips. "Need you."

The rasping quality of his words barely registered. She was lost in a haze of thrumming desire, focusing on the feel of his hands, but the way he looked at her, the way he watched her. He saw too much.

Remembering the scarf she'd worn, she tugged it loose and pulled it from her neck. Shelby bent low and kissed him, slipping the material into place over his eyes.

"Sweetheart, I want to see you."

She kissed him harder, her hands tightening the scarf around his head and making it clear he was to leave it on.

Almost immediately Luke leaned forward in the chair and she gasped and held his shoulders, everything off balance, until he readjusted their positions and entered her. Aching and ready, knowing she'd secretly waited all day for him, Shelby bit her mouth to keep from releasing a moan and held on to him while he settled himself more comfortably in the chair. Blinded by the scarf, he traced her body with his hands, relearning the shape of her, the feel of her. Like he'd been gone years instead of days. She watched him, touched him, ran her hands over the bulging biceps to the leanness of his stomach. She felt freer, liking it that he couldn't see her reaction to him.

A moment later Luke pulled her flush against him and used his hands to rock her. The chair creaked with their movements, loud in the quiet house.

Shelby lifted her legs and tried to find an anchor by putting her feet on the lower rungs. She held on to his shoulders, tried to catch her breath. Why was it so hard to breathe when he was near?

"Trust me." He growled the words into her skin. "Relax, sweetheart. Just trust me," he repeated huskily. "You like what we do. But you don't want to like it, do you?"

Was she so transparent?

"But every time we do this?"

Below the blindfold his lips pulled up in a wickedly sensual smile that curled her toes, his hands locking down on her hips to hold them still on his when all she wanted to do was move.

"We get closer."

No. She didn't respond verbally, but she tensed. She couldn't help it. She wasn't going to argue because she knew it would be easy to prove her wrong.

After a second passed, Luke began rocking her against him again.

"We're going to be okay, sweetheart. You, me and the bab—"

"Shut up."

A chuckle rumbled out of his chest and his grip tightened as he reestablished the ebb and flow of them. "She speaks," he growled, nibbling on the supersensitive skin of her neck. "Ah, honey, you're going to have to learn what it means to trust me because trust and love go hand in hand."

The words had barely left his mouth before Luke widened his legs in a sudden movement and the shift dislodged her feet from the rungs. Her body sank lower on him and they both moaned at the sensation.

"Shelby...I trust you."

Shelby tried to get her feet back into position but he set up a rhythm that made it impossible. All she could do was hold on to him, let the pressure within her build. She wanted to scream, but she couldn't. Her lungs lacked air, and she couldn't focus on anything but Luke and what he'd said, how he made her feel, until they both cried out.

Her forehead on his shoulder, Shelby gasped. Luke trusted her...meaning he *loved* her? But that was crazy. People didn't fall in love that fast.

Alex was right, though. You've always had a connection with Luke. Maybe he's telling the truth?

Friendship, her mind argued, not love. Trust, yes, but not *love*.

She didn't return it. Didn't feel it, didn't believe in it.

But you want it.

And that, she decided, was the most frightening thing of all.

FIRST THING MONDAY morning, John Watkins met Luke at the door of Galaxy Games and pulled him aside.

"You're not going to believe this."

Whatever it was, Luke knew he didn't want to know. After blurting out his feelings to Shelby during their kitchen tango, she'd withdrawn more than ever. Maybe Anne-Marie was right because only a stupid computer geek would tell a four-time pageant winner he loved her like that. Trust and love go hand in hand? How lame could he get?

Way to go, Romeo.

Luke shrugged off his exhaustion and focused on John. "What's up?"

"I had a revised version of Mystic Magi on my desk this morning, courtesy of Tony Giovanni, that new hire in programming. Word has it he and Anne-Marie started chatting it up last week after her brainstorming session and over the weekend they apparently decided to have a private party. Those changes you had programming remove because they were screwing things up? The idiot did them—and her."

Luke swore, anger racing through him faster than a runaway train. He could only imagine how John knew that last fact. If there were no secrets in small towns, there certainly weren't any in small offices. "We're a week away from presenting and she's letting a kid *play* on it?"

"Luke—" John glanced around to make sure no one was around to hear "—it's gone. The magic is gone. She didn't just let him play with it, she gave him free rein. The details we worked three years to perfect? The things that made it our breakout? *Gone.* The version on my desk looks like a poor quality bootleg."

"We have backups. We can use one of them for the presentation."

"Not unless Anne-Marie agrees."

"Hello, boys. Is there a problem?"

Luke turned to find Anne-Marie walking across the white, black and red tiled floor toward them, her hips swinging in a confident strut that didn't quite go with the look on her face. One glance told him John hadn't exaggerated. She'd partied hard over the weekend. And if his suspicions were correct, the party hadn't only included alcohol and sex.

"Is there a problem?" she asked again, not quite meeting his eyes.

Luke handed John the messenger bag with his computer inside and jerked his head toward the hallway leading to their department. "Would you mind putting this in my office for me, John? I need to speak with Anne-Marie."

"Sure thing." John took one last look at Anne-Marie and bolted.

"He's always reminded me of a nervous little squirrel. The pocket protector doesn't help. Who wears those things anymore?"

Luke stared at Anne-Marie, remembering when he'd found her sexy and attractive, and how tempted he'd been to ignore his business ethics and accept her advances. Something had always held him back. Instinct, timing. Reasons he couldn't put his finger on but he thanked God for now.

But John was right. Anne-Marie was the owner of the company. Creator or not, she called the shots on what Sony saw.

"So, what was that all about? Or do I need to ask?"

Luke shook his head, having a hard time comprehending her thinking. "What did you do?"

"What do you mean?"

Luke took her arm and began walking toward her office. "What's going on, Anne-Marie? The game was as close to perfect as it could get and you're screwing with it? Why? Were you that mad at me for turning you down? Did you sabotage the project to get even?"

CHAPTER SIXTEEN

ANNE-MARIE LAUGHED. "My, my, how your ego has grown. I let Tony have a little fun. I wanted to see what he was capable of. What's the big deal?"

"So the demo you gave John was an edited copy? You don't intend for us to present that to the purchasing team?"

Her gaze sidled away. "Tony has potential."

"I'll decide that for myself. That is part of my job."

"When you do it." She said that with an expression he couldn't read. What was going on?

"Pay close attention to the changes Tony incorporated. They were very good."

"Not that good. They can't be. He's fresh out of school and still too green."

"Scared he'll take your job?"

Another threat? He didn't like where this was headed, didn't like how nervous she seemed to be. Almost…panicked. "Why are you doing this? What are you trying to prove?"

Her chin lifted. "I'm looking at all the possibilities. Tony made Aiya sexier. She's more appealing to our audience of teenage boys and old guys with no life."

"The heroine was perfect. She was beautiful but flawed."

"Too flawed. All that angst was boring. Look at the lake

scene. Aiya has no money, nothing to barter. There is only one way for her to get what she needs."

He blinked, unable to believe what she hinted at. "Not every woman would sell themselves," he said tightly. "She has to work with the Magi and learn how to get what she wants, *fight* for it. Doing it that way allows the player to go underground in the Magi's kingdom. It gave us a whole other dimension to explore."

"Tony's version is more modern."

"I don't believe this."

"Tony's onto something, Luke. There's a whole untapped market for this type of game, one we could cash in on."

"You're not turning Aiya into a prostitute."

"Perhaps we should leave it up to Sony. Present it both ways."

"What?" Luke struggled to control his temper. "From the beginning, we agreed the game was to be rated for teens because the fighting involved wouldn't let us have an everyone rating. I designed a clean game, something my nephew could play."

"Designs change."

"The lake scene would rate it mature. We'd lose a huge portion of sales because parents won't buy it for their kids. I wouldn't buy it for mine." He glared at her. "Anne-Marie, don't waste everyone's time on creating a second pitch when you know Sony will like the teen-rated version due to the higher revenue potential."

She crossed her arms over her chest. "Don't worry, Luke. I'm putting Tony in charge of the mature version."

Luke blinked. "He's a kid. He isn't ready to be in charge of anything."

"I think he is. What's the harm? We're simply adding a few scenes here and there."

Luke swore. What's the harm? It wouldn't be his game then, wouldn't be something he could be proud of. But his hands were tied and she knew it.

He hated the restrictions and problems placed on him by working for a business not his own.

"Luke, relax. Try to think of it as a little creative competition. We'll present both versions and see what happens."

"You're not going to sell sex to kids."

"Of course not. We'll sell it to their fathers and older brothers. As Tony so astutely pointed out, gamers do get older," she murmured, studying her fake nails. "Tastes change. They can't play kiddie games forever."

Frustration ate at him. All his hard work, time and energy. Years. Down the drain. What kind of self-destructive move was this? Why would she take his work and turn it into an X-rated game for adults?

Luke wanted to shout the place down, but one glance at Anne-Marie's set expression told him it wouldn't do him any good. He could talk until he turned blue but she would still do whatever she wanted. "Anne-Marie, I want what's best for the company. I've worked my ass off for this company," he said. "You and I both know Tony's version might have some splash and sensationalism that would draw attention, but it isn't what's best. G-rated movies outgross R movies for a reason. Games are no different. I know you're pissed at me and think I'm nuts for marrying Shelby, but do you really want to proceed with this?"

Anne-Marie nodded once. "It's already done."

Luke turned on his heel and headed to his office. It was going to be another long, hard week. No matter how hard he worked, he wouldn't be able to fly to Beauty to see Shelby this weekend.

He was sick of this. The politics, the manipulative, self-indulgent behavior Anne-Marie was displaying. If he was smart he'd walk away. So why didn't he?

There are other jobs out there.

But if he walked, his game stayed behind. Luke dropped into his office chair and rubbed both eyes with his palms. He couldn't walk away but if he did, where would he go? Tennessee? Nothing changed the fact that California was the hot spot for what he did. Sony had a branch office not far from where he sat.

No, even if he left, it would have to be to another company, a competitor. He couldn't go back to Tennessee.

The saying was true. Once a person left home, they couldn't ever go back.

LUKE WASN'T coming home that weekend. During last night's late-night phone call, he'd broken the news to her, regret clouding his voice. She'd squelched the stab of disappointment she felt, knowing it was a warning.

Shelby settled herself in the chair at her mother's shop and waited for her to finish up with a client, her thoughts on all the reasons why Luke had decided to stay in California.

"He might've told you the truth. He said he had to work on his presentation."

"What did you say, Shelby?"

She blinked and her mother's reflection came into focus in the station's mirror. The bell on the door dinged as her mother's previous client left, and Shelby refrained from rolling her eyes at her mother's lack of smock. But how else would the guy have seen her mom's hot-orange wrap dress that showed too much cleavage and leg? "Just talking to myself."

Pat settled the cape around Shelby's shoulders then turned to grab the smock she normally wore from a nearby hook. "Have you talked to Jerry?"

Shelby set aside the boatload of hurt baggage weighing her down and opted for forgiveness. Sometimes a person had to make up their mind and act accordingly. "Yeah. The job is nearly done. He'll be home in a week or so and can start working on the mill house full-time." Thank goodness. Finally some real progress could be made.

"Has he said anything about me?"

Shelby stilled, her thoughts flying back to her wedding day and the suspicions over her mother's stunt. "Why do you ask?"

"Oh, it's nothing." Pat's layered bracelets jingled as she sprayed Shelby's hair to wet it.

Whatever "it" was, it was something. Shelby could tell. *Oh, crap.*

"Baby, I want to apologize again for not telling you. I should have when you were old enough to understand."

Shelby plucked at the cape, glad the shop wasn't busy because of the early hour. Only one of her mother's station renters was there and she was waxing someone's eyebrows on the other side of the large room, out of hearing range. "I've been thinking about that. In a way, I'm glad you didn't."

"Really?"

Her mother spun the chair around with a jerk and Shelby's stomach whirled. *"Mom."*

"Sorry. Do you mean it?"

Swallowing the quick surge of queasiness, Shelby nodded. "I can't imagine growing up knowing that he was here, in town, and didn't want to know me or admit he was my father.

I don't know. I guess now that I've had time to adjust to the thought of having a baby, I've been thinking about what I would've done. I wouldn't want my baby to grow up thinking it wasn't wanted and I wouldn't have wanted to grow up thinking that about myself in regard to him."

"Oh, baby. Thank God you don't have to worry about that. Why, I never paid much attention to Luke before because his other brothers have always been so…well, delicious—"

"Mom." Shelby shook her head and grabbed the station counter to turn slowly back to the mirror. She didn't want to face her mother when she said things like that.

"But Luke looks all grown-up now. California's been good for him. And he couldn't seem to take his eyes off you on your wedding day. It was very sweet." She picked up her shears and comb and set to work. "Shelby, I know you think I'm too bold and I know I'm the last person to give you advice on marriage under the circumstances."

Shelby braced herself for the *but*.

"But marriages aren't bulletproof. If you give your man the cold shoulder for too long, for whatever reason, things *will* fall apart." Her passionate-pink-colored lips twisted, the wrinkles around her mouth prominent. "I pushed Jerry away time and again because he wouldn't do what I wanted. Still, I never stopped loving him. I guess for us the timing was never right."

She hadn't exactly pushed Luke away, Shelby mused. At least not sexually. But wasn't she doing that emotionally? *Self-preservation,* she reminded herself. "You never put Dad first. It wasn't timing, it was immature choices."

Her mother finished the trim and ran her fingers through Shelby's hair, checking the length. "I suppose you're right about that. And I should've put him first, after all he'd done for you and me both. I just couldn't get over the fact that Zacharias owed us."

"Mom, you didn't get pregnant with me on purpose, did you?"

A sad smile tugged at her mother's mouth. "No, Shelby. Not with you."

Shelby stiffened. "What do you mean, not with me?"

"I miscarried once when your father and I were trying to get back together. I'd seduced him, hoping a baby might help him see what we had. When it was gone all the problems with Zacharias were still there." Her mother's gaze lifted to hers in the mirror. "Have you given any more thought to California?"

"No. Why would I?"

"Because when you thought no one was looking, you couldn't take your eyes off Luke, either."

"It's not like that. We only married because of the baby."

"Are you sure? I'm asking because when a man looks at a woman like that, he loves her. Jerry used to look at me like that. Maybe one day he will again."

She blinked, her suspicions confirmed. "Five times wasn't enough?"

"Who knows? Only time will tell." Pat removed the cape, careful to keep the damp trimmings clinging to the plastic away from Shelby's clothes. "Your father told me what you said about love."

Her mother had to stop and clear her throat. The tears were back, the trembling chin, but unlike all the other times before where her mother blubbered noisily, this time the tears fell with no sound.

"I'm thinking a man like Luke might be the kind of guy to make you take a look at your life and want more. If you want the truth, I saw an awful lot of Jerry in Luke on your wedding day, and if I could go back in time…"

The bell jingled and one of her mother's longtime, elderly clients walked in, sporting a cast on one arm. Her mother blinked away her tears and turned.

"Oh, my heavens! Oh, honey!" Her mother jogged across the room on her heels and wrapped her arms around the woman, fussing over her something fierce. "Oh, bless your heart, would you look at that? What happened, Bea?"

Watching her mother interact with the woman gave Shelby pause. Beneath the big hair and overdone makeup, beneath the flashy clothes and melodramatic persona, her mother had a heart. Sometimes it was hard to see, but it was there. She'd have to remember that when her mother was driving her nuts.

Shelby put her hands over her stomach and rubbed the bulge starting to form. Her personality might be opposite her mother's; she might be moody and picky and controlling, but she hoped her son or daughter always remembered she had a heart, too. Broken from childhood, tattered from life, but there and beating, and wanting so desperately to trust that everything really *did* happen for a reason.

SHELBY PRESSED the tape onto the mill house floor and frowned. She'd talked to Luke every day. And on Friday evening when he should have boarded a plane to come see her, she couldn't shake the anxiety she felt because he hadn't. It was as though she had to see him, wanted to see him. Needed contact with him to know everything was okay. Was he avoiding her because she hadn't responded when he'd told her he trusted her? Her mother's words had given her a lot to think about this week.

"Here you go. Water on the rocks. Shelby? You okay?"

She smiled at Alex and motioned toward the area now marked off by bright blue tape. "I'm fine. Just wondering how my tarts are doing at the club and if this is enough room for a dance floor. What do you think?"

"Dance floor?" Alex eyed it with a frown. "Yes, I think so. Dancing is best when it's close quarters. As for the tarts, does Mr. Long know they're yours?"

"He does now. He saw me bringing them in this morning. More surprisingly is that he told me he'd heard about my plans for this place." She spun the roll of tape on her fingers and walked over to the freshly de-junked kitchen. Her appliances had been delivered earlier in the week and she and Alex had spent the evening cleaning up the packing materials. "He actually told me if I wanted him to, he'd come take a look at the layout and give me his thoughts."

"That's great. You wanted that job because of what you could learn from him. Having him offer up help voluntarily is fantastic."

She nodded, pleased but wry. "Since the mill house is really close to the country club I think he wants to scope out what will be the competition. The sixth hole is through the woods behind the house. I let him off the hook by telling him I'm sticking with more traditional food. Sort of Paula Deen's style of cooking. That way it'll be totally different than the Old Coyote, and less expensive and more casual than the club."

"Sounds like you've got a plan. But does that fit with a dance floor?" Alex took a drink of the water she'd carried in for herself.

"I'd like to do special occasion type stuff, too. Birthday parties and anniversaries."

"Ah. So…Luke isn't coming in tonight?"

Shelby finished putting the last of the tape down and smirked at Alex. "Nice transition there."

"I thought it was subtle." Alex grinned. "So are things okay?"

"Don't you have to go to Rosetta's?"

"I'm already late. A few more minutes won't hurt. Well?"

Shelby shrugged. "They're…fair."

"Fair? You're getting along? Having sex?"

"Alex!"

"Welllll? I don't want details, just reassurance that you're both okay. You know Gram is going to ask me since she knows I came here first."

Just what she needed. Luke's grandmother involved in their sex life. "Things are progressing as well as can be expected."

"Uh-oh. That sounds ominous."

"We need time to get used to things."

Alex set her glass aside and grabbed her purse and keys. "Do you miss him?"

Shelby paused by the refrigerator and fingered the stainless steel front. Luke's words to her last weekend and her lack of response could have been awkward afterward, but he'd acted like he hadn't basically said he loved her during sex.

But now he wasn't coming home. Bruised ego?

You think? You know it's what he meant. Some guys might say that as often as they belch because they think it's expected, but Luke? He wouldn't say it unless he meant it and why did that give her the warm fuzzies? Could he really *love* her?

"Sometimes." Like at night when the house grew chilly and too quiet. Or when she hung up the phone after one of their many talks in the dark and she wanted him to be there instead. She even liked the stupid songs he sang in the shower. Air Supply. Get real. But it was sweet and sexy in a really weird way.

"You know, my parents are counting on you to be the one to bring Luke home."

She turned to face Alex. "What do you mean?"

Alex frowned. "Remember when Nick was really getting into trouble a lot in school? Skipping classes and flunking out?"

"Vaguely. I remember it happening but that was around the lead-up to divorce number four."

"Yeah. Well, Luke would blow off classes and tests, too, to share the punishment. Anyway, long story short, Nick began to resent Luke dumbing himself down because of him and they started fighting, too. I remember once Nick said something along the lines of he hated looking at Luke because he saw himself without the brains."

"That's awful."

"Yeah. Luke took it hard. They were really, really close until Nick began to struggle. Luke already felt bad enough because the schoolwork always came easy to him, but to hear Nick say he hated looking at him." Alex grabbed a piece of Bubble Wrap and began popping the tiny bubbles.

"I thought everything was fine now."

Alex shrugged. "It is on the surface, but deep down? I think it's why Luke stays away."

And why wouldn't he? Shelby pulled the strips of tape off the drawers and containers that went into the fridge, needing something to do so that Alex wouldn't notice how Luke's story was affecting her. She knew drama and upset, and even though she knew Marilyn and Alan would do anything for their children, how could they not have seen the impact Nick's problems had had on Luke? Did they even know? This was the first she was hearing about it and she'd practically lived there.

You're not a parent yet, don't be judgmental.

"Luke's always felt guilty, I think. Wouldn't you, knowing the person you shared a womb with couldn't keep up? Anyway, that's why everyone thinks you and the baby will bring him home. Thank God Jenn figured out what Nick's problem was and he's one of us again, but now we have to get Luke back."

That was a lot of pressure. "I don't know what you think I can do about it."

"You can make him want to be here. If he spends more time with us and sees that things are okay now, Luke will know he can come home. You can convince him for us."

Did she want Luke to be here? Getting along on weekends was a lot different than spending every day with someone. And it definitely put a more permanent spin on things. *Still thinking short-term?* Luke's chiding voice sounded in her head.

"You've got the weekend off, don't you?"

Shelby knew where this was headed. "Yeah, but I'm working here. I'm not spending my weekend off on a plane."

"Luke does it for you."

With the container free of tape and padding and ready to slide into place, Shelby gripped the pull bar on the fridge, her palm sweaty. "You'd better go before Rosetta sends out a search party. You're never late."

Alex sighed and jingled the keys in her hand. "Okay, okay, I get the hint. Think about what I said? Wouldn't it be great if you and Luke could have a real marriage like everyone else?"

Wouldn't it? After Alex had driven away Shelby was still asking herself that question. She locked up the mill house and set the newly wired alarm system, taking no chances that her expensive kitchen equipment would disappear. Inside her house, she seated herself at her computer and checked her e-mail, not finding anything more interesting than the usual spam. She moved the cursor to exit out and decided to check flights to California. Just to see what was available. She wasn't going to book one but it wouldn't hurt to know how much one would cost.

Seconds later she stared at the discount airfare listings page. "Crap." Airlines didn't like flying with empty seats, as was evident by the price listed in front of her. One she could afford if she wanted to go. It wasn't a declaration of love, but it was something that might show Luke that she liked his brains and wanted him to be himself with her. She nibbled her lower lip, her hand hovering over the mouse. To go or not to go, that was the question.

CHAPTER SEVENTEEN

LUKE COULDN'T BELIEVE his eyes when he saw Shelby sitting propped up against his apartment door sound asleep. Pleasure filled him as he set his messenger bag aside and squatted down in front of her. "Shelby? Sweetheart, wake up."

She mumbled something like, "Too tired."

She had to be exhausted. The baby, the flight and time difference, a hard day's work. But she was here and he couldn't stop grinning because of it. "Let's go inside and go to bed. Come on, up you go."

He scooped her up in his arms, carried her inside and laid her on the bed before he went back to the door to get her overnight bag and his computer.

Luke locked up, stripped and then set to work on making her more comfortable, hating the dark shadows he saw beneath her eyes, the way she never fully awoke because she was so drained.

He couldn't stop kissing her, though. She'd flown to California and he knew what a concession it was on her part to come to him. Luke dropped another kiss to the soft, sensitive skin of her neck and shoulder, chuckling softly at the chill bumps that arose on her skin. Pure, soft skin. Her hives were gone?

That more than anything had him squeezing her close and

burying his nose in her hair. Her hives were gone. Maybe she was getting used to him. Their marriage. The idea of being pregnant.

Snuffling softly in her sleep, Shelby rolled and flung her leg across his thighs, snuggling close to his chest. She inhaled and released a contented sigh.

Tired though he was, the feel of her made him hard and achy. His hands began to roam and before long Shelby's head rose, her thick lashes lifting to reveal the glimmer of her eyes. "I thought I was dreaming," she complained. "I didn't think you were ever coming home."

"If I had known you were here, nothing would've kept me away. Why didn't you call me?"

"Knew you were busy." She yawned and pressed her nose to his shoulder, her eyes closed. "Don't know why I came."

His arms tightened and drew her closer, hoping he knew why. "I'm glad you did." He'd left her T-shirt and underwear on, but now his hands slid over her rump, pushing the material away.

Unlike the times before, this mating was slow and lazy, both of them tired but needing that intimate connection. And when it was over Shelby fell asleep on his chest, their bodies still joined.

Luke stared up at the ceiling, completely and totally exhausted but unwilling to miss the pleasure of holding her in his arms, praying he was one step closer to her heart.

"So," SHELBY SAID around a mouthful of Chinese greens, "I get that your job is great and you like it here, but why does it seem like there's more to the story?" Propped against the footboard of his bed, she tilted her head to the side and waited for him to respond.

Luke stiffened slightly and swallowed the food in his mouth. "You fishing for my parents, Alex, Gram or for yourself?"

Shelby shrugged. "Just me. That day at the country club I felt…tension. And since you know all my embarrassing, humiliating stuff about my mother and my paternity, I think it's only fair I get some insight to you."

"Insight? Or dirt?" One corner of his mouth curled and brought out a rarely seen dimple. She leaned forward over the boxes of takeout to kiss it, drawing back in surprise when she realized what she'd done. "You, um, had some sauce there." She lifted her hand and used her thumb to wipe the imaginary spot. "Got it." Shelby had to force herself to look away. Oh, those eyes of his. And the way he looked at her. Was her mother right?

"Thanks."

She cleared her throat and tried to remember what they were discussing. "Sure. Um…so?"

He shifted his position on the bed and poked at the contents inside the box he held. "I get tired of being the kid who never grew up. When I go home, an awful lot of people look at me and shake their heads because they think I'm bumming in California, surfing and playing video games."

"Does it matter what they think?" She knew Luke valued his parents' opinions, but she'd heard Alan state more than once that Luke needed to get a real job. That had to hurt.

"No. But I don't like defending what I love to do."

Or the way it probably made him feel, she mused. "You're not playing, you're designing. There's a big difference."

"Shelby, my own father doesn't get what I do. Why should I spend so much time explaining myself when here, I can do, think, act and *be* who I want to be?"

Shelby snagged a pillow, lying on her side as she regarded

him. "That sounds like it's about more than your dad. Like maybe you're not comfortable with someone else?"

"You're not subtle." He stretched out one of his long legs and set their food aside, lacing his fingers over his lean stomach. "Where are the questions coming from?"

"Alex."

"Ah."

"I didn't know you had a thing about Nick."

"I don't have a thing."

"Yeah, well, Alex said to make sure you knew things are better now, and you shouldn't feel like you couldn't come home."

"Maybe they are from Alex's point of view. Is that why you came?"

"No. Luke, *no.* I came because…" She bit her lip, shoved her hair out of her face and tried to figure that out herself. "Because I wanted to."

"Because?" His eyes dared her to be brutally honest.

"Because," she drawled as she crept up the bed to lay her head on his shoulder, "I *might* have missed you. Just a tad."

"Is that right?" His arms wrapped around her and tightened, his mouth finding hers as he rolled on top of her. "Let's see if I can make you miss me more."

SHELBY WENT TO WORK on Monday morning feeling more hopeful about the future. For the first time since they'd said their vows, she felt a stronger connection with Luke, one not based on sex but actual communication. Her confession about missing him had set off a five-alarm fire in him. He'd pressed a kiss to her lips and the next thing she knew, she was naked and panting. What a way to spend the weekend.

Lying in bed and watching the apartment complex's

pool reflect moonlight onto Luke's bedroom ceiling, they'd talked about everything. Their childhood dreams, favorite things. When she'd mentioned their playtime in the attic, Luke had started laughing and the movement of his chest bounced her head until she'd lifted it to see his smile. He'd immediately rolled with her, kissing her, making his way down to her stomach and acting silly by talking to the baby. According to him, the baby was going to be called Gigabyte. He said Garret had referred to Darcy's baby girl as Spike so their baby needed a nick-name, too.

It had been a great weekend, one that made her think that maybe she and Luke might have a chance. Maybe they could split their time between California and Tennessee. Lots of people had two residences; maybe they could, too? It was definitely something to think about—after she got rid of the headache plaguing her.

"Jeez, stop already," she muttered to her aching brain. Her head had begun to pound like a teenager with a new drum set and her lower back felt tight and achy, her legs weak. *You're probably sick from breathing in the recycled air on the plane and sore from being stuck in those tiny* little *seats.*

Heaven knows it wasn't from anything else. She'd flown all the way to California and all she'd seen was the airport, the city lights and the inside of Luke's apartment. Not that she would have changed a thing. This weekend had been sur-real. Perfect, just the way it was.

Shelby rubbed her back as she walked down the club-house hall toward the dining room. Along the way her stom-ach cramped and she made a detour to the bathroom, only to shake her head at herself and whatever was causing the tremor in her hands. Her stress level had risen but why? A panic attack? She'd had them before, mostly in childhood, though. Shelby stared at herself in the mirror and searched for signs of those stupid hives. Yup, there they were. What was going on?

Luke's presentation. She inhaled and sighed in relief. That was it. Sheesh, of course that was it. Luke was scheduled to step before Sony's purchasing team in an hour or so, and he'd told her about his boss's underhanded deal with the mature game. When she'd asked Luke about the reasoning behind it, he'd shrugged it off, but she could tell that his employer's actions had undermined Luke's confidence. Stupid woman. "He'll be fine. You just need to—"

Her stomach cramped again and she bit her lip. Had she eaten something bad? The cramps sort of indicated that, like she had an upset stomach.

"Ms. Brookes, are you okay?"

She forced a smile at the club's secretary. "I'm fine, Wendy. Just a stomachache."

"Oh, I hope you don't have that virus that's going around. I was down all last weekend with it. Nasty stuff."

Sweat broke out on her forehead. "Do you, um, know if Mr. Long is going to be in today?"

"It's early yet, but I doubt it. He mentioned something about a movie with his grandson. If you're not feeling well and need to leave, I'd be happy to keep an eye on things for you. I can call you at home if there are any problems."

"You wouldn't mind?"

"Not at all," the fortysomething woman said with a concerned expression. "Nothing's on the books and it's raining so it'll be a slow day. You go on home and take care of yourself. Would you like me to call someone to drive you?"

Shelby shook her head and shoved herself upright from

where she'd stood gripping the sink. "No, thank you. I'll be fine."

Minutes later Shelby was on her way home, her windshield wipers and air conditioner both on high. She felt so hot. How ironic would it be to get the flu now?

She made the twists and turns toward home on autopilot. Her heart pulsed in her ears and nausea threatened to overwhelm her more than once. Almost home.

She rounded the curve in the road before her house when a particularly hard cramp stabbed her from deep within. Shelby gasped, barely able to breathe for the pain, then something seemed to pop within her before hot fluid gushed between her legs. Dizzy, Shelby looked down, shocked at the bright red slowly spreading through her white linen slacks. She stared at the growing stain, uncomprehending.

Her hands on the wheel, she looked up, belatedly realizing the car was still moving and she'd gone left of center, the curve mere feet ahead. She jerked the wheel and hit the brakes, tires squealing, but it was too late. The car kept sliding out of control on the water-and-leaf-covered asphalt, spinning two full circles before she hit the deep ditch just short of her driveway.

LUKE ENTERED Galaxy Games's conference room and wished he could remove the suit coat he wasn't used to wearing. Jeans and T-shirts were standard attire at the company, except when the bigwigs came to town. And Sony definitely qualified as *big*.

On the far end of the rectangular room, a sixty-five-inch LCD screen took up most of the wall, the cover of Mystic Magi in full detail. He stared into the summer-green eyes of Aiya and smiled. This was it.

"You ready for this?"

He gave John a confident nod. "Ready as I'll ever be."

The team from Sony entered the room and Luke stepped forward to shake hands with the men who would decide his future, noting that Anne-Marie's boy toy was late to the show. Luke made small talk, aware that Anne-Marie was growing more nervous by the second. Why she pushed this, he didn't know.

"Well, gentlemen, shall we get started?" Luke indicated the chairs with a wave of his hand. "I think you're going to like what we have to show you."

The door burst open and Tony hurried inside, looking like the too-young but cocky wannabe he was. He flashed a cool smile and nodded, but didn't offer an apology.

Anne-Marie glared at Tony and made the introductions. Luke graciously offered to let Tony show his creation first. He wanted to know what he was up against.

Luke's version of Mystic Magi disappeared from the screen, replaced by a raven-haired vamp in thigh-high boots, a bikini top and boy shorts. The presentation consisted of loud rock and Tony's version of Aiya sashaying through the forest. The game teaser showed the kid's immaturity and lack of finesse, and Luke watched the Sony reps glance at each other and their watches. Only one seemed mildly interested. The rest were not even curious.

Then it was his turn. Luke gave his pitch, quoting the higher sales stats for games rated more family friendly. He was deep into his spiel, pointing out all the ways Mystic Magi surpassed old-school techniques, when his iPhone vibrated in his jacket pocket. He ignored it and kept going, not about to lose momentum.

While the screen clearly depicted the higher quality graphics and details of the game versus the dark, S and M dungeon look Tony had tried to evoke, he had begun to cover the specs of the game when the door opened again.

"Lu—uh, Mr. Tulane, you have a call."

"Cassandra, we're in the middle of something." Anne-Marie jerked her head toward the receptionist's desk on the other side of the clear glass wall. "Hold *all* calls."

"It's an emergency."

Luke frowned, knowing his family of doctors wouldn't toss around the word carelessly. "Who is it, Cassandra?"

"Your brother, Nick. He said to interrupt you, that you'd want to take his call."

Luke's heart stopped, then began to pound out of his chest. "Gentlemen, if you'd excuse me?"

Anne-Marie jumped to her feet. "Luke, what are you doing? It can wait until we're finished. Cassandra, *take a message.*"

Luke turned toward the table. He noted the wedding rings on several of their hands. "I see most of you are family men. My family isn't one for dramatics so I'd like to get this. I'm sure you understand." Remembering the way his father spoke to his patients, Luke made eye contact with every one of the team and gained their nods of support before ignoring Anne-Marie and leaving the room.

He took the call at the receptionist's desk. "Nick?"

"I'm sorry to call you right now. I know this is your big day."

"What's wrong?"

"I got a call at the garage for a tow. State police. It was Shelby, Luke. She hydroplaned and hit the embankment not far from her house."

His gut knotted, his lungs refusing to work. "Is she okay? The baby?"

Silence, then Nick said, "Shelby's fine."

Shelby. But not the baby.

"I'm sorry, Luke. EMS was pretty clear about that, I don't think there's any mistake."

Luke closed his eyes against the burn and fought the vise closing around his chest. He hadn't seen it, hadn't held it, but he'd loved his baby. Now it was *gone?* The pain was there, sharp and deep. But it would have to wait. "How is Shelby handling this?"

"I got there late, but the EMS guys said she was dazed and quiet. She'd hit her head and probably has a concussion. I towed her car to the house and put it behind the shed for now so I could head to the hospital. When I get there, I'll give you another call."

"I'll catch the next flight out."

"Don't you even think about it." Steel lined Anne-Marie's voice and he heard the hurried click of her heels against the tile behind him.

Luke ignored her. "Stay with her, Nick."

Nick murmured goodbye and hung up the same time Anne-Marie stepped in front of him. She opened her mouth but he held up a hand, needing a moment—one freaking moment without her shrieking at him—to grieve for his baby.

"Whatever it is, I'm sorry. I am, Luke, but it has to wait." Anne-Marie gripped his arm. "You can't walk out of this presentation. They were eating out of your hands."

He headed down the hall to his office to grab his computer and keys. "I don't care."

"You don't— Luke, get back in that conference room and do your job. Please!" Anne-Marie ran to keep up.

"Tell your boy toy to do it. My child just—" He had to stop, take a breath. How did Shelby stand feeling this way all the time? Damn, but his chest hurt. "Shelby was in an accident. She miscarried."

Other than a flicker of her lashes and a slight pause, Anne-Marie's expression didn't falter. "I'm sorry."

He snorted. Yeah, he could tell.

"I mean it, Luke, but you are hours away and it's done. What can you do about it? *Nothing.* Why ruin your career? Your future? This is *it.* Some of those men in that conference room flew halfway around the world to meet with us, *you.* Don't blow it."

"You're laying all this on me? *Now?* Go give Tony another shot." He packed his computer and a couple personal files, but left the rest. He'd pick them up later. "The presentation was nearly finished. If Tony can't man-up to the job, John most certainly can."

"Neither of them know the game or have the passion for it like you do. You proved that without a doubt in there."

"You're only just figuring that out?" Sick to his stomach, frustrated as hell that Shelby was so far away and needed him and he couldn't get to her within a reasonable amount of time, Luke turned on Anne-Marie. "Why are you suddenly gung ho on having me back in the game? Did you finally realize your precious bottom line might suffer?" Luke frowned when tears filled her eyes. He'd seen Anne-Marie in a lot of moods. Happy, angry, sad, but never teary.

"I did something stupid, okay? *Really* stupid. And to keep people from finding out—" she looked away from him "—I agreed to Tony's demands that he get a chance to show his version."

Luke straightened. "What did you do?"

Anne-Marie twisted her hands in front of her, the move reminding him of Shelby. "I went to a party with him. I knew better than to mess with the crap they had laid out as favors, but I was feeling low and I did it anyway. When I woke up…Tony had taken pictures."

"Nice guy you chose there."

Hot color filled her face. "You don't see the resemblance?"

He stared at her blankly.

She smirked, her expression sad, old for her thirty-four years.

Shock came first, then anger. "Don't you dare blame me. I never let you think we were more than friends."

"I know. But after my divorce when you were so nice…I guess I got it into my head that we could be."

He grabbed his bag. "I'm sick of feeling guilty for things I'm not responsible for."

Anne-Marie wiped away the tears and nodded. "It's my fault. I know that. I was just… Never mind. Tony said all he wanted was a chance and if Sony liked his version over yours, that was it."

Luke grabbed his jump drive and portable storage to take with him for safekeeping. "You know as well as I do he's lying."

"I know. Luke, please believe me. I regretted it, but by then it was too late. I didn't want to tell you what I'd done so I went along with him. I didn't *mean* for it to happen."

He was so tired of hearing that excuse. "But it did happen. Anne-Marie, you need help. Counseling. Something. Those pictures are probably online somewhere."

The trickle became a steady flow. "I know."

He couldn't stand to see a woman cry. "Look, I know it's tough but in today's world, nobody will care."

"You do."

He thought that over a long moment, then shook his head. Maybe he would have cared once, but not anymore. When was it time to say enough? Time to walk away from a job and an employer who took advantage of him? She screwed up and it became his fault? He'd worked his ass off and because Sony had liked the presentation, Anne-Marie would reap the benefits. That was just messed up. "Do yourself a favor and call the police. Come clean, get Tony out of here, and get yourself some help. But whatever you do, leave me out of it. I'm done."

"Luke, please. You can go as soon as the team leaves, but—"

"No *game* is worth putting my family second and not being with my wife when she needs me. I'm going back to Tennessee. It's time I became the husband I should've been from the beginning."

CHAPTER EIGHTEEN

SHELBY STARED at Dr. Clyde and nodded her understanding at what the doctor had told her.

"Shelby, I wish you'd let someone come in to sit with you. What about your mother?"

"No." She shook her head firmly, unable to deal with her mother's drama now. Pat would need to be comforted, and at the moment Shelby didn't have it in her. "Please, I need some time alone."

"Luke's family is outside as well. They're very worried about you."

"I'm fine." Shelby moved the IV lines and tried to scoot up in the bed but gave up the effort when her head and body protested with a multitude of aches and pains. "Just really sore."

Dr. Clyde nodded. "You will be for about a week or so. You took a hard plunge into that ditch." The doctor set the chart aside and sat on the bed at Shelby's waist. "Right now you're probably feeling overwhelmed, maybe even a little numb, like it didn't happen. That's all normal and part of grief. But I want you to understand that the miscarriage wasn't your fault. Nothing you did made you lose the baby. Sometimes these things just happen. I know we only met briefly to confirm your pregnancy, but I've gone over your chart carefully. Your history doesn't look conducive to getting pregnant easily *but,* with bed rest and special care, I see no reason why you couldn't carry a baby to term."

But everything happens for a reason.

Shelby stared down at the polka dots on the gown she wore, tired and angry and sick to her stomach. Did the gowns have to be so ugly? Why wouldn't they let her leave? She'd already gotten up to go to the bathroom. If she could do that here, she could do that at home.

"Do you have any questions?"

She shook her head. Dr. Clyde had been very thorough. The pregnancy had happened once and it could happen again, but the odds were still against it. Scar tissue, her previous problems. She'd cleaned Shelby's insides up as much as possible, but the endometriosis would come back, the same with the cysts, and the tumors lining her uterus were still there. Only a hysterectomy would rid her of the painful conditions.

"We can give you something stronger for the pain. The local anesthesia has worn off."

"No. I don't like feeling drugged." And this was a pain she felt she deserved.

Dr. Clyde frowned her disapproval. "What about the hives? I understand they're your normal stress reaction, but maybe some Benadryl would help?"

She shook her head. "I'm used to them."

Shelby could feel the woman staring at her, trying to judge her state of mind. What did Dr. Clyde want her to say? Did the good doctor want her to freak out?

"Shelby, listen to me. You will be okay. It might not seem like it now, but one day you'll feel like your old self again."

She highly doubted that. She hadn't wanted the baby, said it was a mistake how many times? It wasn't until Luke had kissed her stomach and named it Gigabyte that she'd really and truly—

"I'm going to do rounds but I want you to have a nurse page me if you need anything. And if you change your mind about the meds, just speak up. I'll leave instructions with them, okay?"

Shelby nodded her head, the pillowcase scratching her bruised cheek. "Will you keep them out?" she asked softly, throat sore from where she'd screamed during the accident. "All of them. Tell them I'm fine. I'll *be* fine. I just…need to be alone."

"I'll let them know."

The doctor left and Shelby carefully rolled onto her side, feeling every muscle and bone in her body despite the after-effects of the medication they'd given her for the procedure. She stared at the wall in the darkened room, the moon high in the sky and visible outside the open blinds.

Rosetta's saying ran through her head over and over again. One thing becoming more and more clear. If everything happened for a reason, she was obviously not meant to be a mother.

Or a wife.

BY THE TIME he arrived in Beauty, Luke had accumulated two speeding tickets and had paid a college kid five hundred dollars for his standby seat from Chicago to Atlanta. Thank God for ATMs.

Phone calls to Nick had kept him posted. He knew about the D & C procedure and Pat Taylor's arrival. Pat had informed Jerry, according to Nick, and Jenn had called the rest of the family to let them know what had happened so Luke didn't need to worry about that.

Now he ran through the hospital, took the stairs because the elevator was too slow, and arrived at Shelby's room out of breath and at a complete loss for words. What do you say after something like this?

"Luke, wait."

He turned and found Nick and Garret hurrying toward him from the waiting area. Beyond their shoulders he spotted Jenn and Darcy still sleeping in the chairs. "Who's in there with her? Her mom? Gram?"

His brothers exchanged a look.

"She wouldn't let any of us in," Nick told him.

Luke swore. "Not even Alex?"

Garret rubbed at his red-rimmed eyes. "She's in a remote part of Canada at a bed-and-breakfast. I got her voice mail. Mom said Alex told her service was iffy there, so we don't know when she'll get the message."

Anger poured through him even though he knew it wasn't their fault. "Shelby's been in there all night by herself?"

Nick's face mirrored Luke's frustration. "Shelby had the doctor post an order to keep us out. She told the doc to tell us she was fine but needed time alone. I snuck in a couple times and she was asleep."

Luke's instincts screamed. He stared at the occupants of the waiting room. "Didn't you say Pat was here? Where's Shelby's mother?"

Nick turned and looked, too. "She was here earlier. Maybe she went for coffee."

"She could've snuck in like we did to check on Shelby," Garret added.

Luke turned and entered the hospital room as quietly as possible, his brothers on his heels.

The bed was empty.

MOST MISCARRIAGES OCCURRED in the first three months of pregnancy. Shelby knew the statistics, knew that the doctors thought the three-month time frame was good because at that stage the mother hadn't felt her baby move. But Shelby had recently passed that three-month mark, the shock had worn off, and it had finally begun to sink in that maybe having a baby wouldn't be such a bad thing.

Wouldn't have been *such a bad thing.*

But now not only was her baby gone, the very reason for her marriage was gone as well. The honeymoon was definitely over.

"Shelby? He's here."

Her mother's voice came from the living room, her words knifing into Shelby's soul. She wasn't ready to face Luke, wasn't ready to see the hurt and pain in his eyes. Her hands stilled on the spatula, the air bubbles in the glob of blueberry muffin batter left in the bottom of the mixing bowl popping in slow motion.

The image of Luke talking to her stomach over the weekend appeared out of nowhere. *Baby Gigabyte.* Something so small and fragile but so very important. How could she not have wanted it?

The kitchen door opened.

Shelby stared at Luke and wished she'd gone to bed like her mother had wanted her to. But why bother when she couldn't sleep? She hadn't been able to close her eyes since she'd woken up from the procedure. She'd lain awake, staring at the wall, and heard someone enter her hospital room during the night, knew it was Luke's family sneaking in to check on her. The second time it had happened she'd waited until they were gone, then forced her feet to the floor and opened her hospital-room door, dressed only in the ugly gown and blanket.

The first person she'd seen was her mother. Pat had opened her mouth to call out, but Shelby had shaken her head, her expression pleading for silence, for *help*. And for the first time in Shelby's memory, her mother hadn't made a scene. Pat had taken a long look at Shelby's face, grabbed her oversize, shiny gold purse, and crept from her chair a slight distance from Luke's sleeping family.

She'd reluctantly driven Shelby home, but her mother hadn't left and Shelby hadn't asked her to. Sometimes a girl just needed her mom and nobody else would do.

"Shelby? Thank God." Luke crossed the floor in three strides and swept her into his arms. She felt him bury his nose in her neck, the trembling deep inside him breaking through her battered senses.

"Luke, why don't you take Shelby in the other room? I'll finish up here."

Shelby pulled away and shook her head at her mother. "I want to do them. Why don't you go to bed, Mom? You look tired." Her mother looked to Luke for guidance, which totally pissed Shelby off. "Mom, it's okay."

Luke nodded, his gaze never leaving Shelby's face. "I'll take care of her, Pat."

She didn't need anyone to take care of her. If she'd taken care of herself in the first place, none of this would be happening.

Her mother wiped her damp eyes and stepped close to give her a hug. "I love you, baby." Her voice dropped. "Please don't do anything drastic. Not right now."

Shelby kissed her mother's cheek. "Thanks for driving me home."

Sending Luke a nervous glance, her mother left the room and headed down the hall.

Shelby picked up her spatula and began stirring the rapidly thickening glob again.

"You should be in bed."

She ignored his attempts to take the spatula away from her and slid the bowl farther down the counter away from him, adjusting her position in the process. "The doctor said the soreness would lessen if I moved around."

"I doubt they meant for you to do it as soon as you stepped out the hospital doors—early, I might add. Do you know how I felt when we realized you were gone?"

"Sorry." She glanced up at him from beneath her lashes and noticed his suit. "You shouldn't have come. I'm fine. You walked out on your presentation, didn't you? You need to fly back tonight. That way you can give it tomorrow."

Luke stared at her and fought for patience, incredulous. They were surrounded by a good six dozen muffins and she was *fine?*

"I mean, the baby's gone."

"Sweetheart, come here."

"So I was thinking," she continued determinedly, "since it's the only reason we got married, there's no reason for us to stay married anymore."

Shock poured through him. "Shelby—"

"We've barely been married a month, and most of it has been spent apart. Phone calls and Internet chats don't really count, you know?" She poured the mix into muffin pans, acting like they were discussing something as inane as the weather, and set the bowl aside. "Garret can handle it without a lot of fuss."

"Handle what?" He had to hear her say it.

"Our divorce."

She said it without any hesitation. Just like that. A part of him wondered how she could be so cold and unfeeling, so detached, but when she lifted her hand to her chest and rubbed hard, he focused on the bright red hives. She wasn't as blasé about this as she wanted to be. She was scared and sad and trying to stay on her feet even though she'd been kicked.

He reminded himself that Shelby had not only lost the baby, but crashed her car, had a medical procedure performed, a slight concussion and was probably still medicated. She wasn't thinking straight. It didn't make her words any less painful, though. "We can talk about this in the morning."

"What's to talk about? There's no reason to be married now."

No reason? He'd told her he loved her. Maybe not in so many words but he'd definitely implied it with that whole trust thing, lame though it was. "I love you." The words came out gruff because his chest was so tight, but he cleared his throat and tried again. "There *is* a reason to stay married, Shelby. I love you."

She wouldn't look at him. "I'm sorry. The baby's gone, Luke."

"Our vows haven't changed."

She grabbed the muffin pan and yanked the stove door open, sliding it onto the racks with a clatter.

"Shelby, it's okay to be sad. It's okay to cry. We lost something precious tonight."

Her gaze lifted to his, completely dry. "We lost something that wasn't meant to be. Haven't you figured that out yet? I didn't want to be pregnant in the first place. Why would I cry?"

Despite the sight of her obvious pain, the words sent shock waves through him. It was one thing to be cold, another to be cruel. "Don't say things like that. You'll regret them later."

"Just stating a fact."

"A fact? You said you liked the name Gabriella for a girl or Gabe for a boy."

She set the timer on the stove, her hands quaking. "And now it doesn't matter. The reason why we got married is *gone*. It's over, Luke. How many times and ways do I have to say it? The pregnancy was a fluke and the odds are it'll never happen again. The night I slept with you? The *only* reason I did it was because I'd been told I needed a hysterectomy. You know that and yet you're still trying to twist the truth into some romantic fantasy when it was sex, simple as that."

Shelby had gone into detail about her health problems over their time together. He'd also spoken with Dr. Clyde before coming to the house. He knew the odds, the risks. Knew they didn't matter to him. Shelby did. "You got pregnant once. If you want a baby, who's to say it won't happen again?"

Shelby washed the mixing bowl in the sink, her whole body moving because she scrubbed it so hard.

"Sweetheart, miracles do happen."

She stilled, her hands in the sudsy water, her body tense and tight, her eyes clear but bleak. "And *everything* happens for a reason." Shelby pulled her hands from the sink and dried them with a towel. "We kidded ourselves into thinking we could make it work, but this is proof that it was never meant to be."

"You're wrong."

"I'm right. You *know* I'm right."

He moved toward her, wished she'd let him hold her. They could get through this together if she'd just let him try.

"Just because things are tough right now—just because the baby didn't make it—that doesn't mean we have to give up on each other."

"What are we giving up on? How does a person give up on something they never believed in in the first place?"

"I believed in it, in us."

Shelby laughed. *Laughed.* And it was her laughter that finally got through to him. Luke stared at her and grew angrier with the sound, the grating edge transporting him back to the days when he'd been the butt of wimp jokes and cheerleader ridicule. After the day he'd had, after what Anne-Marie had done and said to him about not being the guy with the pretty girl, he felt like a fool. Was it all a fantasy in his head? A game he couldn't win?

"Luke, you need to know something about me. When the going gets tough? I get going. I have a lot more of Jerry Brookes in me than good old Zacharias. That's the truth. Whenever the guys I dated wanted more? I dropped them, just like that. A few dinners, some nights out, some fun," she said suggestively, her tone sending Luke's blood pressure soaring because of the images it evoked, "and I was done. The moment they so much as started describing their family, I ended things, no matter how nice they might have been, no matter how much I might have liked them."

"Alex always said you didn't want to be tied down, but she thought it was the guys you dated."

A bittersweet smile touched her mouth. "Alex thought that…or you? Did you hope *you* were special?"

A hot flush rose in him. She was striking out, hurting. He was hurting, too.

"What we had was a few fun weeks that life just shattered all to hell. We were playing at marriage, playing at being a family but…it wasn't real." She made her way to the door, slow but with measured, decisive steps. "Go home to California, file for divorce and sign the papers as soon as you get them." She held his gaze, not so much as a flicker of regret in her eyes. "Goodbye, Luke."

SHELBY LEANED her full weight against the door the moment she heard Luke start his car. That had to be the hardest thing she'd ever done in her life. But he'd survive—better off for not having her to deal with.

"I never realized what it must have been like for you."

Shelby froze at the sound of her mother's voice. Luke's vehicle raced away with a roar of the engine and she felt dizzy from not being able to breathe. Why wouldn't they all leave her alone?

"No matter how quiet we tried to be, you heard, didn't you? How many times did you sit in your room listening to me and Jerry fight?"

Too, too many times.

"I know what happened between you and Luke. I heard it and I still can't believe it. But you…you were a child." Her mother lifted her hand and wiped her nose. "You heard us, but you didn't understand because you didn't know the truth. Oh, baby. I'm so sorry."

"I survived." Her hand hurt where it grasped the knob but she couldn't let go. She'd fall if she did. "If you taught me nothing else, it was how to survive."

"Is that why you're doing this? Is that why you're shoving a good man away?"

Luke was better off without her. "It's for the best."

"The best thing to do would be to call him up and ask him to come back. Shelby, don't do what I did, don't lose someone you care about because you're focusing on things that aren't important."

Aren't important? Shelby released the knob and walked across the floor, pausing by the entry. "Why did you stay quiet?" She shifted her gaze to her mother. "Tonight when you saw me, why did you help me leave the hospital without making a fuss?"

Pat wiped her eyes, frowning at the sight of the black streak on her fingers. "Because I've felt that emptiness inside," she whispered. "I guess I figured you'd had enough drama for the night. It's also about time I try to make you proud of me instead of embarrassed."

Shelby's heart constricted. She retraced her steps and stood in front of her mom, letting her mother pull her into a hug. "Thank you."

"You're welcome, baby."

She inhaled the scent of her mother's perfume, tired and achy and hurting in places that time couldn't fix. "Remember when it would storm really badly and you would climb into bed and sleep with me?"

Her mother's arms tightened. Without a word, Shelby found herself ushered into the bedroom, into bed. But after turning off the light, her mother climbed in beside her.

"I love you, Mom."

"Oh, baby." Pat stroked Shelby's hair. "I love you, too."

"YOU LEFT? Are you serious?"

His little sister's anger traveled the miles separating them. Still at the bed-and-breakfast, Alex's cell hadn't worked, but Jenn had gotten a text message through. "Shelby wants a divorce."

"She's reeling from a miscarriage. *Hello?* She wouldn't

be Shelby if she collapsed into your arms and begged you never to leave, now would she?"

"She told me to go back to California."

"And what did you say?"

"Nothing. I left. I didn't even tell her I quit my job." Silence. "You quit? Seriously?"

"Yeah."

"Because you love Shelby? Wanted to be with her?"

"Yeah."

"Then go to her. I know it sounds messed up and juvenile and maybe it is, but everybody has their hang-ups, including Shelby. This is one of hers, okay? I can't spell it out more clearly to you. You have to prove to her she can count on you."

"I've told her that."

"And then you walked out. You can't tell someone they can trust you, you have to *show* them. By leaving, you did what Jerry did every time he and Pat had a fight."

He closed his eyes. "Dammit."

"Oh, Luke. You just wiped out any progress you made with Shelby by not sticking around and fighting to prove you're not like her parents."

Dammit!

Alexandra released a soul-deep sigh. "Think about it. Shelby's Shelby. Do you think, *really* think, if she didn't want you there, she'd have ever agreed to marry you? She might not have had much experience with kids but, come on, she kicks butt at everything she does. She always has because she's such a perfectionist. It's all or nothing with her, but she could've hired a lawyer and fought to raise the baby on her own."

Luke pulled to the side of the road and stopped, shoving the rented vehicle into Park and letting the motor idle.

"Alex, she only slept with me that first time because she'd received bad news."

"I know. But I'll tell you what I told her that day. She *chose* you. Do you really think that doesn't mean something? In the time you've been together, haven't you connected at all? I got the impression you had from the way Shelby talked."

He thought of them sexually first, her need to control their lovemaking, her favorite position of power. But then he thought of the way Shelby had come to California to see him. The way she'd curled her arms around him and let him make love to her for a change.

Her protective walls had started to come down, meaning she was starting to trust him. Love him?

And was running scared, afraid to believe that without the baby he could love her anyway.

Because he'd proved her right by leaving.

Luke hit the steering wheel with his palm. Why did women have to make things so complicated? Why not say what they meant? "What do I do?"

How embarrassing was it to have to ask his younger sister for advice? But if anyone had any gems of hope, Alex was it.

"Well…things happened kind of fast, right?"

"Yeah."

"So since the baby is gone…" Her voice cracked saying the words. "Maybe you should start over?"

Start over? He stared out the windshield. He had already started over by quitting his job. But how could he go about convincing Shelby he wanted more than a part-time marriage?

CHAPTER NINETEEN

"GLARING AT LUKE hasn't made him go away yet. Come eat some of this soup your mother made."

A week after the accident, Shelby turned her back to the window and tried to get the sight of Luke sitting on the porch of the mill house, looking tired and sad and lonely, out of her mind and off her conscience. She had nothing to feel guilty about.

Except for making it clear he isn't welcome to eat lunch with you.

Sighing, Shelby made her way to the fridge. "I'm not hungry, Dad."

"You're losing weight and looking scrawny. And if you don't take something for those hives, you're going to turn into a great big one."

"I'm fine."

"She keeps saying that like we're going to believe her."

Alex simply raised an eyebrow when Shelby turned her glare on her so-called friend. "Shouldn't you be packing up to go somewhere?"

"Be nice. I worried myself sick about you while I was in Canada. Now I'm home for one whole day and I'm spending it with you."

Lucky me. Is the rest of Luke's family going to show up, too?

"Think I'll go get the rest of the supplies we talked about if Luke's here to help unload them. Might as well put that boy to work if he's going to be hanging around all the time," Jerry said.

"I don't want him hanging around. I want him gone." Shelby's head throbbed. "It's been a week and every time I turn around, he's here. He mowed my lawn, used the Weed-whacker on everything—including my late-blooming daisies—took the car you loaned me and had Nick check it out and gave Biggun a bath."

Alex wrinkled her nose. "Biggun?"

Shelby waved toward the back door. "A stray pup showed up. His paws are almost as big as my fist but he's keeping the deer out of my garden. The point is," she continued, "I went back to work three days afterward. Why doesn't he make up with his boss and go back to California? He'll never be happy here."

Jerry frowned and turned to Alexandra. "Didn't you say Luke quit his job to stay here with Shelby?"

Alex nodded, hurt apparent on her features. "Why wouldn't Luke be happy here? It's home."

Arms across her chest, Shelby clenched her teeth so tight pain shot up the side of her jaw. "Is that why you never stay around for more than a weekend?"

"Now, don't be a witch. I'm home between assignments. And maybe Luke would be happy if you'd talk to him."

"He left."

"But he came back."

That he had. But why? "Which one of you gave him your key?" she asked, knowing they were arguing in circles.

"I did," Alex confessed. "He's your husband and you wouldn't give him one." She fiddled with the strap of her purse. "You're being unfair, Shel. You're angry about losing the baby and no one blames you for that. But you shouldn't be taking it out on Luke."

Shelby was. She knew she was but she couldn't help it. She couldn't handle Luke's sudden return on top of everything else. "I've asked for a divorce. Why sleep on the couch when he can stay at Nick's old apartment above the gym?"

"Why stay there and drive out here every day to putter around?" her father countered gruffly. "Gas is expensive. Besides, he's building that wine rack you wanted. You should be thanking him."

Her wine rack? "But…I didn't have enough in my budget for that."

Jerry set his coffee cup down on the table. "Luke saw it on the plans and asked where it was. I told him and then he went and bought the materials. He said that wall wouldn't look as good without it."

"You let him do that? Why didn't he take that money and file the divorce papers?"

"I guess because the boy doesn't want one." Her father pointed a finger at her as he stood. "Maybe you should pay attention to that. I'm heading back out. Too much tension in here."

"Tell him I'll repay him. And ask him to leave!"

"You want to talk to him, you do it yourself. But if I were you," Jerry continued, pulling his hat on his head, "I wouldn't be too hard on the boy. It was his baby, too, Shelby Lynn."

Guilt stirred. Luke had been much more excited at the pregnancy. Was he handling the miscarriage okay?

"Besides, I happen to relate to his side of things."

"Dad."

"It's true. Women might carry the babies, but how helpless

do you think a man feels when something's happening and he can't do anything about it? Then you try to kick him out and divorce him. You're takin' after your mother there."

Just what she wanted to hear. Shelby moaned and turned toward the cabinets, pulling out her pots and mixing bowls.

"And there you go again." Her father cursed. "At least Luke is being productive in his grief instead of moping around starving himself to death. For all those muffins you bake, you sure ain't eatin' them."

"I'm fine."

"And I'm the president. Alex, see if you can talk some sense into her."

After her dad walked out, Shelby stalked to the table to grab up his soup bowl, carrying it to the sink.

"He's right, you know."

"Don't you start, too."

"How can I not be concerned? Shel, the doctor told you to take at least a week off to recover from your injuries, but did you? No, you went to work days after even though you were so sore you could barely walk. And look at you. Your clothes are hanging on you. You're trying to work yourself senseless to keep from thinking about the baby and Luke and everything that happened."

Shelby flipped the handle of the faucet and grabbed the dish detergent, squirting enough for five sink loads. "What good is dwelling on it? Especially when it's probably the best thing that could've happened for everyone concerned?"

Alex scooted back her chair with a screech. "I hope to God you don't mean that. I hope it's your upset talking because if not, you don't deserve to be married to Luke."

She didn't turn to look at Alex, couldn't after her shameful remark. "Stop saying his name like he's a saint. Luke has his own problems."

Alex shoved the chair in with a bang. "Yes, he does—with his wife, not that you're acting like one."

Her whole body ached. "This is exactly why I refused Luke in the first place, why I *didn't want* to get married. Alex, what do you want me to *do?*"

Alex stomped to the door. "I want you to see what you're doing by being this way. You think you can protect yourself from being hurt, but you can't. Shel, love hurts. It sucks, it's messy, it's painful and—" she yanked her purse strap over her shoulder "—when you care for someone you give them power over you and it's scary as hell. I get that. But I've been watching you and I don't think you feel anything. Your baby *died*. Have you cried?"

Shelby flinched. "That's cruel."

"Is it? I can't tell by the stony look on your face. My brother lost his baby, too. Have you comforted him? Given him an ounce of compassion? I never thought I'd say this to you of all people, but you're being completely selfish."

The door slammed shut behind Alex, leaving a deafening silence.

FOR THE NEXT couple of weeks Luke worked around the house or the mill house every day, rain or shine. Whether Shelby worked or had the day off, whether she wanted him there or not. Each day he watched her with that sad expression on his face and her heart broke a little more. It was so hard not to respond to him, not to want to comfort him. She could tell he was hurting.

She could also tell that Luke was getting tired of her silence, of the treatment he received from her, and even though she told herself to talk, to speak up, something held her back. No doubt her selfish nature.

She liked listening to Luke, liked the things he said to her. He always asked how she felt, if she'd eaten. Did she see that her mums were blooming? The leaves were gorgeous this year. The mill house was coming along nicely. She'd be open ahead of schedule.

She looked beautiful.

What woman didn't want to feel beautiful? She didn't want to encourage him, but she still shivered every time Luke caught her unaware and brushed the hair from her face, stroked his knuckles down her arm or placed his hand on her back to gain her attention and show her something.

She even made lists of reasons they couldn't be together. *Children.* Luke's joy in thinking he was going to be a father indicated how very much he wanted children, something she might not ever be able to give him. But she also knew his love would never be restricted to a blood child. Luke was like Jerry in that aspect, and he'd love any child, no matter where it came from.

Job. She had to be realistic. Luke's future in gaming meant being close to the action, and that meant residing in California. To her this was a huge obstacle. But before she'd lost the baby hadn't she already thought of dividing their time in the two places? Her father was a foreman used to managing people. Maybe he'd run the restaurant for her during the winter months when his construction work ground to a halt?

Luke's family. She loved them but could she really put up with them butting in whenever they felt? Alex was her friend but her comments hurt. Having to listen to that kind of bluntness would take more patience than Shelby possessed. But she had put up with it since kindergarten and, in truth and until now, she'd liked having that constant in her life.

That's it? Three things? That's all you could come up with?

Throwing the last of the trash she'd dragged out of the mill house into the commercial Dumpster, she jumped back when a bumblebee buzzed so close to her face she felt the breeze created by its wings. Her heart thumped hard in her chest and the air left her lungs in a gush, and she laughed at her silly reaction.

But it was a similar reaction to how she felt with Luke. She'd never admit to the belly-clenching, spine-tingling, heart-in-her-throat rush she got whenever he was near. Still it was true, and if weeks of closeness with Luke left her feeling so out of her depth, what would a year be like? Two? She had to stay strong, not let him wear her down. He'd get fed up with her moods and her baggage and stupid issues and walk away for good. It was only a matter of time and she'd best stop thinking he meant what he said, that he'd changed his mind and regretted walking out.

Call her a coward but she'd spent her childhood in limbo twenty-four/seven over just this type of thing. Coming home from school had always been an adventure of whether or not her parents had had a fight and were still together. No way would she live her adulthood worried and afraid of the same thing happening. Maybe Alex was right about some things, but she was definitely wrong about others.

Nothing was worth the fear of loving something you couldn't control.

LUKE FELT Jerry's stare and braced himself. "Whatever it is, just say it."

The man Shelby considered her father took his ball cap

off and wiped a red patterned hanky over his head. "Just commiserating, son. I've been in your shoes many a time."

Luke stilled, the wood trim piece forgotten in his hands. How much longer could this go on? "Any advice?"

Four weeks had passed since the accident and miscarriage and even though he'd spent every morning and evening with Shelby, she kept him at arm's length. She wouldn't go anywhere with him, wouldn't attend church or family functions. He'd resorted to using any excuse to touch her, talk to her—and for a guy better with a computer than words, that took a lot of effort.

"None worth taking. I seemed to always do the wrong thing with Pat. I guess if I did offer up something, it would be to remember some people have to lose a good thing before they appreciate it."

"Shelby and I have both learned that lesson the hard way."

"No, son. I didn't mean the baby. Shelby's testing your sticking power. She did the same thing to me whenever her mother and I got back together."

Luke wasn't about to thank Jerry for the events that contributed to Shelby's abandonment issues.

"Some people learn quick, but others take longer," the man continued. "Shelby's one of them."

Jerry held the trim piece in place with one hand and motioned for Luke to grab the nail gun to fasten it to the window's frame.

"Shelby Lynn might not be my true blood daughter, but she gets that from me. You love her. I can tell. Hell, I knew it the first time you drove the girls home after one of their sleepovers. You couldn't take your eyes off Shelby even though you blushed every time she glanced your way."

Luke put his head down with a groan. Those weren't his best years.

Neither is this one.

"I guess what I'm saying is that some people have to hit rock bottom before they wake up and swim. You're fighting, but Shelby's still floating through the muck of what her mother and I did to her."

Luke pulled the trigger and the blast of compressed air shooting the nail into place filled the mill house.

"She's afraid to try because if she doesn't, she can't be disappointed again. Her mother and me, losing the baby...you."

Luke set the gun aside and grabbed another piece of precut trim. "How do I fight that fear? She's afraid of failing, but not trying to make it work is failing." He didn't like the look in Jerry's eyes.

"You can't beat it, son. You're not a boy with a crush anymore. You see Shelby's faults and you love her anyway, but that fear in her is bigger than you and until *she* gets control, nothing you do is gonna win her over. Son, I never thought the day would come when I would say this to the man married to my daughter, but sometimes a man has to know when to walk away and hope what you're wanting comes after you."

LUKE WAS ABOUT READY to pack up for the day when he heard slow, measured footsteps approaching the mill house. He hesitated, then continued what he was doing.

"I'll repay you everything I owe you for materials as soon as I can."

"Consider it all a wedding gift." He turned to look at her and had a hard time biting back the words that came to his lips. He hadn't seen Shelby much in the past couple days but she looked even worse than before—gaunt and exhausted and wound too tight. He stared at her, hating the situation they were in, knowing it could be easier if she'd bend a little and realize the baby wasn't the end. But first he had to acknowledge that Jerry was right.

He'd walked away from Anne-Marie to be the man he needed to be. He needed to do the same here. Staying so close to Shelby certainly wasn't helping her face what had happened. They'd grown close and it had been acceptable to her so long as the baby was a buffer, but without it she was too scared to trust his feelings for her—and perhaps hers for him?

Heart heavy and aching, Luke finished staining the last section and wrapped the brush up to clean later, then headed out onto the porch for the fresh air he needed to do what he had to do. "The fumes are getting to me," he said as he seated himself on the steps.

After a minute or two, Shelby followed.

"Beautiful night, eh?" Fireflies danced over the grass, the sight bringing memories long buried. Smiling sadly, he got up again and stepped off the porch, headed out into the darkness of the yard that would soon be a parking lot for Shelby's dream come true.

"What are you doing?"

Luke reached out and caught one of the fireflies in his palms, carrying it back to her. She wouldn't take it. "You remember now." He heard her swallow, the sound audible over the crickets and frogs and whip-poor-wills in the woods behind them. How many nights had his brothers and sister, Gram and Granddad, and Shelby spent out under the stars like this?

His grandfather had loved to tell stories and he'd told them fireflies lit up because they were promises someone had made but hadn't kept. So many promises.

Careful of his winged friend, Luke snagged her hand in his and opened her fingers, gently pressed so that the lightning bug crawled into her palm. "I made you a promise. And I want to keep it. But day after day you won't give me anything in return. No friendship, no thought of reconciliation. No hope. I need more."

"I—"

"Let me finish." Luke stared down at their hands, his chest tight. "We got close for a while. That last weekend before… It was everything we should've been. I know you need time to recover from the miscarriage, but *I* need some kind of sign or signal, something to hold on to right now. I'm tired of beating my head against the wall, Shelby. I'm tired of the way things are between us."

"The baby is *gone*."

"Yes, it is. But I married you because I love you." Luke lifted his head and looked her square in the face, letting her see everything he felt.

She closed her eyes. "No."

"Yes," he countered softly. "Maybe the circumstances weren't ideal and maybe we rushed things, but I love you. And I don't ever want you to doubt that. Especially now when…"

"When what? Why are you saying this?"

"Because I'm tired of settling. I want a wife who loves me as much as I love her. I want to be with someone who trusts me and wants me enough to share her fears and her secrets and know I'd never deliberately do anything to hurt her. Shelby, I want a marriage like my parents have and my grandparents had. But this isn't it."

She tried to pull away but he wouldn't let her. His hands tightened over hers, the bug inside lighting up every few seconds. "This is my promise," he stated roughly. "But you have to decide right now if you're going to keep it or throw it away. The choice is yours."

Luke released her hands, staying close because he wouldn't take that step unless he had to. He saw Shelby's throat work as she swallowed, heard the rasp of her breathing and still he waited for her to speak, to say something, to fight. For them and their marriage, for herself and the future they could have if she'd only try.

But without a word she opened her hands and he watched as the lightning bug lit up and took flight, joining the others around them.

Luke watched it go, his gut in knots, his lungs burning. Then he turned and walked away from the woman he'd always loved.

CHAPTER TWENTY

"YOU LOOKING for something?"

Shelby turned and saw her father staring at her with a knowing glint in his eyes. Two days had passed since Luke had left. Two long, lonely, horrible days. So why was she still waiting for him to come back? "No. Just noticing the windows need cleaning."

"Might as well wait. They're just going to get dirty again." He set down the wheelbarrow he pushed and began loading the last of the boxes that had accumulated from installing the many light fixtures. "Luke has an interview today. If you're interested."

An interview? Just like that? She feigned indifference. "Good for him."

"I'm checking out early today."

"Oh?"

"I got a date with your mother."

Shelby shook her head, so lost in her thoughts she wasn't sure she'd heard him right. "Huh?"

Jerry lifted his shoulder in a shrug. "We're like two old shoes, I guess. One's no good without the other."

"But...*again?*"

"You think I'm a glutton for punishment."

"Most definitely."

"I think I'm a fool for love." A low rumble left his stocky chest. "Your mother isn't all that bad, Shelby."

She shook her head, dazed. "I know that. I love Mom. She's loud and needy and a pain in the butt, but I love her. She's been great ever since the accident." They'd gotten closer, like a mother and daughter should be. But a part of Shelby still held back, afraid to be burned by her mother again.

"I know."

"So…*why?*"

"It hit me after all this with you and Luke. That accident you had could've killed you. If that airbag hadn't deployed and your seat belt hadn't held, you could've flown right through the windshield. Every day I see that tear in the ditch and the tarp covering your car out back, and I think about what could've happened. It's made me realize I've wasted a lot of years because of stubborn pride and foolish jealousy."

"You accused her of cheating while you were married."

He stared at the newly waxed concrete floor beneath their feet. "I was angry."

"So? What about trust? You know what a flirt she is. Are you going to trust her, or walk out every time you and Mom fight?"

He thought that over a moment. "I trust her. And walking out and cooling off is better than saying something else I might regret. Besides, I don't recall seeing you let Luke off the hook when he was sticking around."

"But he's not sticking around now, is he? He left and you just said he had an interview. Considering the kind of work he does, it's probably with some company in California." Even as she said the words, even as she dared her father to answer honestly if he knew, she felt her lungs seizing up. She really wished she hadn't been proved right, but she'd known all along that he'd leave.

You drove him away. There is a difference.

"It is. Some competitor of that place where he used to work." Her father gave her a pitying stare. "Shelby Lynn, you can't expect a man to go jobless when you won't give him the time of day." He grabbed his tool belt. "Sometimes a man has to leave to prove he's worth wanting."

Shelby blinked, shock ripping through her. "You *told* him to leave me? What kind of father does that?"

Jerry gave her his strictest look, one reserved for missed curfews and swearwords. "The kind who wants you to be better than me and your mama raised you to be. That boy is a fine man. And if you can't be a wife, you need to let him go find someone who can. I see the love on your face when you look at him but your damn pride and fear is getting in the way, just like mine always did. You pushed him away but you want him. Be woman enough to admit it."

He waited, then shook his head at her silence. "Shelby Lynn, I've picked more than my share of the fights. I was always so sure your mother would leave me for Bennington that I pushed her away. She couldn't hurt me that way. Sound familiar?" he asked dryly. "But now Bennington is gone and I'm going to get my wife back, once and for all."

"Let me know when the wedding is. What *do* you get for a sixth marriage?" Sarcasm laced her words, unearthed from deep inside. Would it be a repeat of the past?

"Stubborn as all get-out," he complained. "Time is wasting, girl. Love doesn't come around often and when it's right in front of you, a person needs to hold on with both hands before they lose it for good. You really want to spend your life alone? Lock up behind you when you're done. I don't want to be late."

LUKE LISTENED to the offer being made and tried to hide the surge of excitement rushing through him. Better money, the ability to build his own team, stock ownership and a vested interest in the company. Partnership after one year in a company that would go head-to-head with Anne-Marie and Galaxy Games. He couldn't help it. There was a huge sense of satisfaction in being able to outperform her, maybe even bring John and some of the others over to his side of things.

"What do you think?"

Luke stared at Jimmy James, a former LCD like himself. Jimmy had started his own company two years ago and made a name for himself from the get-go, possibly because of his ability to predict trends. As far as companies went, Jimmy's Doghouse Games was a great move profession-ally—under the right circumstances. "I think I—"

Jimmy's cell phone vibrated against the battered wood table where they sat at the Old Coyote, cutting off Luke's response.

"Sorry. These things are evil, aren't they?" Jimmy picked up the phone to see the number. "It's my wife. I left her at her parents' house in Nashville. She misses home so much we come to visit a couple times a year. Mind if I take this?"

Luke shook his head. "No, not at all. Go ahead."

"Be right back." Jimmy stood and answered the call, holding a finger to his ear to block out the sound of the jukebox as he walked away.

Luke stared at the offer in front of him but jerked his head up when a chair thumped against the table.

"Do I want to know what that is?" Nick asked, straddling the chair and crossing his arms over the back.

"Don't get comfortable. You can't stay, I'm in an interview."

Nick's scowl deepened. "Didn't recognize him. Is he from Nashville?"

"No." Nick waited for him to elaborate and Luke sighed. "The company is in California. Look, the guy took time out of his family vacation to meet with me, and I'd appreciate it if you didn't say anything to the family. I'll tell them myself."

"So you're taking the job?"

He'd be the world's biggest idiot if he didn't.

"What about Shelby?"

"She wants a divorce."

Nick released a deep sigh. "I'm sorry to hear that. But why leave? Luke, listen…I came over here because I saw the guy and guessed you had something going on. But now I have to know if you're leaving because you still feel weird about how things were between us."

"I'm good. You?"

Nick looked ready to knock his block off for his flippant answer. "No, I'm not. I owe you quite a few apologies."

"You don't owe me anything."

Nick shook his head. "I do. Look, that day when Matt was thrown from the horse, I was…angry. You probably felt like I blamed you for the accident but I didn't—I don't. The horse reared, there's nothing you could've done about it. I was worried about Matt, and the hospital wanted me to fill out paperwork and— I'm sorry, okay?"

Luke nodded, accepting the apology.

Nick rubbed his neck and squeezed. "I should've called after Jenn and I got back from Paradise Island, especially since you and your passport were the only reasons I was able to go after her."

"It's okay."

Nick's silver-blue eyes pierced him. "But it's not. Not according to Alex. You still have hang-ups about us and all the stupid stuff I said and did as a kid."

Luke wiped a hand over his face and propped his cheek on his fist. He didn't want to do this now. "Alex needs to keep her mouth shut."

"Is it true?" Nick didn't give him a chance to answer. "I saw your gear at the apartment. I know you've slept there the past couple nights. But now you're interviewing with that guy. Are you seriously thinking of going back to California?"

"Why not? Shelby and I are over."

"What's that got to do with you leaving town? Leaving us?"

Luke flipped the offer over until it was facedown on the table. "That's almost funny coming from you. What's the difference if I live here or in California?"

Nick leaned closer to him. "The difference is that I was a hotheaded kid too stupid to know better, but you're a grown man about to walk out on everything he ever wanted. You carry that computer around like it's surgically attached—why can't you use the damn thing to have a life with your family? Do what you need to do here and go there every once in a while?"

"Live here—and see Shelby every day?"

"Are you really ready to let her go?"

He didn't answer.

"Luke, if you two are through, it's going to be rough, but we're still here and we want you around. Especially me. I know I'm the one who drove you away."

"I went away to college, then got a job."

"If I did badly in school, you'd flunk a test. I couldn't play ball worth a damn so you quit the team even though you were good."

"I wasn't that good."

"You kept sacrificing your happiness for me. I know why you did it, but I didn't like it."

"I didn't like it that I could do the stuff and you couldn't."

"Yeah, well, I can now. I couldn't handle it as a kid, but things have changed." A grin tugged at his mouth. "Don't say anything to the parents, okay?" When Luke nodded, Nick glanced around and leaned toward him even more. "I'm getting my GED."

Luke drew back in surprise. "That's great."

"It's not a big deal."

But it was. Anyone could see that. Pride was stamped across Nick's face, and Luke knew his brother had turned a corner in his life.

"Luke, regardless of what happens with you and Shelby, I'm asking you to not take the job."

"Sorry about that— Whoa." Jimmy stopped in his tracks and grinned at them, then stuck out his hand. "You've gotta be one of Luke's brothers."

Nick flashed Luke an irritated glare, obviously upset that they'd been interrupted. He stood. "I'm his twin, Nick Tulane."

"Nice to meet you, Nick. Jimmy James."

Luke watched as Nick reluctantly shook hands.

"I'll let you two get back to business. Luke—" Nick's silver-blue eyes were filled with meaning "—remember what I said. Things have changed."

Luke stared at Nick, torn. Changed? They had, obviously, but he knew what he had to do in order to be able to live with himself. Being in the same town, seeing Shelby and wanting her but not being able to be with her would kill him.

So did that mean he wasn't ready to let go? Give up? What about his family? He'd loved getting those phone calls from his mother. But hearing the details of what his family was doing and knowing he could be a part of things if he wanted had gouged deep and made him homesick.

"So…" Jimmy waited, a wide grin on his face. "Did you tell your brother about the offer? Are we gonna celebrate tonight or what?"

Luke hesitated, then nodded. "I think we are—after we work out a detail or two."

Glowering at him, Nick stalked away.

SHELBY SAT in her darkened living room when she heard the squeal of tires and a low *thump*. She set the cup of tea aside and got up to look out the window, barely catching sight of the vehicle crawling along before it took off with a rev of the motor. What had they hit? The steady rain obscured any sign of movement by the road.

It wasn't the first time an animal had been injured in or near her yard. With all the deer, rabbits, raccoons and forest creatures, it was inevitable that something was hurt or killed. It was probably one of them. Which meant another burial. She couldn't stand to see them lying there day after day.

Better hope it's not Biggun.

Her stomach clenched. What if it was? She hadn't seen him this evening when she'd filled his food bowl. He could have been on his way home. Was that the thump she'd heard?

Shelby searched for the flashlight. If nothing else it would distract her from thinking about what her father said regarding Luke. What if he took the job and went back to California? *It's what you wanted.*

But was it? Really? Her father's words had hit home. She'd always known that despite their differences, her parents loved each other. Maybe with Bennington gone, they'd make it this time. Who knew? They hadn't dated or married anyone else in all the years they were apart. Deep down, she knew they loved each other, screwups and all.

Shelby grabbed a jacket off the hook by the door, hurrying out into the rain. She dodged mud puddles as she walked around the side of the house and down the driveway. "Biggun?" She whistled softly. But the only sound she heard was the rain on her roofs and the creek rushing down the mountain.

Then she saw it. Shelby's breath froze in her lungs when she saw the fawn lying beside the ditch where she'd wrecked. The force of the impact had knocked the baby deer clear across the divide and into her yard. It wasn't moving.

Chest hurting, she knelt beside it and put her hand on its tiny form. Dead. Shelby gulped in air, unable to get enough. Anyone who lived in the country knew this was a fact of life. It happened all the time. But the little fawn…it was so tiny. Still spotted and soft and small. Rain swept into Shelby's eyes and stung and even though she told herself to wait, to let her father bury the deer tomorrow morning, she couldn't leave it there. It wasn't more than a week old, maybe not even a few days old. She could carry it.

Shelby ignored the sickening twist of her stomach and lifted the baby deer in her arms. It was all legs, no weight, and she sludged through the mud of her yard, down to the shed in back. The coons and rabbits and feral cats were buried in the field away from the house. But the big pine tree in back of the shed already shaded Rascal, her longtime pet feline who'd had to be put down not long after she'd moved in, and it could shade one tiny deer.

Shelby picked a spot, retrieved the shovel and set to work. The rain-softened ground made it easy. The fawn was so small it didn't need a big grave, but before she had a hole dug, her back ached, she felt blisters on her hands and every inhalation was a struggle.

She finally tossed the shovel aside and placed the fawn into the grave, her chest so tight and full she could only take shallow breaths. "There you go. Nice and snug." Thunder rolled in the distance and the wind and rain picked up, cold where it hit her cheeks. Shelby ran her hand over the rain-slicked fur of the animal's neck, then set to work with the shovel again, every movement quicker than the last because she couldn't stand the sight of it, half-covered in mud.

Deer were considered stupid animals but would the mother miss it? Feel its loss? She hadn't felt the baby move but—

Shelby shut down her thoughts but it was too late. The pain came, fast, stabbing, stealing what was left of her breath. When the last shovel of dirt was in place, she turned to go back to the house and the soothing tea she'd left behind, but along the way the light from her flashlight caught a gleam of red.

Nick had towed her car up the driveway to the house so that he could rush to the hospital. He'd put it behind the shed where it still sat. Luke had just recently told her that Nick would be by to get the vehicle and take it for scrap parts but right now, the bright red Beemer mocked her, visible from beneath the tarp.

Shelby stared, uncaring that the rain beat down and soaked her hair and coat, ignoring the thunder blooming louder, closer. Wind tore through the trees around her, but the storm was nothing compared to the one that raged within her. How could this happen? Why?

Unbidden, her shaky legs carried her toward the carport where she pulled the canvas off the hood, off the car entirely.

Fifteen years old, the impact had totaled the vehicle. But as she stared at that bright red paint, a different kind of red appeared in her mind. Red on white linen, on white leather seats.

She didn't remember dropping the flashlight or lifting the shovel, but as another big boom exploded overhead and the skies opened up, she hit the car as hard as she could. Her hands went numb when the handle vibrated from the blow but she did it again. And again. *Again*.

What did it matter? The car was ruined. A gift from the man who'd never wanted her enough to claim her. Zacharias Bennington's dirty little secret. Now he was dead. But what happened to men who never cared about their children?

What happened to women who said they didn't want them?

She moaned, the sound raw. She'd said that. She'd actually *said* that about her baby. Her *baby*.

Shelby staggered and stared over to where the fawn lay in the too-small grave. Images flashed through her head. That night in June, her wedding day, the trip to California. The bright spot of red.

The baby was gone. Luke was gone. Gone, because she hadn't wanted it. Gone, because she'd pushed Luke away and because she was too afraid to hope and dream and *trust*. She stared at the car, at her ruined dreams, her father's words echoing in her head. "What did I do?" Her chest squeezed tighter, harder. "What did I *say?*"

She closed her eyes, the pain too much, ripping her apart, shattering her from the inside. "Oh, God, why. *Why?*" She choked on the rain, the words, anger surging through her so strong, so swift, she lifted the shovel over her head again and hit the car with every ounce of strength she possessed. The side mirror cracked on the first blow, broke on the second. "I didn't mean it. I didn't! I want my baby. *I want my baby!*

Please, give it back. I didn't mean it. I'm sorry! Please, please, give it *back!*"

The mirror fell to the side of the car and hung there—like the limp head of the baby deer. Sliding in the mud, she struggled to plant her feet and lift the shovel again, her arms shaking. "I want my promises. I want *all* of them! I want my *baby,* and I want L-Luke. I want our *marriage!*" She hit the door, wishing and praying and hoping for the impossible. "I want my husband," she sobbed. "Please, God, I want my promise back. I want them back, please, please, please give them *back!*"

Strong arms surrounded her and tried to pull the shovel from her numb hands. Shelby screamed and fought for control. "No!"

"Shelby, stop!" Her father's voice was choked and hoarse. "Honey, please, let go. It's all right. Shelby-girl, it's all right. It's going to be all right."

Her father's crooning voice released the remaining flood inside her. She turned in his arms, pressed her face against his chest and sobbed. "*Dad.* Dad, help me. I screwed up. I screwed up so bad."

"It's okay. I've got you now. Shh…"

"Why did I do it? Why did I say those things?" She gripped her father's shirt until her fingers hurt. "I don't want him to go. I don't want Luke to leave." She sobbed the words, huddled in her father's arms.

Another arm surrounded her, and Shelby smelled her mother's perfume.

"Oh, baby. If you don't want Luke to leave, *tell him.* It's not too late for you to tell Luke how you feel."

Shelby choked on a laugh when she lifted her head and saw her mother standing in the mud in three-inch heels and her hair plastered to her face despite the umbrella Pat tried to hold over all three of them. Her family, there when she'd needed them most. "But…I don't know where he is."

Her dad kissed the top of her head. "You don't, but I do."

PEOPLE STARED as Shelby walked through the Old Coyote, but she didn't care. She'd seen Luke's dark head the moment she'd stepped through the door, her parents at her back. Finally she made it to the table where Luke sat and he glanced up, his eyes widening when he saw the state she was in, soaking wet, covered in mud and a smudge of the baby deer's blood on her coat. She didn't care. Some things were more important.

"Shelby? What happened?"

"Luke, is there a problem?" the man with him asked.

"I changed my mind." Her words came out choked and thick and tears immediately filled her eyes. Now that she'd started crying it appeared she couldn't stop the flood. Some might think she was having a breakdown but she knew she was simply discovering twenty-eight years of pent-up emotion, locked away inside of her.

Luke stiffened at the sight, stood, but for once in her life Shelby didn't try to hide what she felt. They were tears for him, for them. Because she cared. Because she—

"About what?"

"My promise." The words emerged raspy and low, and Luke had to bend closer to hear her. "I want it," she continued. "You gave it to me and you have to keep it. You have to because I trust you and I—I—" She gulped. "I don't want you to go."

Luke's blue gaze sharpened and burned. "Why don't you want me to go?"

Because she loved him. Because she didn't want to spend her life wishing she'd been brave enough to fight for what she wanted. Because he was sweet and sexy and tender and knew exactly how to push her buttons and drive her nuts, and because she needed him to keep her grounded. But how could she say all that?

"Because…*I love you,*" she said simply. "I couldn't say it before because I thought I didn't believe in it or want it but I *do.* I want you, I need you. Please don't go." She used her dirty sleeve to wipe her face, but more tears trickled down her cheeks as she waited for him to respond.

Shelby heard murmurs behind her, felt the heat of bodies crowding close behind her in an attempt to hear her words, but she kept her gaze on Luke, waiting for his reaction. Was she too late?

His expression dark, tense, Luke stepped closer. Without a word, he cradled her face in his hands and lowered his head, kissing her until her body warmed from the inside out and her toes curled in her soggy shoes. The crowd erupted around them, catcalls and whistles, applause. But then everything faded when the kiss went on and she didn't care what they thought, didn't care that she'd made a scene. By the time Luke let her come up for air, all she could do was hold on to him.

"I love you," he murmured against her lips.

She whispered the words right back, happier than she'd ever been in her life. "You'll say no?"

"Shelby, I already took the job."

Then, just like that, her smile fell. "What?"

"Luke," Nick said from somewhere behind her, "so help me I'm going to—"

"I'm not going anywhere."

Shelby blinked up at him, confused. "But—"

"You just said you took the job," Nick reminded him grumpily.

"I did." Luke turned her so that she saw the man he'd been sitting with when she'd arrived. "Sweetheart, this is my boss, Jimmy James. He has family in Nashville and since we both have ties here, I added a few conditions of my own to the offer. The first of which was that I get to stay in Tennessee." His gaze returned to hers, warm with love.

"You're staying? Here?"

"I couldn't stand the thought of giving up on us."

Her father, mother and Nick spoke at once, asking Luke questions. Shelby buried her head against her husband's chest and fingered the buttons of his shirt, doing her best to ignore the stares boring into her back due to the spectacle she'd made of herself. Turned out, she was her mother's daughter after all. Not that she'd ever admit that.

"Shelby? What were you doing before you came here?" Luke asked softly.

Her laugh was more of a groan. "Beating up my car." She smiled at his perplexed frown. "It's a long story."

"Must be a good one."

"Why do you think that?"

Luke kissed her again. "Because your hives are gone."

* * * * *

The TULANES OF TENNESSEE *continue!*
Look for Ethan's story
by Kay Stockham.
Coming in Fall 2009
from Harlequin Superromance.

*Celebrate 60 years of pure
reading pleasure with Harlequin®!
Silhouette® Romantic Suspense is celebrating
with the glamour-filled, adrenaline-charged series*
LOVE IN 60 SECONDS
*starting in April 2009.
Six stories that promise to bring
the glitz of Las Vegas, the danger of revenge,
the mystery of a missing diamond, family scandals
and ripped-from-the-headlines intrigue.
Get your heart racing as
love happens in sixty seconds!*

Enjoy a sneak peek of
USA TODAY *bestselling author
Marie Ferrarella's
THE HEIRESS'S 2-WEEK AFFAIR.
Available April 2009
from Silhouette® Romantic Suspense.*

Eight years ago Matt Shaffer had vanished out of Natalie Rothchild's life, leaving behind a one-line note tucked under a pillow that had grown cold: *I'm sorry, but this just isn't going to work.*

That was it. No explanation, no real indication of remorse. The note had been as clinical and compassionless as an eviction notice, which, in effect, it had been, Natalie thought as she navigated through the morning traffic. Matt had written the note to evict her from his life.

She'd spent the next two weeks crying, breaking down without warning as she walked down the street, or as she sat staring at a meal she couldn't bring herself to eat.

Candace, she remembered with a bittersweet pang, had tried to get her to go clubbing in order to get her to forget about Matt.

She'd turned her twin down, but she did get her act together. If Matt didn't think enough of their relationship to try to contact her, to try to make her understand why he'd changed so radically from lover to stranger, then to hell with him. He was dead to her, she resolved. And he'd remained that way.

Until twenty minutes ago.

The adrenaline in her veins kept mounting.

Natalie focused on her driving. Vegas in the daylight wasn't nearly as alluring, as magical and glitzy as it was after dark. Like an aging woman best seen in soft lighting, Vegas's imperfections were all visible in the daylight. Natalie supposed that was why people like her sister didn't like to get up until noon. They lived for the night.

Except that Candace could no longer do that.

The thought brought a fresh, sharp ache with it.

"Damn it, Candy, what a waste," Natalie murmured under her breath.

She pulled up before the Janus casino. One of the three valets currently on duty came to life and made a beeline for her vehicle.

"Welcome to the Janus," the young attendant said cheerfully as he opened her door with a flourish.

"We'll see," she replied solemnly.

As he pulled away with her car, Natalie looked up at the casino's logo. Janus was the Roman god with two faces, one pointed toward the past, the other facing the future. It struck her as rather ironic, given what she was doing here, seeking out someone from her past in order to get answers so that the future could be settled.

The moment she entered the casino, the Vegas phenomena took hold. It was like stepping into a world where time did not matter or even make an appearance. There was only a sense of "now."

Because in Natalie's experience she'd discovered that

bartenders knew the inner workings of any establishment they worked for better than anyone else, she made her way to the first bar she saw within the casino.

The bartender in attendance was a gregarious man in his early forties. He had a quick, sexy smile, which was probably one of the main reasons he'd been hired. His name tag identified him as Kevin.

Moving to her end of the bar, Kevin asked, "What'll it be, pretty lady?"

"Information." She saw a dubious look cross his brow. To counter that, she took out her badge. Granted she wasn't here in an official capacity, but Kevin didn't need to know that. "Were you on duty last night?"

Kevin began to wipe the gleaming black surface of the bar. "You mean during the gala?"

"Yes."

The smile gracing his lips was a satisfied one. Last night had obviously been profitable for him, she judged. "I caught an extra shift."

She took out Candace's photograph and carefully placed it on the bar. "Did you happen to see this woman there?"

The bartender glanced at the picture. Mild interest turned to recognition. "You mean Candace Rothchild? Yeah, she was here, loud and brassy as always. But not for long," he added, looking rather disappointed. There was always a circus when Candace was around, Natalie thought. "She and the boss had at it and then he had our head of security escort her out."

She latched on to the first part of his statement. "They argued? About what?"

He shook his head. "Couldn't tell you. Too far away for anything but body language," he confessed.

"And the head of security?" she asked.

"He got her to leave."

She leaned in over the bar. "Tell me about him."

"Don't know much," the bartender admitted. "Just that his name's Matt Shaffer. Boss flew him in from L.A., where he was head of security for Montgomery Enterprises."

There was no avoiding it, she thought darkly. She was going to have to talk to Matt. The thought left her cold. "Do you know where I can find him right now?"

Kevin glanced at his watch. "He should be in his office. On the second floor, toward the rear." He gave her the numbers of the rooms where the monitors that kept watch over the casino guests as they tried their luck against the house were located.

Taking out a twenty, she placed it on the bar. "Thanks for your help."

Kevin slipped the bill into his vest pocket. "Any time, lovely lady," he called after her. "Any time."

She debated going up the stairs, then decided on the elevator. The car that took her up to the second floor was empty. Natalie stepped out of the elevator, looked around to get her bearings and then walked toward the rear of the floor.

"Into the Valley of Death rode the six hundred," she silently recited, digging deep for a line from a poem by Tennyson. Wrapping her hand around a brass handle, she opened one of the glass doors and walked in.

The woman whose desk was closest to the door looked up. "You can't come in here. This is a restricted area."

Natalie already had her ID in her hand and held it up. "I'm looking for Matt Shaffer," she told the woman.

God, even saying his name made her mouth go dry. She was supposed to be over him, to have moved on with her life. What happened?

The woman began to answer her. "He's—"

"Right here."

The deep voice came from behind her. Natalie felt every single nerve ending go on tactical alert at the same moment that all the hairs at the back of her neck stood up. Eight years had passed, but she would have recognized his voice anywhere.

* * * * *

Why did Matt Shaffer leave
heiress-turned-cop Natalie Rothchild?
What does he know about
the death of Natalie's twin sister?
Come and meet these two reunited lovers and
learn the secrets of the Rothchild family in
THE HEIRESS'S 2-WEEK AFFAIR
by USA TODAY *bestselling author*
Marie Ferrarella.
The first book in Silhouette® Romantic Suspense's
wildly romantic new continuity,
LOVE IN 60 SECONDS!
Available April 2009.

CELEBRATE
60 YEARS
OF PURE READING PLEASURE
WITH **HARLEQUIN®**!

Look for Silhouette®
Romantic Suspense in April!

Love In 60 Seconds
Bright lights. Big city. Hearts in overdrive.

Silhouette® Romantic Suspense is celebrating
Harlequin's 60th Anniversary with six stories that
promise to bring readers the glitz of Las Vegas,
the danger of revenge, the mystery of a missing
diamond, and family scandals.

**Look for the first title, *The Heiress's 2-Week Affair*
by *USA TODAY* bestselling author
Marie Ferrarella, on sale in April!**

You're invited to join our Tell Harlequin Reader Panel!

By joining our new reader panel you will:

- Receive Harlequin® books—they are FREE and yours to keep with no obligation to purchase anything!
- Participate in fun online surveys
- Exchange opinions and ideas with women just like you
- Have a say in our new book ideas and help us publish the best in women's fiction

In addition, you will have a chance to win great prizes and receive special gifts! See Web site for details. Some conditions apply. Space is limited.

To join, visit us at
www.TellHarlequin.com.

REQUEST YOUR FREE BOOKS!

2 FREE NOVELS PLUS 2 FREE GIFTS!

◆ HARLEQUIN®

Super Romance®

Exciting, emotional, unexpected!

Harlequin® Historical
Historical Romantic Adventure!

Undone!

THE RAKE'S
INHERITED COURTESAN
Ann Lethbridge

Christopher Evernden has been
assigned the unfortunate task of minding
Parisian courtesan Sylvia Boisette.
When Syliva sets off to find her father,
Christopher has no choice but to follow
and finds her kidnapped by an Irishman.
Once rescued, they finally succumb to
the temptation that has been brewing
between them. But can they see past the
limitations such a love can bring?

Available April 2009
wherever books are sold.

HARLEQUIN®
Super Romance®

COMING NEXT MONTH

Available April 14, 2009

#1554 HOME AT LAST • Margaret Watson
The McInnes Triplets
Fiona McInnes finally has the life in the Big Apple she'd always wanted. But when her father dies, she's forced to return home to help settle his estate. Now nothing's going as planned—including falling back in love with the man whose heart she shattered.

#1555 A LETTER FOR ANNIE • Laura Abbot
Going Back
Kyle Becker is over any feelings he had for Annie Greer. Then she returns to town, and suddenly he's experiencing those emotions again. But before he and Annie can share a future, Kyle must keep a promise to deliver a letter that could make her leave.

#1556 A NOT-SO-PERFECT PAST • Beth Andrews
Ex-con Dillon Ward has no illusions about who he is. Neither does his alluring landlord. But Nina Carlson needs him to repair her wrecked bakery—like, *yesterday*. And if there's one thing this struggling single mom knows, it's that nobody's perfect....

#1557 THE MISTAKE SHE MADE • Linda Style
Tori Amhearst can't keep her identity secret much longer. Ever since she brought Lincoln Crusoe home after an accident took away his memory, she's loved him on borrowed time. Because once Linc knows who she really is, she'll lose him forever.

#1558 SOMEONE LIKE HER • Janice Kay Johnson
Adrian Rutledge comes to Middleton expecting to find his estranged mother. He doesn't expect to find Lucy Peterson or a community that feels like home. Yet he gets this and more. Could it be that Lucy—and this town—is the family he's dreamed of?

#1559 THE HOUSE OF SECRETS • Elizabeth Blackwell
Everlasting Love
As soon as Alissa Franklin sees the old house, she knows it will be hers. With the help of handyman Danny—who has secrets of his own—she uncovers the truth about the original owners. But can a hundred-year-old romance inspire her to take a chance on love today?

HSRCNMBPA0309